The Eagle and the Weasel

The Slater Ibáñez Books

That First Heady Burn

True Vermilion

The Dark Shill

A Stack of Sawbucks

The Hillside Roble

The Peroxide Pomp

The Incidental Twin

Brawl in Bardo

The Window-Shade Job

The Convenient Patsy

The Artisanal Grifter

Shrink in the Shadows

Project Chartreuse

From a Desert Playa

The Tired Canary

A Desperate Frame-up

Trail of the Blue Agave

The Saucer-Heads

The Satin Squeeze Play

Chiseler in Jade

The Eagle and the Weasel

Subscribe to the Slater
Ibáñez Books newsletter:

slaternews.dagmarmiura.com

The Eagle and the Weasel

The Eagle *and the* Weasel

George Bixley

Published by Dagmar Miura
Los Angeles
www.dagmarmiura.com

The Eagle and the Weasel

Copyright © 2024 Dagmar Miura
All rights reserved. No part of this book may be used or reproduced in any manner whatsoever without prior written permission except in the case of brief quotations embodied in critical articles or reviews. For information, address Dagmar Miura, dagmarmiura@gmail.com, or visit our website at www.dagmarmiura.com.

This is a work of fiction. Names, characters, businesses, places, events, and incidents are either the products of the author's imagination or used in a fictitious manner. Any resemblance to actual persons, living or dead, or actual events is purely coincidental.

cover image inspired by the art of William Blake

First published 2024

ISBN: 979-8-89195-031-3

ONE

A GREEK RESTAURANT IN THE Valley was an odd place for a meeting, Slater knew, but Svetlana must have her reasons. She'd summoned him here with little explanation, and he relied on her too much for his surveillance tech to say no. He hated being that dependent on anyone, but he'd be hobbled if she ever cut him off, so he'd come running when she called.

He nosed the Continental into the lot behind the strip mall, half empty at the moment, and pulled into a stall, the sleek cloudy-blue machine bouncing gracefully on the uneven asphalt. That was the one upside about the Valley—there was lots of parking.

As Slater climbed out, a dark-haired guy paused as he was getting into an SUV in the next space. "Sweet ride."

"I know." Slater glanced at him as he slammed the door and stuffed the keys into the front pocket of his jeans.

"What year is it?"

"It's a '73."

"You want to sell it?"

Slater walked away, not responding to that. It was such

a stupid fricking question, and he heard it all the time.

As he walked toward the back entrance to the restaurant he saw there was a burly guy in a dark suit standing outside, a sidearm bulging under his jacket, his feet planted apart, studying his phone screen. Bald on top, he wore his beard neatly trimmed with some gray in it. Totally fuckable, Slater decided. As he approached the door, the guy held up the phone toward him. He'd just taken his photo, he realized.

"What the hell, man?" Slater demanded.

Ignoring him, he looked down at his screen. Slater stepped up to him and slapped him hard, left and then right, a rapid kovac.

"Why do you make me do this to you?" Slater growled.

Baldy hadn't been expecting that, and planted a palm on his chest to shove him off.

"You do this when you know I'm armed?" he said, his eyes wide.

That Slavic accent—this was one of Svetlana's guys, her driver, or her security detail, or both.

"Are you seriously threatening to draw down on me?" Slater said. "Why did you take my picture?"

He huffed. "Identity check. Facial recognition says you're Ibáñez."

"I could have told you that, toots."

The guy glared at him. "You're expected."

Slater scoffed and walked past him, pulling open the back door. He should have figured out who he was. Svetlana was all about tech. Of course her security thug would use facial recognition.

Walking past the kitchen, he caught a whiff of hot cooking oil and spices. The dining room was almost empty, not a surprise in the middle of a weekday afternoon. Svetlana was sitting at a table with her back to the wall, strategically positioned with a view of both the door to the street and the back way in. Her hair was down today, and she had some weight on her frame, wearing a red jacket over a bright fuchsia print blouse.

"Dobre den," she called to him, and he repeated the phrase back to her as he leaned in to briefly grasp her hand. "Such fine pronunciation," she said, and chuckled.

She had a demitasse cup and a plate of baklava in front of her, and Slater sat opposite, eyeing the server as she stepped over.

"Bring me a Greek coffee," he said.

Once the woman had stepped away, Svetlana spoke, her Russian accent flattening the vowels. "Thank you for coming, and thank you for being on time. So many people show up half an hour late and say 'traffic.'"

"I usually build in extra time for the drive."

"I want to introduce you to someone. A potential client for you. She's my customer." She raised her eyebrows. "Not as good a customer as you are. You should feel no obligation from me to work for her. This introduction is just a courtesy. I saw some potential work for you among her problems."

"Got it. What kind of business is she in?"

"She'll tell you about it. From me it would sound like gossip."

"I met your security guy," Slater said. "I almost never see you outside your workshop. Do you always have him around?"

Svetlana waited while the server set a little white cup in front of him, then waved a hand in a helpless gesture. "Any successful business has its detractors."

More like enemies, he thought, if she had an armed guard outside a business meeting. But he didn't need to get into that.

As he sipped the coffee, a woman walked in from the back, by the kitchen, and Svetlana smiled in recognition. Slater turned to look. Clad in jeans and a mustard-yellow top, with a briefcase dangling from one hand, her wild black hair was tied back. Like lots of Angelenos, her vibe was Latin.

Leaning in, the woman greeted Svetlana with a kiss on each cheek. No way could he even imagine doing that with her. Slater rose as she turned to him.

"This is Elvaine," Svetlana said.

Elvaine smiled, revealing even white teeth. "Don't get up for me. That's so old-school." She turned to the server. "Is that Greek coffee? Get me one of those."

Svetlana rose then and looped the strap of her handbag onto her shoulder. "I'll leave you two to talk."

"Thanks for the intro," Elvaine said.

"You're both so frugal, drinking only coffee and eating nothing but air. It's on me." She paused at the register to hand the server some cash, then walked toward the back door.

Setting her briefcase where Svetlana had been sitting, Elvaine took the chair adjacent to him, shifting close to the table once the server set down her coffee. She tapped the edge of the plate of pastries. "Are these yours?"

"Svetlana must have ordered them," Slater said. "Go nuts. So what do you need my help with?"

Munching on a chunk of baklava, Elvaine wasn't shy about talking with food in her mouth. "Sveta said you're a field person. I'm more of a desk person. A journalist by trade. I've gone as far as I can in my research, and I wanted to get some help."

"Are you related to Svetlana?"

Her brow furrowed. "I'm not. I buy equipment from her. Stuff to record interviews and for music. Why do you ask?"

"You called her Sveta. I've only heard her relatives do that. What exactly are you researching?"

"A guy named Boris Brooks. He was a freshman at Live Oak College, and he disappeared. He was last seen on campus. In his dorm room."

"I know Live Oak. It's on the east side of the Valley."

"Right up the road," Elvaine said. "One night Boris just evaporated."

Slater sipped his java. "What do the cops say?"

"They investigated, and looked for him, and interviewed lots of people, but they couldn't figure out what happened. They never officially closed the case."

"When did this happen?"

"The spring of 1988."

"Are you kidding me?" Slater demanded. "It's too long ago. I'm not a historian."

"I just need a fresh pair of eyes. Maybe you'll have insights into things that I missed."

"I can't see how."

Elvaine set down the baklava and held his gaze. "Hear me out, Slater. Just for a minute. Let me lay it out for you before you say no."

He folded his arms. "What's your ultimate goal in finding this guy?"

"It's not about finding him. I want to find out what happened, and then I want to write about it. The case needs a resolution. I've been obsessed with it for a while now."

"Have you seen the police file?"

"I was able to make copies of it, and I interviewed almost everybody they interviewed, plus other people they hadn't bothered with." She reached for her briefcase and zipped open the top, pulling out a tablet and tapping at it.

Slater reached for a piece of baklava and took a bite. It was crisp and flaky and perfect. He waved to the server and waited for her to step over. "Can you box up half a dozen of these to take with me?"

"Sure." She smiled and stepped away.

Elvaine handed him the tablet. "These are some photos of Boris. You can swipe through."

The first image was a studio portrait, taken from the chest up against a mottled sky-blue background. Boris looked to be a basic white dude, but he was handsome. His dark hair was styled thick like they did in the eighties, and his front teeth were slightly misaligned. The next image was another portrait, Boris in a royal-blue gown and a mortarboard, with the same smile. Unlike the first image he had a little acne on his cheeks.

Slater turned the screen toward Elvaine. "High school graduation?"

"Right."

The next few photos depicted Boris standing with a group of people, some of them holding red plastic cups, at a party maybe. They all looked to be college age. His skin had cleared up. Dressed in a baggy shirt and pants, Boris stood next to a guy in a jacket with oversize shoulders, both of them with skinny little neckties. One of the women wore a dress in blocks of neon pink and green, another had exaggerated shoulder pads like a linebacker, and everybody had big hair.

"They're all dressed like it's the 1980s."

"Those were taken on campus," Elvaine said. "You can tell it's in the dorm by the cinderblock walls."

Next was Boris's driver's license photo. Those were never flattering, but he looked hot, with that solid jaw and his pale brown eyes.

"Boris was a smoke show," Slater said.

"Maybe he still is, if he's alive. He'd be in his mid-fifties." She set down her cup. "The night he disappeared was in the middle of exams. Everybody was stressed out. In the dorm, Boris shared a room with a guy named Jeff. That evening, another guy on their floor put a dead fish in Boris's bed."

"Gross." He furrowed his brow. "Was he trying to send a message? Like a threat? 'I'm going to send you to sleep with the fishes?'"

"It was just a prank. Apparently they used to do things like that to each other. Boris did too. Anyway, Boris went to the desk downstairs to get clean sheets for his bed around 8 p.m. Jeff was in the library and came back to their room around 9 p.m. Boris's textbook was sitting open on his desk. His keys and his wallet with his driver's license were there, and his signet ring and his watch were in the drawer. The police report said his toothbrush was still in the bathroom, and his car was in the parking lot."

"What did he drive?" Slater said.

"A 1982 Dodge Aries sedan. Kind of a warm cream color. The Aries was one of the K series."

"K-cars were sweet. Are you a car whack?"

Elvaine raised her eyebrows. "I drive a car. I'm not really into them."

He watched her for a moment. The fact that she remembered tangential stuff like that, the fine detail, meant that she was invested in this.

"And nobody ever heard from Boris again," Slater said.

"The cops got involved the next day, and local media covered the story. The fire department got a bunch of students to help search the Sepulveda Dam. It was like wilderness back then, trees and brushland. They also dragged the Encino Reservoir." She sipped her coffee. "In the weeks after he went missing, there were some sightings. One woman up in Big Bear said Boris knocked on her door one night that summer, and asked to use the phone, but she didn't have one. When it happened, she didn't recognize him, but later she saw his photo on a poster or a flyer some-where. She said the guy who'd come to her door looked just like Boris."

"Did the cops follow up on that?"

"How could they? The woman didn't report it for a couple weeks, and nobody else saw him up there. All they could do was record the incident and ask around." She raised her eyebrows. "The most compelling sighting was a year later. A woman who taught at Live Oak was in New York, and she spotted Boris or his doppelgänger at lunchtime in a restaurant in Midtown. He was sitting at a table with other people. She said they were dressed like office workers. She knew him from the flyers and the media coverage, but he wouldn't have known her—Boris wasn't in her classes. She said she sat at another table and couldn't help but stare at him, and then it felt like the guy picked up on it, and soon after, he walked out."

"Did she follow him?" Slater said.

"She didn't have the nerve to do that, but she was certain it was him."

"And since then, nobody's seen him?"

"Nobody who's gone on the record." Elvaine sipped her coffee.

"Was there any other evidence of what might have happened?" Slater said.

"That night in the dorm, the night he disappeared, Boris's psych textbook was left open on his desk to a page about psychotic breaks."

"Was he majoring in psych?"

"In the first year he was doing a general arts program," Elvaine said. "He hadn't declared a major yet. The textbook thing was odd because he'd already written his psych exam, so he was done with the book. He would have been study-ing for other exams. Leaving it open to that page implied he was concerned about having a psychotic break. To me that seemed suspicious."

"Too on point," Slater said. "Like it was staged."

"Exactly." Elvaine waved a hand. "Who reads up on a mental health problem right before they have a mental health problem?"

"So the last potential sighting was thirty-five years ago," he said. "What about John Does in the morgue? Did the cops check?"

"They monitored those for a while, around LA and in other states. A few times out-of-state agencies requested details on Boris when they had an unidentified body that kind of fit his description, but they were never able to match his fingerprints. That hasn't happened in at least twenty years."

"If he was spotted at Big Bear," Slater said, "he could be up there fertilizing the pine trees. A person could wander into the forest and never be found."

"He's not at Big Bear," she said intently. "I've done so much research—into his professors, his connections, his friends. Have you heard of MKUltra?"

"That sounds like a superhero movie."

"It was a CIA program that hired academics to do research on brainwashing and psychological torture. They wanted to use it for interrogations. It was totally secret, but the details came out in the 1970s. Supposedly they shut down the program then, but why would they just stop? There's no real oversight of those agencies, and by design everything they do is shrouded in secrecy."

Slater frowned. "How is Boris connected to MKUltra?"

"Boris's psychology professor, a guy named Cameron, was deep into the program. He's dead now. In an interview he once claimed he'd only worked on interrogation research until MKUltra got shut down, but I have records showing that he still took money from the agency into the 1990s, right up until he retired. I'm talking lots of money. The book Boris left open on his desk was the text from Dr. Cameron's class."

Slater folded his arms, watching her talk. It seemed so tenuous, so long ago. "What do you think happened to Boris?"

"Boris was gay. That's partly why Sveta thought you were the man for the job."

"It takes a queer to track down a queer?"

"That might be it." Elvaine chuckled. "Sveta's a *chingona*. She put us together for a reason."

"I don't know that word."

"I mean she's a badass." She leaned toward him. "I think Boris's psych professor was involved in some secretive government program. The extension or the descendant of MKUltra. I think they used it against Boris to recruit him into something nefarious."

"Like what?"

She sat back. "I have no hard evidence. Just inferences. But when you stack them all together, they feel like evidence. There's interviews and documents that explain how the spy agencies recruited gays and lesbians for covert intelligence work."

"Boris was hot," Slater said. "He would have been perfect for that. A honey trap to seduce closeted Soviet men."

"The Cold War ended a few years after Boris disappeared, but I'm sure the spy shenanigans never even slowed down."

Slater thought about it for a minute. "So why would they want him to make a total break from his family, and from his school? Why not wait to hire him until he'd finished his degree?"

"I think they were using psychological manipulation

to get total control of people. MKUltra was literally about brainwashing. The perfect employee has nothing else to do but work for you—no family obligations, no distractions. If it was about down-low stuff like intelligence gathering, he'd have no one to gossip with." She threw up a hand. "We know the feds do all sorts of shady stuff, and they have capabilities to make people disappear. Like the whole witness protection thing."

"Why would Boris go along with a total break like that?"

"I'm not sure. People who knew him portray him as an ordinary kid. But nobody knows what's going on inside someone else's head."

Sipping at his coffee, room temperature now, Slater drained the last of it, down to the muddy grounds. "I'm going to have to pass. If I took your money, I'd be ripping you off—I just can't see any possible positive outcome."

Elvaine huffed. "Will you at least look at my research files? I'll pay you to do that. If you go through everything and still can't see any way forward, I'll accept your refusal."

He had to grin. "I guess tenacity is a useful quality for a journalist."

"I'm thinking you're a mutt like me, right? Latin and something else."

"My father was Latin, and my mother's white, if it matters."

"I'm Latin and Malaysian. From my dad. He says his people were go-getters. Tenacious types. That's where I get it from." She raised her eyebrows. "I have copies of my files for you. In my car."

"They're on paper?"

"It's how I work. I find it easier to organize paper than peering at a bunch of digital files on a little screen."

"You're putting a lot of trust in me, believing that I'll take your money and actually do the reading."

"Svetlana trusts you. She says you're smart. Do you need cash up front?"

He pursed his lips for a moment. "Let me look at what you've got first."

"Great." She smiled. "Journalists aren't big earners, but I do have the money. I got a grant to write a book about the case."

"Who gave you that?"

"A philanthropic literary organization."

That felt cagey, but their identity probably didn't matter, he decided. "Do they have an agenda for Boris's story?"

"They want to see a book." Elvaine held his gaze. "Nonfiction. But they're not invested in specific outcomes, and neither am I. I just want answers."

"I get that. Unanswered questions are like an itch that you need to scratch."

"No matter how ugly or unwanted or improbable it is, the truth is the truth," she said. "It always has a beautiful consistency. The pieces all fit."

"I understand that too. It's satisfying because it knits the world together."

Elvaine leaned in and slapped his forearm. "You see? You already know where I'm coming from."

Elvaine got up and zipped her tablet into her briefcase. Slater pulled out his wad of cash and stepped over to the register to pay for his pastries. He carried the little pink box out to the parking lot and watched as Elvaine opened the lift gate of her SUV. She pulled out a banker's box, lifting it with both hands.

Slater set the pastries on top of it and grabbed the handles. It was heavy. "This is a lot of freaking paper."

"Let me know if you have questions. I'm sure you will." As she closed the lift gate, she added, "I never got your number."

He recited it as she tapped it into her phone, then walked over to the Continental, and put the box in the trunk.

TWO

ONCE SLATER WAS BEHIND the wheel he headed to the freeway and through the Cahuenga Pass to his place. It was an obnoxious modern box on a hilly street that was still mostly houses from the last century. Built by some idiot gentrifiers, he'd had to buy it when he got involved with Pike, to make room for what they needed to build. He didn't actually call it a relationship, as the word was too limited, too square. It was better described as a multidimensional narrative complex.

Pulling into the garage, he opened the trunk as the door rolled down and retrieved the heavy banker's box and the baklava. He carried them up the stairs, past the floor above the garage, where there were a couple of bedrooms, to the top floor, with the kitchen, and a big room that was mostly empty except some lounge furniture at one end, and the French doors to the deck.

Slater set the box on the dining table that sat just past the kitchen, and pulled the lid off, and started to lift out the stacks of documentation. Elvaine had it sorted in bundles bound with oversize spring clamps. He started to pile it around him on the table, scanning the top pages to assess what they contained. Interspersed with the stacks were loose photos. Some of these he'd seen on Elvaine's tablet, but others were new. They were all images that included Boris, sometimes with other people, sometimes on his own, posing with a birthday cake or sitting at a desk, always clad in bland eighties clothes. In many of the shots the guy seemed distracted, sometimes smiling and energetic, but often looking like he wasn't really present.

Sometime later he heard the sound of the front door. That was Pike. Slater's heart pounded at the very thought of him. Finally. He'd been out of town for work for a couple of days. Soon Pike appeared at the top of the stairs and flashed that easy smile. Built thick, with a perfect bit of flab, Pike wore his dark hair slicked back, today clad in black chinos and a dress shirt.

Slater rose to wrap his arms around him, and ran his hands over his back, and briefly kissed him. "I missed you."

"Me too," Pike said squeezing the back of his neck. "You're warm."

"Are you done for the day?"

"Oh, yeah. Too much time behind the wheel." He pulled back and gestured to the dining table and the banker's box and the stacks of paper. "What's all this?"

"A new gig. I'm not even sure if I'll do it. I have to do some reading first."

"It looks like there's lots of that." Stepping over to the table, he picked up the pink pastry box and flipped open the lid. "I love baklava. Are these reserved, or can I have one?"

"They're for you," Slater said intently. He raised his voice. "Everything is for you. The sun and the moon and the stars. Everything orbits your white-hot Pikeness."

He chuckled and fished out a piece. "Just the one,

then." Pike bit into it, and through a mouthful mumbled, "It's good."

Slater stepped close to him, and cradled his head in his hands, and met his mouth, tonguing a bit of flaky pastry on his lip. Putting his hands on the sides of his belt, he pulled him closer, and ground his burgeoning woody into his thigh.

"You're getting me revved up," Pike said, squeezing his biceps. "You should fuck me. It's been too long."

He pulled back. "So hop to it, son."

Pike ate the rest of the baklava as he walked through the kitchen to the head of the stairs, and down to the bedrooms. They slept in the one facing the street, and the one in back had a bed and a desk that Pike used when he worked remotely. He'd dropped his overnight duffel on the floor next to the closet, Slater saw, and watched as Pike pulled off his shirt and dropped his trousers.

"You're going to have to do all the work," Pike said. "I'm wiped out."

Slater sat on the side of the bed to untie his boots, and kicked them off, and soon they were both naked. Stretching out next to him, Pike folded his arms behind his head. Slater shifted beside him and grabbed his cock, hard now, and met his mouth as he stroked it.

From the bedside drawer he grabbed the lube, then reached between his legs and worked a thumb into him. Watching Pike's shifting expression, the look on his face, got him rock hard. Moving up, he pressed into him, pausing when Pike grimaced.

Despite his claim of not having any energy, Pike got into it as Slater started to pound him, looming over him and grabbing his shoulders, then moving close to inhale the scent of his hair. As he climaxed he strained into him, then sank on top of his body for a minute, catching his breath.

When he pulled back, he took Pike into his mouth, and worked him hard. Pike ran a hand into his hair, gently guiding him, and soon yelped and spasmed as he came. Slater pulled away and flopped onto his back.

"That was so damn hot," Pike said.

"You're so damn hot," he mumbled. It was such a good feeling, right afterward, when he was satiated. Sleep felt close, and he knew he could easily drift into it. Instead he forced himself to sit up. "I need to get back to work."

Once he'd washed up and pulled his clothes on, he went upstairs and carried a pile of Elvaine's files out onto the deck, setting them on the patio table. The marine layer had retreated and the sun was out now. May gray and June gloom were LA's fifth season, between spring and summer, when the days were overcast until the afternoon. It never rained, and it never got very warm, it was just gray, and it made everything feel muted and languid.

Slater sat for a minute and absently eyed the California fuchsia he'd planted in boxes spaced around the low wall that surrounded the deck. They were starting to bloom in brilliant red. A lone hummingbird flitted around one of them. It needed to be cut back a little. But not today.

Scanning the documents in the stacks of paper, he saw that Elvaine had gone down some deep rabbit holes. One thick collection wasn't even about Boris, but covered MKUltra and the allegations that there were similar degenerate programs ongoing. He pulled off the big binder clip and started going through the pages.

Boris's psychology professor, Dr. Cameron, had definitely worked for the military. Elvaine had compiled quotes and statements from his grad students about the work he'd done. There were transcripts of interviews and copies of articles by other journalists about other topics, but Elvaine had connected the dots, highlighting the salient sentences and paragraphs in fluorescent yellow.

One of Cameron's colleagues had said that very little of their actual research was ever made public. Other pages showed that Cameron had published several journal articles in the field. One stapled sheaf of photocopies was an article he'd written about interrogation, dated 1991. Slater read the summary on the first page, but more interesting was the handwritten note in red ink in the top corner:

The feds paid Cameron $40K for this.

Elvaine's handwriting was sharp, and dense, and clearly legible. Below the note she'd written a file number. All these documents bore numbers, he realized, in the top right corner of each front page. She'd carefully catalogued all her research.

Deeper in the stack was a document that cited Cameron's payout for the 1991 research. This one had a sticky note in Elvaine's distinctive handwriting:

MIBs noticed this FOIA request.

He knew that FOIA was the Freedom of Information Act. It allowed regular slobs who weren't part of the bureaucracy to request documents from the feds. This page actually did bear a bunch of stamps and record numbers and initials—that implied it had been filed in some government archive. The strange part was the reference to MIB. That had to mean the men in black. Slater had come across them before, when he'd been dealing with the saucer-heads. They were shadowy types that tried to intimidate UFO witnesses, but there was no agreement on whether they were the Navy, or aliens, or something else. What the hell was Elvaine talking about? Dr. Cameron and his mind games had nothing to do with flying saucers.

Slater reattached the binder clip and picked up the next

stack. This was a collection of interviews done with Boris's parents. There were a lot of pages. Some of them were on police department letterhead, written in terse language, and another was titled "Interview by S. L. Hughes, *LA Daily Bugle*." It wasn't a piece that had been published in the newspaper, he saw, but rather a raw transcript. Somehow Elvaine had convinced this journalist to share their source files.

Also in the stack were a dozen or so news clippings that covered Boris's disappearance. They came from the *Bugle* and other local newspapers, most of them long defunct. Elvaine had organized them in the order they'd been published, and he got absorbed in reading them. Right after Boris had gone missing the tone of the stories bore the urgency of a missing persons case, but as the months went by they took on a feeling of resignation. The last article in the stack was a ten-year revisit of the story. It had nothing new to add.

The next heavy stack of paper was titled in thick black pen in Elvaine's handwriting: "Evidence that Boris is gay." As he got into it, he realized she'd spun this part of the story to him, presenting it as established fact. But this collection made it look more like an informed conclusion. The first page was a summary of the evidence, in bullet points, with cross-references to the subsequent documents.

The first was "Boris dated only one woman in college: Heather." When Slater flipped to that page, it was a transcript of an interview by the initial investigators with Heather, asking what she knew about Boris. Elvaine had highlighted a paragraph several pages in, where Heather had said, "We went out a couple of times, but there was nothing romantic." A few paragraphs below that, she denied flat-out that she'd ever slept with Boris. The cop had asked her that directly, and then rephrased the question twice more, as if he didn't believe men and women could hang out together without having sex.

The next document in the list was "The girl Boris took to high school prom." Elvaine had interviewed her many years later, and in the transcript she said, "It was just a date to prom. We were completely platonic."

Another page in the stack of evidence was a set of printed notes with no sources listed. These had to be Elvaine's own musings:

> Boris didn't sleep in his room the Saturday before he disappeared. He wasn't at his parents' house. No one ever said where he was. The police assumed it was a hookup, but no one ever came forward. If it was a woman, even off-campus, she would have heard that he was missing and she would have stepped up and said something. A closeted gay man would have kept silent to protect himself.

Slater sat back and thought about it, closing his eyes for a moment and turning his face to the warm sun. In aggregate it did paint the picture that Boris was a closet case, but Elvaine was still making an assumption.

The next note in the list was about smoking:

> Boris didn't smoke. People who confirmed that: his roommate, Jeff; his mother; his sister, Bettina; Mike from the dorm. But he always carried a pack of cigarettes with him, according to the roommate and to Heather. Why did Boris carry cigarettes?

Elvaine hadn't answered her own question, not on this page at least, but she'd included this with the evidence that Boris was gay for a reason. It felt like a canny insight: Carrying smokes was an easy way to meet other guys, and lots of gay guys smoked. When you lit someone's cigarette, it let you get close to them for a moment, long enough to figure out if you might get some action.

At the bottom of the stack were the first few pages of another journal article, with the publishing details and the summary on the front. Dated 1984, it had been authored by Boris's psych prof, Dr. Cameron: "Psychological Profiles of Men Discharged from the Armed Forces for Homosexual Activity." Elvaine's only analysis was DATED, written in caps in red ink at the top of the page. She probably meant it was outdated thinking, as gay sex wasn't a psych diagnosis anymore, and they didn't kick queer people out of the military these days.

Pike stepped out through the French doors. "It looks like you're deep into it."

Leaning back in the chair, Slater set the stack on the table. It was getting late, he realized. The sun was still out but it was casting the golden light and long shadows of the end of the day. "I got lost in the flow of it."

"Should I get tlayudas from that Oaxacan place?"

"Suits me."

Pike went back inside, and a while later, when he heard the doorbell, Slater scooped up the stacks of paper and carried them inside, setting them with the others on the dining table.

When Pike brought the food up, they ate outside. He talked about his road trip, about him and his colleague Hopkins interviewing people in pawn shops in small towns in the Central Valley.

"You do that a lot," Slater said. "Hitting the hock shops."

"Tracking down firearms is the ATF's bread and butter."

After they'd eaten, Pike folded up the wrappers. "Are you going to take that case? All the paper makes it look like there's a lot to it."

"I feel like I'm getting sucked into it," Slater said. "I'm just not sure if there's anything I can do. It's about a guy who went missing forty fricking years ago."

His eyebrows shot up. "Who wants you to work on that?"

"A journalist. She's writing a book."

He told him about meeting Elvaine, and eventually they went inside, and Pike pitched the food wrappers in the trash. Dusk was setting in, and Slater sat at the dining table to read more of the files.

One thick stack was a copy of the police file, and he started flipping through it. The original notes had been produced with some ancient technology that capitalized every letter, like the whole document was shouting. Each of the letters was made up of visible little dots. Elvaine had highlighted a couple of lines: "Dr. Cameron says that during the spring semester, Boris saw him three times during office hours for hypnosis treatment." In the margin, Elvaine had written in red: "Why was Cameron treating Boris? Why did no one ask Cameron that?"

He tossed the sheaf onto the pile he'd already been through. The next stack was a fat bundle of paper with the top page titled in Elvaine's handwriting: "Spy agencies use gay men for intelligence work." Going through it, he found photocopied pages from published books, a couple of journal articles, and transcripts of several interviews Elvaine had done herself. Taking a breath, he set to reading.

From World War II on, it seemed, the government recruited gay men to be spies. Early on they used blackmail techniques to sign them up, threatening to out them in an era when that would mean losing your job, or getting locked up in a psych ward, maybe even going to jail. The military and the three-letter agencies never officially admitted it, but they never officially admit anything, Elvaine noted in the margin. She had found dozens of tangential references to the practice. Many were interviews with guys who'd been roped in and then talked about it much later in their lives, when they had less to lose, less fear of breaking a nondisclosure order.

Eventually he set the stack down and rubbed his eyes. Dr. Cameron had profiled gay men that got turfed from the military, and he'd researched brainwashing and interrogation techniques. If the feds needed someone to coerce gay guys into one of their spy programs, this knucklehead would be a perfect fit.

It was getting late, and Pike had gone to bed a while ago. Rising, he went to the kitchen, pulling open the cupboard where they kept the booze, his cheap-ass quotidian bourbon and Pike's tonier scotch. The booze rules said he could have half an inch, but he was bleary-eyed from all the damn desk work. Pulling out a tumbler, he poured his ration, but let it flow a little longer, adding another finger.

Walking over to the French doors, he looked out at the glittering lights of the Financial District in the distance, and lifted the glass to savor the heady fumes. As he took that first sip, he relished the burn in his throat, coughing a little at the intensity of it.

Boris fucking Brooks. He'd been sucked into it now. Giving him that banker's box was an effective gambit— Elvaine knew it was too tantalizing to turn away from. Slater slammed the rest of the bourbon and went downstairs.

Pike was in bed, his lamp still on, his nose in a hardback. Once he'd ditched his clothes, Slater climbed in with him, and sidled up to him, inhaling the scent of his armpit.

"What is wrong with you?" he demanded.

Pike frowned. "What are you talking about?"

"You smell amazing. Your skin feels so damn good. It's like electric dope, and I'm a helpless junkie in your thrall. Why do you do this to me? I can't keep my paws off you."

He chuckled and shifted to shove his arm under Slater's neck. "You're done with your reading?"

"Not yet. I did figure out that my client is running a gimmick on me."

"She lied to you?"

"Not that I know of. But that box of paper is like those irresistible monsters who sang sweet songs for Odysseus. When he tied himself to the mast but then he struggles to escape so he can swim over and get with them."

"The Sirens."

"That's Elvaine. She knew I'd totally get sucked in."

THREE

S LATER WOKE TO HIS phone buzzing on the night-stand. It was morning, he saw, with the usual May gray outside the windows. Pike was already gone. It wasn't an alarm, he realized—his phone was ringing. Scrabbling for it, he struggled to focus his eyes on the screen. Elvaine.

"There's no moss growing on you," Slater said when he picked up, his tongue thick.

"Your voice is weird. Are you still asleep?"

"I was just eating some peanut butter."

"So what are you thinking?" she said.

"My eyes are messed up from all the reading, and I need to get out of the house. Can you swing by my office? It's in the Fashion District." He rattled off the address.

"I actually live close to there," she said. "I can probably walk."

Forcing himself out of bed, he got dressed and went upstairs, and ate a chunk of baklava, then slurped at the tepid coffee Pike had left in the pot. Once he'd loaded all the files and stacks of paper into the banker's box, he carried it down to the garage and put it in the trunk of the Continental.

Slater backed into the street and waited for the door to roll down, then drove to his office. It was in a century-old building that had once been white-collar space but now was almost all sewing factories in the bustling clothing-industry neighborhood.

Parking the Continental in the surface lot across the street, he retrieved the banker's box and carried it over to the lobby. A couple of day laborers were studying the sticky notes on the wall advertising gigs in the factories upstairs, sewing and carting rolls of fabric and delivering garments. Riding up on the poky ancient elevator, he walked around behind the shaft and admired the lettering on the door as he twisted his key in the lock:

SLATER IBÁÑEZ

MAXIMILLIAN CONROY

INVESTIGATIONS

The suite had a small office for him and one for Max, plus a front office between them with a desk that their operatives sometimes used. The place looked a lot more professional since their operative Etta had put some color on the walls and updated the furniture.

As he stepped in and flicked on the lights he double-clicked his tongue to greet Rey Pascual, a little plaster statue that sat on the front desk, a skeleton holding a scythe and wearing a crown.

He stuck his head into Max's office to make sure he really was here alone, then in his own office set the banker's box on his desk. A knock came at the door, and he stepped out to pull it open. Elvaine was dressed in jeans and a white shirt, today with a tweed jacket over it, her black hair tied back. She had two paper coffee cups in hand.

"You like espresso?" she said.

"I'm not going to lie to you, Elvaine. I like it a whole lot."

She smiled and handed him the smaller one, and Slater waved her in.

"I love the deco furniture."

"One of my operatives did the renovation. Apparently it's all vintage."

"Who's this?" She pointed to the statue on the front desk.

"His name is Rey Pascual," Slater said. "He's not the narco saint, even though everybody thinks he is. He's actually pre-Columbian."

"I know about the narco saint. Santa Muerte. She's female. Can you text me this guy's name? I want to read up on him."

Slater led her into his office, and sat behind his desk, and waited for her to take the guest chair across from him.

"Who's Maximillian Conroy?"

"My business partner." He reclined and laced his fingers behind his head. "You're good, I'll give you that."

"You mean my research?"

"I mean the old bait and switch. You hand me this box and say, 'Just have a look.' Of course I got sucked into it. It's like getting caught in a riptide, and now I'm thirty miles from shore."

Elvaine laughed. "I'm glad it's compelling to anyone besides me. It's hard for me to be objective about any of it."

Sitting up, he pried the lid off the little paper cup and sipped the coffee. It was still warm. "How long did it take? All this research."

"Years, Slater. I've been at it on and off for over a decade."

"How many of these witnesses are still alive?"

"Some of them. The roommate and the sister are both here in town. Boris's parents are dead, and Dr. Cameron is dead. That's actually a good thing—I think the world is a better place without him."

"Preach, sister. From what I read here the guy was a trash bag."

"So you're in?"

"I'm not done reading all the paper in that box," Slater said, "but I'm basically hooked."

She beamed. "That's such good news."

"You wrote somewhere in this stuff that the MIBs noticed your Freedom of Information request. What did that mean?"

"MIB means men in black."

"I know who they are. They try to shut people up when they know too much about flying saucers. You think Boris got taken to Zeta Reticuli?"

"I didn't mean it literally. After I pulled those documents, about Professor Cameron's connection to the military, I noticed that I was being surveilled."

Slater frowned. "By who?"

"Good question. I worked at a radio station at the time, a regular nine-to-six. I'd see these guys in ghost cars parked outside my office, and parked on the street at my apartment, and then sitting there watching me walk out of the grocery store. They were always men, and they were always in pairs. They dressed like suburban dads on Saturday, chinos and polo shirts, but I'm sure they were military. They were fit types and had super short hair. It wasn't really aggressive, but I know they meant to be intimidating."

"OK," he said evenly. Maybe he'd committed to this too soon—she was starting to sound delusional.

"Eventually I confronted one of the guys," Elvaine went on. "He followed me into a shop, a little *tiendita*, and I asked him why he was following me. He pretended like I was the crazy one." She mimicked a deep voice: "'I don't know what you're talking about.' Things got shouty, and the shopkeeper eighty-sixed us both. Out on the sidewalk, the guy said, 'Why don't you just let it go? Write about something else.'"

"That sounds like an admission that they were interested in what you were doing," Slater said.

"After that they stopped bugging me." She shrugged. "It's hard to believe, right? It sounds so paranoid. I bet you don't believe me either. And who could I possibly complain to? I think their assignment was to try to unnerve me for a while, then give me that warning, and then move on. It's effective, right, because when I talk about it, I sound crazy. They weren't really the flying-saucer men in black, but it was the same kind of operation." She raised her eyebrows. "And when someone tells me to back off, I only want to dig deeper."

"When you're running an investigation," Slater said, "if nobody's pissed off at you, you're doing it wrong."

"You know what I'm talking about." Elvaine shifted in her chair. "About the next steps. I have a research session set up tonight. The results might impact how you proceed. I can fill you in tomorrow, and get you some money."

"What kind of research session?"

She held his gaze. "You can't judge me."

"You're paying me, ostensibly. You'll get better results if you tell me the whole truth. No spin and no varnish." He raised his voice. "Sing, sister."

"Dude—chill." She frowned. "It's a séance."

"To talk to Boris? You think he's dead?"

"I'm not sure. The session is just to gather more information. It might not even happen tonight. I have to round up a couple more bodies before we can do it."

"I'd be down for a séance. How many people do you need?"

"The psychic said it takes five total, so I'm short two."

"Text me the details," Slater said. "I can bring my boyfriend. He loves all that psychic bullshit."

Her eyes narrowed. "I said no judgment. You can't be part of it if you're a debunker. You'll inhibit the ethereal channels."

"I can behave." He briefly held up his palms. "Maybe you'll educate me. And I'm not a debunker—I've actually seen some inexplicable stuff myself."

"Like what?"

He raised his eyebrows. "I saw bigfoot. Out in the Great Basin in Nevada."

"Well, that's just bullshit," she said, holding his gaze, then rose, and scooped up her coffee cup, and walked out.

Slater had to chuckle at that. Elvaine seemed to be on the ball, but then the men in black, and now a séance. What had he signed up for?

Lifting the box off his desk, he locked up the office and carried it down to the street, lugging it across to the Continental. Once he'd slammed the trunk, he walked back out to the sidewalk and up the block, scanning the side streets until he found a *lonchera* parked at the curb. Most of the menu was tacos, but he got a basic burrito, and ate it over the gutter, then threw the wrapper in the trash.

Back at his house, once he'd pulled into the garage, he carried the box upstairs and set it on the dining table. With a deep breath he pulled the lid off and got into it, heaving out a stack of files he hadn't been through yet. Carrying them out to the deck, he sat in the muted gray daylight and started to read.

Elvaine had transcribed her talk with Boris's sister, Bettina. Her interview technique was effective, pulling out lots of detail, and actually read like some of the cop interrogations. But he could see some things that she missed, questions she should have asked. Pulling out his phone, he did a search for Bettina.

There weren't many people with that name, and even though her last name wasn't Brooks anymore, he quickly tracked down a Bettina who looked to be about the right age. On her website she called herself an herbalist, and she ran a shop in Venice that specialized in magnesium supplements.

That was trendy right now, he knew, one of the current health crazes to separate people from their money. Plants needed it, and when he'd done horticulture he saw magnesium deficiency once in a while, evident in a specific pattern of yellowing in the leaves. They treated it by mixing a fertilizer that contained magnesium compounds into the soil. He texted Elvaine:

Does your Bettina run Mondo Mg on Abbot Kinney?

Her response came almost right away:

That's her place.

A moment later came a second text:

Who's the skinny guy with the scythe on your front desk?

He'd forgotten about that, but clearly Elvaine hadn't. He texted back:

Rey Pascual. He's the king of the graveyard.

Next he read through Elvaine's interview with Boris's dorm roommate, Jeff, and what he'd said about the days leading up to the disappearance. There were no details in it that he hadn't seen before.

Another sheaf of stapled pages bore the police department's logo. He'd been through the police file already, but this was another part of it—notes from the cops who processed Boris's car. They enumerated the contents of the vehicle: a jacket on the passenger seat, identified as Boris's, and some junk-food wrappers on the floor. The unusual thing they'd found was his violin. One of the investigators had added a note:

> The violin case was on the back seat, visible from outside. Most students wouldn't leave anything of value because of the risk of it getting stolen. Campus PD reports the dorm parking lot was well-known for vehicle break-ins.

Downstairs he heard the front door—Pike on his way in. It seemed early, but when he checked the time on his phone, it was later than he thought, well into the evening.

Pushing himself out of the chair, he went in through the French doors, and dropped the stack of paper next to the box on the dining table, then descended the stairs to the bedroom. Pike was at the closet unbuttoning his dress shirt.

"You're so fricking beautiful."

"Let me get my pants off first, forty-niner. Then I can maul you."

"I don't think there's time for that. I may have signed us up for an event this evening."

Pike raised his eyebrows. "A three-way with some guy you met at the car wash?"

"I wish. It's a séance."

He laughed as he stepped out of his pants. "Why are you going to a séance?"

"For my case. You don't have to come if you're tired."

"How could I ever be too tired for a séance? Maybe we can talk to the victims of Flight 370 and find out where the plane went down."

Slater put his hands on his hips. "That's the first thing that comes into your head when you hear the word 'séance'?"

"What bigger international mystery is there? It's pretty compelling."

"You are such a weirdo." Grasping his waist, he pulled him close, and nuzzled his neck.

"But you love me anyway."

"I love the weirdness," he murmured, and mouthed his jaw. "Every weird cell in your body. Your weird-ass pheromones. I love everything about you." Eventually he pulled back. "We should head out."

"So what do you wear to a séance?" Pike said.

"No idea. I'm wearing this."

Pike pulled on a pair of tan chinos, and a fresh shirt, and they trooped down to the garage. Once they'd climbed into the Continental, Slater put the address Elvaine had sent into the navigation on his phone, then backed into the street, flicking on the headlights. By the time they got to the psychic's place, the gray sky of dusk had faded to full darkness. The shop was on the east side of Hollywood, the less gentrified part, in a strip of tired retail storefronts.

Once he'd parked at a meter farther up the block, they walked back. In the front window was an unlit neon sign, a big lurid eye with a few spiky lashes surmounted by blocky letters that read PSYCHIC.

"This must be the place," Pike said quietly.

A sign hanging inside the glass door said CLOSED, but when Slater tried the handle, it was unlocked, and they stepped inside.

The lights were down low, and there was a lot of open floor space. Farther back were five chairs at a round table draped in black cloth.

Elvaine called out a greeting, and they walked over to where she was standing, at a table against the wall. It bore an array of candles, the kind in tall glass jars with colorful renderings of the saints. All of them were lit and flickering.

Once Pike had introduced himself, and Elvaine told him who she was, she gave them the once-over.

"You two make a cute couple."

Pike laughed. "I'll take it."

"Cute?" Slater said. "Seriously?"

Pike put a hand on his shoulder and gently squeezed. It wasn't a warning, exactly, more a tacit admonition: *Cool it.* Not many people could tell him what to do and not get punched in the face. From Pike it landed differently. It didn't even make him mad.

"We're just waiting for the boyfriend," Elvaine said, "and of course Tanya. She's the psychic."

"I'd say Tanya is Catholic." Slater gestured to the candles.

"Who's the kid?" Pike pointed to the small painting propped against the wall in the middle. Barely taller than the jars, it depicted a child holding a staff and carrying a basket. "She's got the golden glow around her hat. That implies she's a saint too."

"I can tell you're not Catholic," Elvaine said.

Pike met her gaze. "I'm Jewish."

"That constitutes a valid excuse." She eyed Slater. "You must recognize him."

"I know Catholic is the default setting for brown folks in this town, but I'm also one of god's chosen people. We do candles but not paintings."

"Well, I don't go to mass, but like they say, once a Catholic, always a Catholic. It's not a little girl—that's Santo Niño. The child version of Christ. He's a big deal in Zacatecas."

"Maybe Tanya comes from there," Slater said. "Lots of Angelenos do."

Elvaine lowered her voice. "It makes me wonder if Tanya was in prison. I don't know her very well."

"Do jailbirds put up pictures of Santo Niño?"

"He's the patron saint of the wrongly accused, and of prisoners."

"If she's out now, she's paid her debt," Slater said. "It doesn't matter what happened before. Nobody's beyond redemption."

She waved an arm. "That's what Santo Niño would say."

"It's not superstition. Just common sense. You can't write people off for their mistakes."

Pike leaned in to study the image. "I wonder why he's wearing a scallop shell on his cloak."

"That means he's been on the Camino de Santiago pilgrimage in Spain."

"How do you know all this," Slater demanded, "if you're not all devout, and thrashing around on the church floor, and speaking in tongues?"

Her eyes narrowed. "Catholics don't actually do that. I wrote a long-form article about that church on the plaza in the pueblo. It's called La Placita. It's one of the oldest buildings in the city. They have a shrine to Santo Niño." She nodded to the painting. "Besides the staff and the basket, you can recognize him because he always has the lace collar and the floppy hat."

Slater put his hands on his hips. "Do you have OCD? Because it seems like when you dive, you dive deep. All the minutiae in your files. You knew that Boris drove a K-car all those years ago, and what color it was."

She laughed. "I've never been diagnosed, but I'm definitely detail-oriented."

"I'm sure that's a useful skill as a journalist," Pike said.

The front door swung open, and a guy stepped in.

"Here's the old ball and chain," Elvaine said.

He was about her age, and had his Black hair in a short natural style, and a neatly trimmed beard. His pecs were visible under his dark shirt, and his jeans revealed the musculature of his thighs. Totally fuckable, Slater decided.

As he stepped over, Elvaine introduced him as Niles,

and he squeezed her around the shoulder as he greeted them.

"So are you a regular séance-goer, Niles?" Pike said.

He eyed Elvaine sidelong. "When you're with someone who has the energy level of a raccoon on bennies, you just have to try to keep up."

"I'm way more functional than anybody on speed," she said, and waved a hand.

A woman stepped out of the back, through a heavy black curtain hung in the doorway, and walked toward them. In her fifties, maybe, she looked Latin, her graying hair tied back, wearing a black cardigan, a faint smile on her face. She had an accent when she spoke.

"Welcome," she said. "My name is Tanya. I see we have quorum. Please sit."

FOUR

NTERESTING THAT TANYA DIDN'T ask their names, Slater thought. Maybe she already knew them psychically. He sat at the round table between Pike and Elvaine, with Niles on her other side, leaving the last chair for Tanya. Once they were all seated, Tanya turned off the room lights, leaving the only illumination in the space the flicker of candles over by the wall. She came to sit with them, her bulky shadow suddenly lit when she struck a match, the brightness accentuating the wrinkles on her face. She reached in to light the broad flat candle that sat in the middle of the table.

"I ask you to keep your palms on the table, no matter what happens," Tanya said. "Focus on the flame. I will form a bridge to the spirit world."

"Is this just about Boris," Pike said, "or can I ask other stuff?"

Elvaine frowned. "Let's stick to Boris. You can set up your own séance if you have afterlife business."

He chuckled. "Fair enough."

Elvaine had slung her handbag over the back of her chair, and she twisted toward it now and dug in it, producing a small piece of paper. It was a photo, a headshot of Boris, and she set it on the table next to the candle. Slater had seen that one before, an image of him grinning and looking into the camera.

"Let's place our hands flat on the table," Tanya said. "You don't have to close your eyes, but try to clear your mind as you watch the flame. Focus your gaze on it, and think about Boris."

Slater planted his palms on the table along with the others. The five sets of hands made stark symmetry against the black cloth. It was vaguely eerie, and definitely created the feeling that something structured and serious was going down. It would be too easy to drift into sleep if he closed his eyes, he realized, so he kept them open, and focused on the photo, then on the little flame.

Staring at the candle, Tanya's eyes glazed over. She closed them for a while, and then spoke, a sudden sharp sound, loud enough to make him sit up straighter.

"We're looking for Boris Brooks."

Tanya tilted her head back and repeated the name. "He was last seen on this plane almost forty years ago."

When she straightened up again, her eyes had changed—they were darker now. Slater could feel the hair prickle on the back of his neck. How had she done that?

Tanya looked at each of them in turn, a vague smirk in her expression now. "We don't know Boris."

"He might have crossed over more recently," Elvaine said. Her tone was matter-of-fact, like she was explaining a transaction to a bank teller or a post office clerk. "He played the violin."

Screwing her eyes shut, Tanya cocked her head to one side, then opened her eyes and spoke. The voice was different again, higher, and without the accent. "There is no Boris here."

Something underneath the table thumped audibly, and Slater felt the surface move under his hands. Had somebody kicked a table leg? But it felt like the table had jumped straight upward. He glanced around at the others in the flickering light of the candle. Niles's eyes were wide, but his hands were still splayed on the cloth.

Tanya turned her head and focused on Pike. "Amsterdam," she said flatly. Next she looked to Elvaine, and paused a moment. "He's still with you." Another pause, and then she met Slater's eye. "Pay attention. Go east." Her gaze moved on to Niles, and a minute later, she said, "Right beside you."

Then she closed her eyes, and tilted her head back, and took a few breaths. When she opened them they looked gray again, the way they had before. Leaning in, Tanya blew out the candle and moved her hands into her lap. "Boris is not on the other side."

Rising, Elvaine went to the wall to turn on the room lights.

"The spirits said that?" Slater said, and waved a hand.

Tanya met his gaze. "You heard them."

"Do you believe everything they say? Maybe they have their own agenda. Maybe they're playing you."

"I have close personal relationships in the spirit world. They have no reason to lie to me." She got to her feet. "I must rest."

Niles stood up and arched his back, and Slater and Pike rose too.

Elvaine walked toward the back room with Tanya. "Thank you for doing this. I know it takes a lot out of you."

"It's my calling," she said, and gestured dismissively. "You can send the fee to my phone number."

They watched as Tanya disappeared through the black curtain.

"That was intense," Niles said.

"It might be a calling," Slater said, "but Tanya definitely gets paid."

Pike gestured at the room. "Candles aren't free, and neither is the rent on this place."

Elvaine stepped back to the table. "I have to hustle. I've got a gig tonight. Can we debrief in the morning?"

"You're reporting on an event?" Slater said.

"I'm playing in a bar. I'm a singer-songwriter." She frowned. "Did I not tell you that?"

"I'd say you're a renaissance woman," Pike said. "Can we come? I'm into live music."

"That would be great. As long as you clap." She told them the name of the bar and the street it was on, and she and Niles led the way out to the street.

Walking back toward the Continental, Slater interlaced his fingers with Pike's. "You didn't even ask her what genre she plays."

"How bad could it be?"

"Well, Tuvan throat singing comes to mind, and yodeling, and thrash punk, where she screams and throws overripe tomatoes at the audience."

Pike laughed. "If you see any tomatoes, we can walk."

Once they'd climbed in, Slater started the engine and pulled out. The bar was on a side street in another part of Hollywood, just a few minutes' drive.

"I didn't even ask the question about Flight 370," Pike said, "but she answered it."

"When she looked at you, she said 'Amsterdam.' That flight went missing over the Indian Ocean, not Europe. How is that a reasonable answer?"

"In the search zone where they think the plane went down, there's a little speck of rock called Amsterdam Island."

"OK, that's odd, I'll give you that," Slater said. "I wondered if maybe she has the room bugged. That's why she kept us waiting, so she could eavesdrop and get some ideas about what to tell us."

"I don't think I said anything about that airplane in her shop, did I? It was only in my mind."

"I guess the spirits already knew what you were thinking."

"And you," Pike said. "You're supposed to pay attention and go east."

"Pay attention to what? It's so damn vague. Like those horoscopes—'You'll encounter someone today, and later on you'll eat something.'"

"You know, both those things happened to me today. You might totally be psychic."

Slater scoffed. "Go east. What the hell does she mean by that? East like the train station, or east like Tel Aviv?"

"I guess you could hire her and find out."

"The whole thing smells like a racket."

He found a meter space around the corner from the bar, on a street lined with businesses that were closed at this hour. A guy was standing on the sidewalk, next to a doorway with the steel shutter rolled down over it. He had a scraggly beard, and wore a grubby jacket, and spoke as they climbed out.

"That's a beautiful car."

Slater glared at him. "It better stay that way."

"Are you going to be here for a while?" Pike said. "Maybe you could keep an eye on it for me."

"For a twenty I will."

"How about a sawbuck now, and another when I get back?"

"Deal."

Pike dug out a bill and handed it over. "What's your name?"

"They call me Digger."

"Thanks for keeping an eye on it, Digger. I'll be back in a while."

As they walked away, Slater briefly squeezed him around the shoulders. "You're smooth, daddy-o."

"Twenty bucks is a lot for parking, but it's cheap for security."

Around the corner and in the next block, Slater gestured to a doorway. "Here's the gin mill."

There was no one on the door, and they walked in to the familiar din of booze-fueled conversations and the scent of stale beer. The place was old, with a high arched ceiling, and bare wooden rafters. It had likely been a film production space in a previous incarnation. This neighborhood had been the center of the film business a century ago, before the studios and their vendors moved farther out when they needed more room.

"This doesn't feel like a hipster place," Pike said.

"That means the booze won't be overpriced."

Most of the tables were occupied, the loud conversations echoing off the concrete floor. The bar ran along the back, and at one side was a low stage. Sitting at a table just in front of it was Niles, and he waved them over, and they sat on either side of him. When the server came by, Pike pointed to Niles's drink.

"Is that draft? I'll do one of those."

"Me too," Slater said.

Once she'd stepped away, Pike eyed Niles. "What did Tanya mean when she told you, 'Right beside you'?"

His brow furrowed. "I've been thinking about that. I'm not completely sure. I've been worried about my life, and money, and whether I should change jobs. The big question is about security. Like, where is my stability going to come from?" He picked up his beer glass. "Maybe the answer is the woman sitting right beside me."

"I wonder if Elvaine slipped the psychic a twenty to say that?" Slater said.

Niles laughed. "I wouldn't put it past her."

When the beer arrived, Pike paid for it, and they clinked their glasses against Niles's. Soon after, Elvaine stepped out on the stage, an acoustic guitar in hand. She hadn't changed clothes but her hair was down now, and her eyes bore darker makeup.

The room got a little quieter, as some of the crowd were paying attention, but lots of people were still talking. Elvaine sat on the stool and adjusted the mike close to her face before she spoke.

"Hey, everybody. My name is Elvaine, and I'm going to play a couple songs for you."

Niles hooted and clapped, his eyes bright. Slater and Pike and some of the others joined him. As she started to play, the sound didn't drown out the bar talk, but they could hear her well enough. Her guitar work sounded crisp, and when she sang her voice was plaintive, the pace slow, nothing like the confident journalist persona he'd seen.

> I walked the darkness looking for you
> But you weren't there in the night
> Stood on the edge and called your name
> To the shadows obscuring the light

The piece had a couple of verses and a chorus, and at the end people clapped, and Niles hooted again. Elvaine played a few more songs, with the same sober and introspective tone. After the set, she rose and made a little bow from the neck, then stepped off.

Once the clapping subsided, Niles said, "Give me your digits. I'll send you a link to her album."

Slater recited his number, and watched as Niles thumbtyped it. A moment later he felt his phone buzz in his pocket.

Niles waved the server over, and ordered another round, plus one for Elvaine. When the glasses arrived, Slater dug out his wad of cash to pay for it, and set the change on the tabletop. Elvaine came out to sit with them, and Pike congratulated her, and asked her some questions about her music. Talking about it, she was more animated than when she was talking about Boris or during the séance.

"I've never heard that name before," Pike said finally. "Elvaine."

Niles leaned toward him and raised his eyebrows. "She was named after an alien."

Pike laughed, his tone deep, and eyed Elvaine. "You need to elaborate on that claim."

"It's true," she said. "My mom was really into UFO lore. Elvaine was an alien who lived on our planet for a while and drove around in a VW Beetle. My mom drove one too. She was kind of an outsider. I think she identified with Elvaine."

"Well, that makes perfect sense," Slater said.

"It doesn't, I know that. But that's how she was. She moved up here from Colombia and lived life like she was in a candy store." She spread her fingers in the air on either side of her head. "Perpetually wide-eyed."

"She sounds like a lot of fun," Pike said.

"It wasn't really fun for me. She'd forget things. Like parenting."

"Was Elvaine the alien real or from fiction?" Slater said.

Elvaine shrugged. "How real are any of those alien stories? Elvaine was in a book from the 1960s. It was published as nonfiction."

"I can usually discredit those early contactee stories when the aliens start talking about Jesus," Pike said.

Elvaine chuckled. "They do that?"

"A lot. In those books from the fifties, they usually save

it for the last chapter."

"I should look again. I have that book on a shelf somewhere."

"We have all the books on shelves somewhere," Niles said. "I'm afraid the floor is going to collapse."

Another musician stepped out onto the stage, a skinny guy with a lot of hair and a tight black T-shirt. His appearance elicited scattered applause, and he squatted at an amp to plug in his electric guitar.

"It's going to get hard to talk when he plays," Pike said.

Slater drained his beer and stood up. "We're out."

"Do you need your change?" Niles said, and pointed to the bills on the table.

"It's for the server."

Once they were out on the street, Slater relished the cool night air. Pike wrapped an arm around his waist.

"I liked her music. I think it's more powerful when it's the person who wrote it."

"She can pull it off. I'm kind of amazed she has the focus to write long-form journalism and to write music. It doesn't jibe with what Niles said, about the raccoon on speed."

When they turned the corner, the Continental came into view up the block. The passenger door hung open, with a bulky form leaning inside.

"Fucking royal fuck," Slater muttered, and hustled over. Reaching in to grab the back of the guy's collar, he yanked him out of the car and heaved him across the sidewalk. His body struck the steel shutter with a loud *bang*. It was Digger, the guy Pike had paid to watch the car. His eyes were wide.

"I didn't take anything."

"Goddamn tweaker schvantz. How did you get the door open?" Slater threw a punch, fast and light, striking him on the chin. "Why do you make me do this to you?" he demanded. "Why do you do it?"

The guy tried to grab him, but he was moving slow, maybe addled by dope or booze. Slater threw up his arms to shove Digger's off and struck him again.

"Stop it." Digger dodged sideways and stumbled up the sidewalk. "I didn't take anything, you bully."

"Spread out," Slater said through his teeth, and watched for a minute as he shuffled up the block.

"He pulled everything out of the glove box," Pike said, leaning in the passenger door. "He must have been looking for stuff to hock."

"There's nothing worth stealing."

Slater stepped around him and sat down, taking a minute to replace the paper and charging cables and napkins scattered on the seat and the floor. Arms folded, Pike watched from the sidewalk.

"I don't think anything's missing," Slater said finally, and climbed out.

"I shouldn't even have talked to him."

"At least you saved yourself another sawbuck."

"Is the door lock broken?"

Slater closed the door, and pulled it open again, then tried his key. "I don't think so. He probably had a slim jim in his jacket. Those work great on classic cars. I wonder why he didn't break in as soon as we walked away?"

"He probably went to the liquor store first," Pike said, "to get crunk on that ten bucks, then came back with the Dutch courage."

They climbed in, and Slater nosed into the street, and drove to his house. Once they were upstairs in the bedroom, he started to undress, ditching his clothes in the bottom of the closet. Pike stepped out of his trousers and then came closer, stroking Slater's biceps.

"*Bam*, right in the chops," he said. "Digger didn't know what hit him."

"You like it rough?" Slater jutted his chin. "I can play rough."

Pike met his mouth, and lingered in it for a minute, hot and intense. He squeezed Slater's cock, chubby now, then pulled back and slapped his face, hard enough to turn his head.

Slater inhaled sharply. He could feel the surge of adrenaline and his heart start to pound. "You shouldn't have done that."

His eyes narrowed. "What are you going to do about it?"

Grabbing his wrist, Slater spun him around and shoved his arm up his back. Pike yelped and let him do it, even though he could easily have pulled out of it. He pushed him onto the bed and climbed up to straddle his hips, then leaned over to grab a pair of handcuffs from the bedside drawer.

"Let me take my shirt off first," Pike said.

Slater climbed off and watched as he sat up to unbutton it and take it off, revealing his beautiful torso.

"Where were we?" he said, and grinned.

Shoving him onto his belly, Slater straddled him again, and grabbed his arms, and cuffed his wrists in the small of his back. Flipping him over, he ground his woody into his thigh, then shifted back, and shoved his knees up, and pressed into him.

Pike winced as he got into it, and Slater paused for a moment, making a show of being aggressive but taking it slow. Eventually he was deep into him, then pounding him. He leaned in to mouth his neck and his jaw, burrowing his nose into Pike's sweaty hair. That heady smell sent him, and he came, then sank into the warmth of his body, relishing the feeling of Pike's sweat-slicked skin.

Pulling back, he squeezed his cock. "You're really hard."

"That's your doing," Pike said, and jutted his chin.

Straddling him again, Slater sank onto him, easing himself down, focusing on Pike and the look on his face, leaning in to massage his pecs and his biceps. Eventually he was rocking back and forth, and Pike was thrusting up into him.

"Hoodlum," Pike said through his teeth.

"Speak up, son, I can't hear you." Slater slapped him, not holding back, hard enough to elicit a gasp.

"You're a psycho," Pike spat. "A goddamn lowlife." His face contorted and his head craned back as he came.

Eventually he climbed off and unhooked him. Pike massaged his wrists in turn, and then stretched out and killed the light. As Slater sank toward sleep, he was momentarily roused by Pike's voice.

"That never gets old."

FIVE

WAKING TO GRAY DAYLIGHT outside the windows, Slater forced himself to roll out of bed. Once he'd showered and got dressed, he went upstairs to find coffee in the pot, and poured himself a mug. He could see Pike out at the table on the deck, so he grabbed a banana and headed toward the French doors, frowning at the sight of the banker's box and the stacks of files cluttering the dining table as he walked past. Outside it was warm despite the gloomy gray sky.

"You're up early." Pike was already dressed for the office. As Slater sat adjacent, he set his phone on the table next to a crumb-strewn plate.

"I've got some work to do."

"So we've got shabbat dinner with Doris tonight."

"Damn it," Slater snapped. "Who's idea was that? She doesn't even do shabbat."

"She didn't actually call it that. But it is Friday."

"It's OK to say no sometimes."

Pike grinned at him. "It's just dinner. You'll survive."

His phone buzzed, and he pulled it out to check. Elvaine.

"We should talk," she said when he picked up. "Do you want to meet at your office or at a coffee joint?"

"It's easier to talk at my office. Give me an hour."

After he'd eaten his banana and gulped down most of the java, he rose and knelt in front of Pike, pressing his face into his chest, then digging his nose into his armpit. "You smell amazing." He was lucky, he knew that. Lucky to have this guy in his life. It made his stomach hurt when he thought about it too much.

Pike ran a hand into his hair, watching him, his eyes soft.

Eventually Slater kissed him and then rose. "Later, pretty boy."

Inside he piled all the paper into the banker's box and carried it down to the garage, loading it into the trunk of the Continental. When he got to his office, Elvaine was walking up on the lobby as he hustled across the street with the box under his arm.

"Wait up," she called, and they got on the elevator together.

"You walked here?" Slater said.

"My apartment is on Spring Street. It's faster to walk than to get in and out of the parking lots." She gestured to the box. "Sorry it's so heavy."

"I'm not worried." Stepping off on his floor, he set the box down in the hallway while he unlocked his office, then heaved it up and flicked on the room lights as they went inside.

Slater set the box on his desk, and sat in the chair behind it, and waited for Elvaine to get settled. She hung her handbag on the back of the guest chair as she sat, then picked up the plaster statue that sat next to his computer monitor, a naked guy standing with a horse.

"Another tchotchke." She read the name engraved

along the base: "Pollux. It looks like a bookend. I bet Castor is the other one."

"You'd win that bet."

She raised her eyebrows. "So where's Castor?"

"On Pike's desk. He gave me that."

"That's so sweet. Castor and Pollux. You know they were brothers, right? They weren't actually sleeping together."

"They also got greased during a cattle rustling incident. I have no intention of doing anything like that either." He sat up. "So the psychic came up snake eyes on Boris. What does that change?"

"It means we're not looking for his grave, or for his bones," Elvaine said. "We don't need to waste time checking out unidentified corpses that turned up through the years. We can still focus on where he might be now."

"I know you've tried to get the feds to squawk. I saw several Freedom of Information Act requests in your paperwork."

"Those are next to pointless. At best they slow-walk them, or claim ignorance."

Slater rose briefly to pull the lid off the box and dig out a sheaf of newspaper clippings. "A lot of these articles that were in the paper had the same byline. Is that reporter still around?"

"I actually talked to him, years ago," she said. "I got some of his original interview notes. But he's dead now."

"Along with lots of the other witnesses." He set the clippings on the desktop. "You said the sister is still around, and the roommate. I read your interviews with them, but I need to talk to them both. What about the friend the cops thought was his girlfriend?"

"Heather. She's here in town too. I can set up meetings with any of them. With Bettina, it's easier just to go to her shop. She's always there."

"First try the not-girlfriend, then the roommate," Slater said.

"When are you free?"

"He gestured widely. I'm working for you now. Anytime you say."

Elvaine nodded. "Can I use your front desk?"

"Knock yourself out."

She stepped out, and he overheard her side of a phone call. Slater half listened as he flipped through the sheaf of news stories. A few minutes later Elvaine stepped back in and sat across from him.

"Heather's working today. She's at one of the studios in Culver City. I set up a meeting for you at that mall with all the steps. She said she'll be carrying a book with a red cover to make her easy to pick out of the crowd."

"Good idea."

"She asked me how to identify you."

"Tell her I'll be wearing a white gardenia."

Elvaine's eyes narrowed. "You're really going to do that?"

"I would, but they're in season, so everybody will be wearing one." He waved a hand. "She doesn't need to spot me. I'll find her."

"I didn't get hold of Jeff, but I left him a message."

"About that night Boris disappeared," Slater said. "I saw in the police file that he left all his personal stuff but he took his student ID card with him."

"That's a supposition." She raised her eyebrows. "What we know is that his student ID card wasn't with the other things he left behind—his wallet and his driver's license, his watch, his keys, the signet ring he wore. Something else might have happened to his student card."

He asked her more questions about other parts of the files, things that stood out as potentially significant but that weren't clear to him. Elvaine had some answers but didn't hesitate to say, "I have no idea." Eventually he sat back.

"You're an excellent respondent," Slater said. "You don't make assumptions unless there's evidence."

"I'd call that solid journalism. It's out of fashion now. These days journalism is more like, 'You won't believe these seven amazeballs things that happened in Congress this week.'"

"Your way works better if the goal is the truth."

"I should give you some money," she said, reaching for her handbag. "What do you need to start?"

"Two grand will keep me rolling for a while."

Digging in her bag, she pulled out her phone. "Can I wire it to your number?"

"Cash is better for me."

Elvaine met his gaze. "I'm not one of your shady down-low clients. I'm going to deduct whatever I pay you as an expense. I'll need receipts."

"Fine," he said flatly. "Zap it to me."

Once she'd tucked her phone away, and hoisted her handbag onto her shoulder, Slater got up and pressed the lid onto the box. He tucked it under his arm as he killed the lights and followed her into the hall.

Once they were down on the sidewalk, Elvaine said, "I'll let you know when I hear back from Jeff."

Slater crossed to the surface lot and loaded the box into the trunk, then drove toward Culver City. The sun was starting to burn through the marine layer, and it was bright out by the time he nosed into the garage under the mall.

At street level it was an open and sprawling pedestrian space. The mall building was tiered on the outside, with steps that led up to more shops. There were a lot of people here, he saw, and most of them looked like desk jockeys and office drones, especially the ones sitting in the restaurants.

Near the stairs up from the garage Slater found a coffee

joint, and bought an oat-milk latte, and stood scanning the crowd as he sipped at it. Before long he spotted a woman with a red book in hand. She was the right age to have been in college with Boris, her faux dirty-blond hair bobbed short, wearing a bland gray suit. Like him, she was scanning the crowd. This was Heather.

"With that book you look like a street preacher," Slater said, stepping up to her.

She didn't smile as she gave him the once-over. "You're Ibáñez?"

He pulled a dog-eared business card from his hip pocket and handed it over. Not looking at it, she tucked it into her jacket.

"The book is for a film project," Heather said. "It's the only thing I could think of that would set me apart."

"I get it. The look you're working is corporate drone." He waved at the mall. "There's plenty of those around here."

She frowned. "I'm actually a department head at the studio."

"I know that's the industry here," Slater said. "Film and TV. It explains why this place is so white compared to the city."

"It's not that white."

"You can't perceive it because of your white privilege."

She raised her voice. "Should we go find a bench?"

"Do you need a coffee or something?" He gestured with his paper cup.

"No," she said flatly, and led the way up the outdoor stairs. The terraces higher up had backless wooden benches built into the layout, where people were hanging out and eating in the sun.

"This is also a city, by the way," Heather said, walking abreast.

"If you say so. Culver always makes me a little nervous.

It used to be a sundown town. Guys who looked like me had to vamoose by dusk."

She sat on a wooden bench in the shade of the building, and when he sat next to her, she set the book between them.

"This place is really poorly designed," he said, looking around.

"People in my office love it. The consensus is that it's fresh and eclectic."

"It's also ugly, and the bulk of the structure blocks the sunlight." He pointed to a wall. "That's south, so the plants aren't loving it. It's stupid to plant *Gaillardia* here. They thrive in big sun."

"I guess you can't please all the people all the time."

"Or the plants." Slater picked up the book. It was thick, with the spine labeled DOSTOEVSKY and CRIME AND PUNISHMENT. He set it down again. "This must be a thousand pages long."

"It was written a hundred and fifty years ago. It's been adapted for the screen nine times."

"And you're filming it again. I'm so glad to hear your industry is embracing innovation."

"You sound like a critic." Her eyes narrowed. "We can't just film anything, you know. It has to make money."

"That explains why movies aren't good anymore."

"I don't actually need feedback from a ..." Heather hesitated, her eyes flicking over his body.

"From a blue-collar grunt?" he said. "A fungible peon? You can say it. Others have." He waved it away. "Tell me about Boris Brooks."

She looked away and took a breath. "Boris was a sweet guy. He worked hard at school, and played his music. It threw everyone off when he disappeared."

"You dated him."

"It was really just once. We went to a family wedding. My family. I asked him to go as my plus-one."

"That's not what you told the investigators at the time."

Heather frowned. "You read their files?"

"Some of them."

"The police never got any traction on the case. I wish they'd just drilled down and looked harder. You'd think their core competency would be finding people."

"You can spare me the corporate double-speak. I'm not part of that world."

She scowled. "It's just the way I talk."

He watched her for a moment as he sipped his java. Even in reacting to him she was guarded, with zero warmth. Why were corporate types always like this?

"What you told the police was that you went out together a few times."

"In hindsight I'd say that was aspirational. I wanted to be Boris's girlfriend. I had a serious crush on the guy. I would have gone for it if he'd shown any romantic interest. And then he was just gone."

"Apparently Boris carried cigarettes with him," Slater said. "Do you remember that?"

"Not really. I'm not sure why he'd have those—he didn't smoke. I would have known."

"You mentioned Boris's music."

She raised her eyebrows. "He was quite accomplished with the violin."

"A natural talent?"

"I'm not sure about that. Technically he was good at it, but a lot of that is just practice. I wouldn't say he was an artist."

"The Saturday before he disappeared," Slater said, "Boris didn't sleep in the dorm. Was he with you?"

"We weren't sleeping together. I don't know where he

was that Saturday. The last time I saw him was earlier in the week. At lunch. Thursday or Friday."

"At the time you told the cops it was Friday."

"Well, there you have it. I remember they kept hounding me to admit that we were romantically involved, but it just wasn't true." She waved a hand. "Boris spent a lot of time in his dorm room. He and his roommate had a Trinitron. They'd watch movies. Most kids didn't have a setup like that. There wasn't much space, and that kind of equipment was expensive."

"What's a Trinitron?"

"A high-end television set. From when they were big heavy cubes."

"Did you ever get the sense that Boris was gay?"

"I never saw him with a man," Heather said, "but I never saw him with any women either. I was attractive enough in college, but he never looked at me that way, so I'd say gay would make sense. It would explain his indifference to me."

"Can you think of any other indicators that he was gay?"

She waved a hand. "I wouldn't know. Gay wasn't as big a deal back then. I assume more people were closeted. If Boris was gay, he was definitely closeted."

"Do you think Boris is still alive, or buried somewhere?"

"How would I know that?"

"When people get taken out, it's usually by friends and family."

She scoffed. "I had nothing to do with it. It was traumatic for me when he disappeared. Shocking. We kept expecting he'd turn up somewhere, and phone somebody. Then the days turned into weeks, and the school year ended, and then it was months, and years."

Slater sat up. "Maybe you could turn it into a script, instead of the tenth reboot of *Crime and Punishment* here."

"So why are you bringing up Boris now? Is there some new information?"

"Elvaine brought me into it. I'm just getting started."

"That woman is obsessed. What is there to be gained? Nobody's going to pay her for all this digging. It was so long ago. It seems hard to believe you'll come up with anything new."

"Is there anyone else I should talk to?"

"His roommate, Natasha. They knew each other well. I bet he'd have a better handle on the gay question."

Slater frowned. "I haven't heard that name before. When was Natasha his roommate?"

"Natasha was a nickname. Just in the dorm. His real name was Jeff."

"Why did they call him Natasha?"

"You'd have to ask Jeff."

He stood up. "You've got my card. Let me know if you think of anything else."

"That's vanishingly unlikely to happen." She rose with him. "I have to say I'm confused as to why Elvaine sent you here, and why she thinks I might suddenly have new information for her."

"Don't feel bad." He shrugged. "Lots of people are stupid." Turning away, he walked toward the stairs, and paused when he got down to street level to check his phone. No word from Elvaine about meeting the roommate, Jeff, or Natasha, but it was still shop hours—he could talk to the sister.

NOSING THE CONTINENTAL UP into the daylight, Slater headed west toward Venice. Culver was already halfway there, but it was slow going in the traffic, even though it was still early afternoon. He found a meter space in front of the address for Bettina's shop. There was no mistaking this was the right place, with a big sign along the top of the building that said Mondo Mg. Naming it that must mean magnesium was their primary product. It wasn't actually an herb, despite what Bettina called herself in her bio.

As he climbed out from behind the wheel, he stretched his back, then walked into the shop. One wall bore shelves of little boxes and bottles, like a mini supermarket, and on the opposite side was a bar, fronted in blond wood, with a row of white stools. Bright-green *Pothos* in ceramic pots sprawled at either end of the bar top. At the back was a counter where a guy in a white polo shirt stood at the register, chatting with a customer.

As he stepped in, a lanky woman called a greeting from behind the bar. Wearing the same white polo, her blond hair was tied back, and she looked to be well under thirty. Stepping over to her, he saw that the tag on her shirt said INTEGRITEE. From the contorted spelling, that had to be her name.

"You look a little harried," she said, and smiled.

"I hate coming to this part of town."

"There's so much traffic. It annoys me too."

"You only have yourselves to blame." Slater put his hands on his hips. "For decades you people kept voting down rail transit. Your maids and your busboys still have to get over here somehow. All that traffic is your reward for your short-sightedness."

Her expression sobered. "I've only lived here a couple years, and I don't have a maid."

"I didn't kill anybody." He raised his eyebrows. "I just loaded them into the boxcars."

"You know, I think you need an em-gee power cocktail. It elevates the mood and smooths out stress."

"What's in it?"

"Soda water, cherry juice, and magnesium powder. The *Mg* in our name is the abbreviation for magnesium." Holding his gaze, she enunciated the word clearly, as if he might not have heard it before. "It's an element that your body needs for its biological processes. Like oxygen or water."

"Lo, you learn something every day. Why do you call it a cocktail if there's no booze in it?" He waved a hand. "Speak slowly, so that I can understand."

"Cocktails don't necessarily have alcohol in them. It's a restorative."

"What's it going to cost me?"

"Twelve dollars."

"A small price to pay to get all smoothed out. Set me up." Sitting on one of the stools, he rolled his shoulders and watched as she started preparing the drink in a cocktail shaker. "Is Bettina here today?"

"She's out for a minute, but I'm sure she'll be back soon."

Integritee poured the contents of the shaker into a martini glass and slid it toward him. It was dark red and tasted like sour cherries and chalk.

"I'm feeling more blissed out already," he said, once he'd taken a slurp.

"I'm glad," she said, and smiled.

Too much magnesium must interfere with the ability to detect sarcasm, he thought, and dug out a twenty, and set it on the bar.

"Unfortunately we don't take cash."

"Of course you don't. Why would you?"

He dug out his phone and raised his eyebrows as he waggled it at her. Once she'd produced a card reader, he tapped his phone to it.

A guy walked in from the street and approached the bar, standing between the stools and leaning on it. Tall and pleasingly muscled, he had his faux blond hair tied in a little tuft on top, and was wearing stretchy black athletic wear.

When Integritee stepped over, he said, "Get me an em-gee brain boost cocktail to go."

She nodded and stepped away. Sipping at his chalky drink, Slater leaned back to check out his butt.

The guy looked at him and frowned. "Have I got something on my pants?"

"I don't think so. I'm just admiring the view."

"Dude," he said intently. "I'm not a piece of meat."

"What, you go to the gym so that people won't look at your ass?" Slater demanded. "And that shirt is tight enough that I can see your tits. You've got the assets, pal. Lean into it."

He scoffed as Integritee stepped over and set down a plastic drink cup with blotchy dark-purple contents. Once he'd tapped a card to pay for it he scooped it up and turned to leave.

"Was he upset?" she said, watching him walk out.

"Some people just don't know how to take a compliment." He rose and drained the martini glass. "I guess he really needed that magnesium boost."

The array of products on the opposite wall mostly looked to be supplements, and he stood reading some of the packaging. They all bore stylish minimalist labels branded with Mondo Mg.

A woman stepped up next to him, facing the shelves like he was, and tapped a little plastic bottle. "This is a spray. You mist it over tense muscles. It's great after the gym. It relieves pain and gives you instant relaxation."

She was wearing the same white shirt and trousers as Integritee, and Slater eyed her name tag—BETTINA. She looked a lot older than in her website photo, despite the makeup, and had her faux-blond hair pulled back.

"Magnesium can do that?" he said.

"It can. All the yoga studios are using it. I have trouble keeping it in stock."

He pointed to a little white tube. "This one looks like toothpaste."

"That's colloidal magnesium. You squeeze it into your morning tea."

"That sounds delicious."

"This is magnesium carbonate." She pointed out a clear bottle of ovoid pink tablets. "It helps you fall asleep. And magnesium bisglycinate relieves stress." She lifted a bottle of green liquid from the shelf. "Ozonated magnesium oxide improves digestion and mineral absorption. And this product helps with cognitive support."

"It sounds like magnesium is a miracle."

"It truly is," Bettina said. "It can really enhance your health, once you quit eating animal products and focus on organics."

"I'm already vegan."

She gave him a subtle once-over, her brow furrowing. "You're vegan."

"You know, Integritee just made me an em-gee power cocktail, so I'm not even going to call you a judgmental dipshit, because I'm all calm right now from the colloidal magnesium."

"That cocktail doesn't actually contain the colloidal form."

"I guess I should have known that," Slater said, "what with my new magnesium-fueled mental acuity. I'm here to talk about your brother Boris."

Her expression hardened. "That story just keeps coming back. Like an allergic rash."

"You should try a spritz of magnesium for that. It'll clear up instantly."

"What's your interest in Boris?"

"I'm working with a journalist. We're going over the case to see if we can dig up any new details."

"Elvaine," she said flatly. "You can tell her I don't have any of those."

"Still, I have a few questions."

Bettina scoffed and rubbed the back of her neck. She looked tired now. "All right. Come on back."

Walking behind the counter, she led him into a small office, and closed the door once he'd stepped in. The cluttered desk, the grubby floor, the haphazard stacks of stuff on the wire shelves behind her were the polar opposite of the sleek white minimalism in the shop.

As he dropped into the plastic chair in front of her

desk, he saw that she was wearing a silver medallion on a chain around her neck. It showed a figure with a halo and a gown, her palms outstretched at her sides. That had to be the Virgin.

"Where were you when Boris disappeared?" Slater said.

She folded her arms on the desktop. "Still in high school."

"What memories do you have of him?"

"We were close in age, so we scrapped a lot when we were younger. He looked out for me in school sometimes."

"Did he smoke?"

"I have no idea." Her brow furrowed. "I never saw him smoking, but he went away to college. Things change fast at that age. Maybe he started."

"What about Boris's music?"

"Our parents wanted him to play folk music. To be a fiddler. We had lessons basically from birth. For me it was the accordion. Boris's rebellion was to learn classical violin instead. It's the same instrument. He was definitely a disappointment to them. We were supposed to be all earthy, and he went for pretentious instead."

"Boris's whereabouts weren't accounted for the Saturday before he disappeared. Do you remember that?"

"The question came up at the time. He definitely wasn't at home. Nobody knew where he'd been."

"Was Boris gay?"

She scowled. "No way."

"How do you know that?"

"I would have known. I never saw any evidence. He took a girl to senior prom, and he had a girlfriend in college."

"You mean Heather?"

"I don't understand why Elvaine thinks I'd have anything new to say." She huffed. "It's the same old story. It's all been said already."

It didn't wash, Slater thought, watching her talk. Heather was never his girlfriend, not even for show. Talking to these twerps himself was definitely worthwhile—they were already contradicting each other.

"Is there anything else you can think of that didn't come up at the time?" he said.

"I hate revisiting this. Every time it's like reopening an old wound." Bettina took a breath. "I've got a box of Boris's stuff. You can look at that if you want to."

"What kind of stuff?"

"From college. As I remember, it's his class notes and essays. I haven't looked at it in decades."

"Did the police go through it back then?"

"Probably." She shrugged. "If they took it, they gave it back. It's sitting on a shelf in my garage."

"I definitely want to look through it."

"Give me your number. I'll text you when I get home. I'm usually there after nine."

Slater dug out a business card and handed it over. "What about tomorrow morning?"

"That works."

The office door swung open and a guy stepped in. Tall and losing his hair, he was wearing a powder-blue shirt and skinny-leg pants. A little nebbishy, Slater decided, but basically fuckable.

"Hey, babe," he said. "Am I interrupting?"

"I'll be free in a minute."

Slater stood up. "I was about to hit the bricks anyway."

The guy stepped back and flashed a little smile as Slater walked past. He was wearing a wedding band, the same as Bettina was—this was her husband.

Once he was out on the sidewalk, he paused to dig out his phone. There had to be a coffee joint around here somewhere. It couldn't all be wellness-industry jive. He'd need the joe to steel himself for the drive—the traffic was only going to get worse.

Checking the map, he found a place up the block, and walked there to get an espresso. He slammed it on the way back to where he'd parked at Mondo Mg. On the sidewalk he found a guy with his hands cupped to the passenger window of the Continental, leaning in, his athletic butt on full display.

"Again," he muttered, and quickened his pace.

Pulling the guy back by the shoulder, he spun him around and slapped his face, left and then right, a firm kovac.

"Keep your grubby paws off my rig," he said through his teeth.

"Get off me." The guy found his balance and shoved Slater back. His face was red. "What is wrong with you?"

He'd just seen this guy a minute ago.

"You're Bettina's husband."

"You can't just smack people."

"You can't just damage the merchandise," Slater said.

"I barely touched it. I was admiring it."

"What's your name?"

"Mark." He took a breath and adjusted his shirt collar. "I don't see classics like this very often. I was thinking it must get about four miles to the gallon."

"And yet it's more beautiful than anything built since. That's on the auto industry."

"Bettina said you were looking into her brother."

"Specifically what happened to him," Slater said. "Were you around when he disappeared?"

"That was well before we met. I heard all about it, though."

"Bettina doesn't seem that worried about it anymore."

"I think she's resigned herself to the fact that he's dead,"

Mark said. "She needed to move on."

"She knows for sure that he died?"

His brow furrowed. "You'd have to ask her."

Turning away, he walked up the block. He really was fuckable, Slater thought, watching him go. More significant, the guy was contradicting his wife, implying that she knew more about Boris's disappearance than she'd told Slater.

He climbed into the Continental and started the engine to get the air blowing. What was Bettina up to? On his phone he searched for her name again. There were lots of reviews and pseudo journalism about her shop, but one of the results was for a class: Life-Changing Vegan Cooking with Magnesium. Bettina was teaching it, and it was happening tomorrow. Tapping at the screen, he signed up for it, using the name John Slade. Eighty bucks seemed pricey, but it would give him a chance to see her in action.

SEVEN

IT TOOK SLATER AN hour to drive back to civilization, and he detoured into downtown so he could stop along Eighth Street, where the flower market was. By chance he spotted an open meter and quickly pulled in.

Dozens of prepared arrangements lined the storefronts along the sidewalk, and he stepped into a couple of shops along the block before he found the right thing, a bundle of daisies and cornflowers. The clerk greeted him in Spanish, and wrapped the stems in damp paper towel, and took his money. Back in his car, he set them on the seat and pulled into the traffic.

Pike was upstairs in the kitchen when he got to his house, still dressed for work. Standing at the counter, he had a knife in hand, and a sleeve of crackers in front of him, and a jar of peanut butter with the lid off. Slater embraced him, meeting his mouth, then pulled back and smacked his lips.

"Peanutty."

"My stomach was growling," Pike said, and wiped the corner of his mouth with a knuckle. "I wasn't sure when we were going to eat."

"You're so fucking beautiful." He raised his voice. "I can't stand it."

"Even with sticky fingers?"

"You could cover them in peanut butter and you'd still be beautiful. It's more than that."

He raised his eyebrows. "Some other dimension in our narrative complex?"

Slater mouthed his neck and ground his thigh into his crotch. Tilting his head back, Pike heaved a long sigh.

"Don't get me wound up. We have to go soon."

"It's your own damn fault." Slater stepped back. "Looking like this, smelling like this, eating crackers in the kitchen like a boss. Who does that?"

He raised his eyebrows. "I can't help it if I render you powerless."

Grabbing his belt, Slater pulled him close. Pike put his hands on his neck and kissed him again. Eventually he pulled back.

"Let's roll."

He put the peanut butter in the icebox, then opened a cupboard to pull out a bottle of red wine.

"You're giving that to Doris?" Slater said.

"I don't want to show up empty-handed."

"I'm not sure you need to be subsidizing her drinking habits. She's family. You don't have to put on the dog for family."

"It's just table wine. Nothing fancy." He waved him toward the stairs, and they trooped down to the garage, and climbed into the Continental. Pike lifted the bundle of flowers as he climbed in.

"These are great."

"They were on sale. Plus they're locally grown, so it didn't take an international cargo jet to get them here."

"You can't take flowers to an Orthodox house on shabbat.

The act of putting them in water is prohibited labor."

Slater put his arm on the seat back to look out the rear window as he reversed into the street. "Good thing Doris is a little more chill."

"You obviously planned this, buying flowers for her, but the wine is too much?"

"I've had a lifetime of figuring out how to manage her and her mishegoss," he said, waiting for the garage door to roll down. "You're new at this. You need to watch your back."

Pike chuckled. "I can handle Doris."

"I hope so. You probably should have brought your sidearm."

He headed to hilly Mount Washington, and onto Doris's street. Her Buick was in the driveway, next to her stupid boyfriend's stupid Boxster.

"It looks like we're going to have to deal with fricking Albert." Slater pulled the Continental up tight to the little car's rear end.

"He won't be able to leave," Pike said.

"Not without going through me."

When they climbed out, Pike paused to look over the row of plants along the front of the house, ground-hugging greenery with a cloud of small red blossoms clustered on stalks.

"These are dramatic."

"They like the shade," Slater said, "so they're thriving here."

Doris stepped out the front door to greet them. With a petite frame, she had some gray in her dark hair, today tucked behind her ears. She was wearing jeans and a Breton top.

"Aren't those beautiful?" Doris said. "Remind me what they're called."

"Coral bells." Slater leaned in to kiss her.

Planting an arm on his back, she led them inside. Albert was standing in the kitchen, his white hair too long for how sparse it was, wearing a fugly brown cardigan. Pike shook his hand, exchanging a loud bro greeting. The guy was such a cornball sometimes. He didn't need to get on Albert's good side. Albert didn't have one.

Pike briefly embraced Doris and handed her the wine.

"Thank you, sweetie," she said, examining the label.

"I figured for the havdalah."

"What's havdalah?" Albert said.

"The end of shabbat," Doris said. "It's tomorrow."

"How can you be dating a Jewish woman and not know that?" Slater demanded.

Albert frowned. "I know what shabbat is."

"I'm not really religious," Doris said, and eyed Slater. "Neither are you."

"It's culturally insensitive," Slater said intently.

She raised her eyebrows. "Are those for me? I love cornflowers."

Slater handed her the bundle. "I know you do. Unlike some people, I pay attention."

Doris embraced him again. "My sentimental son." Handing Albert the wine, she said, "We don't have to wait. We'll drink this tonight."

As Albert stepped to the counter and started to peel the foil off the top of the bottle, Doris waved them into the dining room. Food was already set out on the table.

"I ran out of time to cook," Doris said as she sat, "so I ordered in falafel."

Pike sat next to her. "This looks amazing."

"She already likes you," Slater said as he sat down, and frowned at him. "You don't have to butter her up anymore."

"Not every compliment has a hidden purpose," Pike

said, and laughed. "It really does look like a great meal."

"He has manners, sweetheart." Doris met his gaze. "Something you managed to avoid learning, despite my strenuous efforts."

He scowled and looked away, then slurped at his wineglass when Albert handed them around.

"What were you up to that filled up your day?" Pike said.

Doris chatted about it, her afternoon of volunteer work organizing for an upcoming election, and Pike asked some questions about it. He was so nice to her, and Slater knew it was authentic, even though it felt grating to listen to it. Pike liked people, and knew how to talk to them. It made his heart ache to watch the guy just being himself.

Doris was animated too, gesturing and laughing as she engaged with him. She would have loved to have had a son like Pike, someone who was sane and stable and connected. Bad luck for her that she got stuck with a hot mess like Slater.

When there was a lull in the conversation, Slater eyed Albert. "So you're allegedly a doctor."

Albert raised his eyebrows as he picked up a napkin to wipe his hands. "It's not an allegation. I'm a certified physician."

"What do magnesium supplements do?"

"You can skip those. Healthy people don't need supplementation. If you have kidney issues, you could actually get sick from getting too much of the stuff."

"So it's not going to help you sleep better," Slater said, "or clear up your skin."

"Supplements are basically unregulated, unlike medications and food. You can say anything you want about them. But saying something has a health benefit doesn't make it true. With no rules it's hard to know what claims have any validity." He shrugged. "There are people who drink their own urine and say it's a health tonic."

"Ick," Doris said.

"I agree." Albert waved a hand. "Your body's getting rid of it for a reason."

"What about spraying magnesium on your sore muscles," Slater said, "or deep magnesium massage?"

Albert shook his head. "There's no point in putting that stuff on your skin. At best it would do nothing, and at worst it would cause skin irritation."

"Magnesium is trendy right now," Doris said.

"It came up in my case. One of the lowlifes I talked to shills magnesium supplements for a living."

"What makes them a lowlife?"

"The fact that she's selling something that's useless," Slater said, "according to the croaker over here."

Pike gestured with a chunk of pita bread. "It's an odd case. A guy who went missing in the 1980s."

"And you're looking for him?" Albert said. "Hasn't the trail gone cold?"

"It has." Slater gestured with his wineglass. "He was a student at Live Oak College. He faded from his dorm one night and was never heard from again."

"I think I remember that one," Doris said, her brow furrowing. "Boris something."

"Boris Brooks."

"Of course. It was a big story in the news at the time. A friend of mine, Hugo, taught him in high school. The year before he went to college. Hugo remembered the kid."

"Is Hugo still alive?" Slater said. "I should interview him."

Doris frowned. "Of course he's still alive. We're not that old. You actually know Hugo, or you did when you were in school. I'll talk to him."

"The sooner the better." Slater raised his eyebrows. "He's not getting any younger."

She waved a hand. "It's at the top of my list."

"So, Albert, how many knees do you do in a week?" Pike said.

"Four or five sometimes. I don't do knee replacements. I work on cartilage and ligaments. ACL repair is a big one."

"What's the survival rate for knee surgery?"

Albert laughed. "It's not risky at all. We do it with local anesthesia and keyhole surgery. Ninety-nine percent."

"Have you done a lot of them?" Pike said.

"Over four hundred. It's hard to believe I've been at it so long."

"So you've killed four people," Slater said.

His eyes narrowed. "It doesn't work that way."

"I'm just saying." Slater lifted his wineglass. "I never killed anybody."

Albert held his gaze. "I actually find that quite surprising."

As Doris stood up, she put a hand on Albert's shoulder. "How about some strawberries? I couldn't resist. They were beautiful and cheap."

"Let me help." Pike rose, and started to collect the plates, then followed her into the kitchen.

Folding his arms, Slater stared at Albert. "Do you have any plans to retire?"

"Not yet. I like what I'm doing."

"When you do, it would be a very bad idea to move in here."

"You don't get to make decisions for me," Albert said, "or for your mother."

"I'm just putting it out there. I'd hate to see you get messed up. Cartilage and ligaments, broken bones, or worse."

"You're such a prick. You can't use threats and violence

to solve your problems."

Slater held his gaze. "On that, Albert, you're misinformed."

Doris stepped back in with some little bowls in hand, and as she set them down, Slater pointed two fingers at his own eyes, then jabbed a finger at Albert, a tacit *I'm watching you.*

———◆———

BACK AT THE HOUSE, as they climbed the stairs from the garage, Pike spoke.

"Are you going to read to me?"

"If you're up for it," Slater said.

"Let me change."

Slater went up to the kitchen, and through to the sofa, and sat to take off his boots and his socks. Under his feet the patch of faux turf felt almost like real grass. You could buy big rolls of the stuff to make a no-water fake lawn, but Pike had bought a chunk of it instead of an area rug to put under the coffee table. The guy was such a weirdo sometimes. He loved that about him, loved the unexpected parts, loved the quirkiness.

When Pike came up he was wearing black drawstring shorts and a T-shirt. "Where were we?"

Slater picked up the thick book from the coffee table. This had become their thing, reading mythology. He never would have done it on his own, but it was about Pike, so it had instantly become compelling. They'd slogged through modern renderings of the *Iliad* and the *Odyssey,* and now they were getting into a dumbed-down translation of *Theogony,* about the origins of the Greek gods.

Leaning back on him, Pike shifted down and rested his head on his shoulder. Once he was comfortable, Slater put his arm around his neck, his palm on his chest.

"It was getting intense," Slater said. "Cronus cut off his father's junk and threw it in the ocean."

"That seems harsh."

"Painful too." He found the page and started to read: "Where drops of Uranus's blood spattered on the earth, the Furies sprang up."

"I remember them from the *Iliad*," Pike said. "They're the goddesses that come to mess you up when you tell a lie."

"The margin note says, 'The number of Furies is not clearly stated in *Theogony*, and it varies in other sources. There were at least three of them.'"

Sometime later, after he'd read a dozen or so pages, Pike's breathing became regular. He folded the book closed and set it on the faux grass, then closed his eyes and leaned in to inhale the heady scent of Pike's hair. There was nothing else like this.

EIGHT

I N THE MORNING SLATER woke to gray daylight. Pike was gone. He had Saturday off, but he'd made some plan with his work friends, something about softball, either watching it or playing a pickup game. At least it didn't involve Davis. That guy wanted into Pike's pants so bad, and they worked together, so there was nothing Slater could do about it. He just had to believe that Pike would be strong enough to fend him off.

Grabbing his phone from the night table, he saw there was a text from Bettina, with a street address. He sat up and texted back:

I'll be there soon.

Once he'd pulled on his clothes, he went upstairs and slurped at a mug of room-temperature coffee from the pot, then grabbed half a bagel and started into it on the way down to the garage.

Bettina's place wasn't as far as her shop, in a sprawling neighborhood along the 10. It didn't feel freeway-adjacent when he pulled onto her block, lined on both sides by towering *washingtonia* palms. They were a symbol of Southern California, but they weren't native, and they were a pain to take care of. The heavy fronds dented cars when they fell, and they needed to be trimmed way too often. They regularly caught fire in summer when idiots launched their illegal fireworks into them. But they still made an iconic streetscape.

This block had only a few oversize gentrified boxes, with older bungalows on most of the lots, including Bettina's. He parked at the curb out front and looked the place over. A black iron-picket fence surrounded a verdant patch of Bermuda grass. That was so damn irresponsible these days. The sight of it made him scowl.

The rolling gate across the driveway was open, and as he walked up, Bettina stepped out the side door of the house and called a greeting. She was dressed in white work drag like yesterday, complete with the name tag and the Virgin Mary medallion. Walking over to the garage, she unlocked the small door and stepped inside. The double-wide vehicle door started to roll open, revealing the back end of a dark SUV next to an empty bay.

When he walked in, Bettina stood surveying the side wall, lined with shelves bearing corrugated boxes and plastic tubs and some lumpy plastic bags.

"That's it," she said, pointing to the top shelf. One of the boxes had BORIS written on it in black marker. "Can you reach it? I can get a ladder."

Slater stepped closer and stretched up, managing to grab the edges and pull it down. It was another banker's box, and it wasn't heavy. Setting it on the concrete floor, he squatted and spent a minute brushing off the cobwebs and the dust, then pulled off the lid.

The box was half full, and he dug through its contents, starting with several spiral-bound notebooks. One was labeled ECON in blue ballpoint pen, and the next was PSYCH. Flipping through them, they were full of notes in handwriting that looked cramped and a little sloppy.

Bettina stood nearby, watching him. "Those are class notes. Before laptops and tablets you'd do it by hand with paper and pen."

Below the notebooks were some bundles of typewritten pages, stapled in the corner—essays that Boris had written. On the front page each one bore a title, and the name of the class, and Boris's name. Under them were a couple of blocky videotapes in cases, and at the bottom of the box were three computer diskettes, hard little plastic squares with a metal shutter over the floppy disk inside. The videotapes were unlabeled, but the diskettes were all marked ESSAYS in the same tight handwriting.

"Can I borrow the tapes?" Slater said.

"Take the whole box," Bettina said, "and don't bring it back. Boris isn't coming to claim this. I have no interest in whatever he wrote to mollify his professors a lifetime ago."

He pressed the lid onto the box, then rose and tucked it under his arm.

"Do you really believe you'll learn anything new?" Bettina said.

He met her eye. "I don't know."

As he walked into the driveway, he saw Mark stepping out of the house. Catching sight of him, the guy scowled in recognition.

"What are you doing here?"

"Ask your wife."

Bettina stepped out of the garage. "You two have met?"

"On the street yesterday at Mondo Mg," Mark said. "This guy assaulted me for admiring his car."

"You damaged it by looking at it," Slater said. "I assumed you were a homeless tweaker prowling for stuff to steal. And an open-handed kovac isn't assault."

He frowned. "A what, now? You slapped me. Twice."

He set the box down on the concrete and put his hands on his hips. "A kovac. Technically it's one fluid movement. It's not meant to inflict pain, just to get your attention. On the East Coast they call it the paintbrush, and in Japan it's *oufuku binta*, a round-trip slap. Film industry people call it the Joan Crawford because she used to do that to people in her movies."

"I don't need to know all that," Mark said. "I expend a lot of energy practicing calm, and mindfulness, and nonviolence."

"No conflict was ever resolved by mindfulness," Slater said. "If someone is coming at you, you need to know how to defend yourself."

"Violence is never the answer, Slater," Bettina said.

"A kovac isn't violent." He jutted his chin to Mark. "Do you want me to show you how to do it?"

Mark watched him for a moment before he answered. "Yeah, I do."

"Are you kidding me?" Bettina demanded.

"Legally, open-handed is a lesser form of assault," Slater said, eyeing her. "Do you really want him punching people out there? He'll wind up in the hoosegow."

Bettina scoffed and walked into the house.

"Start with your hand low," Slater said, stepping in front of him. "That way you have the element of surprise."

As he brought his hand up, Mark flinched.

"Don't slap me."

"I'll do it at low speed. Just to demonstrate." Slater mimed the action, bringing his palm up and touching it to his cheek. "My hand keeps going, whether your head moves or not. Then the return is a backhand. Like a tennis swing." He touched the back of his hand to Mark's other cheek, then demonstrated the movement once more, a little faster, but not using force. "Now you try it on me."

Mark frowned and shifted on his feet, then went through it slowly, touching his palm to his face, then the backhand.

"Great," Slater said. "Now use full power."

"You can't hit me back."

"Just do it, man."

He took a breath and made a half-hearted slap and return.

"Not enough force, and way too slow," Slater said. "Speed it up. Put your shoulder into it, like you're pitching a baseball."

His brow furrowed and he struck again, harder this time, enough to turn his head.

"Yeah," Slater roared, and then laughed. "Again, only faster. The backhand needs to be quick enough that your target can't grab your arm."

Mark slapped him again, fast and hard, the sound of the skin contact a loud *snap*.

On the backhand, Slater grabbed his wrist. "You have to drop your hand quickly too, so that I can't do this."

"Your cheeks are all red."

"Totally worth it." It was making him chubby too, the proximity to this guy, the feeling of his hands on him.

"Thanks, I guess," Mark said.

"Use it wisely, big guy."

Tucking the box under one arm, Slater adjusted his crotch with his free hand as he walked down the driveway. When he loaded it into the trunk of the Continental, he took out one of the videotapes and photographed the label with his phone.

There was a giant thrift shop in Lincoln Heights that would have what he needed, and he navigated onto the 5 and into that neighborhood. Inside he soon found the room with all the used electronics. There was a whole shelf of old video recorders, and looking them over, there seemed to be several different formats. Digging out his phone, he studied the photo he'd taken of the videotape.

"Can't find what you need?" a guy asked him. He had one of the machines in hand, and set it on a shelf.

Slater looked him over. In his thirties, he had luxy Latin hair and was wearing jeans.

"You work here?"

"I'm just a hobbyist." The guy gestured to the shelf. "Checking out the new arrivals."

"I don't know what format I need. I have some old tapes I want to watch."

"Are they VHS tapes? Almost everything was."

Slater held the photo out to him, and he leaned in to look at the screen.

"That's totally a VHS tape. It says it on the case. One of these VCRs will play that for you."

"VCR is the brand?" Slater said.

"That's what the machines are called, regardless of the manufacturer or the tape format."

Slater grabbed the smallest one and pulled it off the shelf. "How do you know if they're working?"

"They don't put them out if they're not." He raised his eyebrows. "You should probably get an old TV set to connect to it. There's a bunch of them here."

"Can't I connect one of these to a new TV set," Slater said, "or a computer monitor?"

"Definitely not a monitor. A new TV might have the right ports, or it might not. Then you'd need an adapter. You can check on your TV." He reached for the bundle of cables on the machine Slater was holding and held up the connectors. "Look for ports that'll fit these."

"Excellent."

"Are they porn tapes?"

"I'm not sure what's on them."

"Back in the day, people had a trick to hide their porn. You'd record ten minutes of something boring, and then record the porn. So make sure you watch the whole thing."

"Got it."

"How old are your tapes?" the guy said.

"Late 1980s."

He clicked his tongue. "They might be blank by now."

"That happens?"

"Things age. Information is stored on the tape magnetically, and magnetic force fades over time."

"Does that happen with floppy disks too?" Slater said. "I'm thinking it's the same technology."

"Totally."

"You really should get a job here."

He laughed. "I hope you find something good on your tapes."

Walking over to the next section, he found a portable TV that had the right ports to connect the player. It was heavy but small enough that it wasn't unmanageable to lug around.

He carried the machines to the register to pay for them, then headed out to the Continental. Once he'd parked in the surface lot across from his office, and opened the trunk, he decided he could manage the electronics and the new banker's box in one trip. He stacked the tape machine and then the TV on top of the box, and lifted it by its handles, and carried them across the street.

Upstairs, when he unlocked his office, he found the lights on. As he hauled in the stack and set it on his desk, Max called to him from his office.

"Whoa—is it 1990 again?"

Slater stepped over to his doorway, and Max leaned back in his chair. The guy was beefy, with mousy hair, his gut bulging over his belt. He'd hung his suit jacket on the coatrack, revealing his sidearm in its holster, strapped over his shirt. Unlike Slater, he was a licensed PI.

"I found some old videotapes that I need to watch," Slater said. "It's a missing-person job."

"When did they go missing?"

"In 1988."

"That technology was definitely relevant then," Max said. "It can't be a job for the insurance company."

Leaning on the door frame, Slater told him a little about Elvaine's ask. "What are you working on?"

"Same old stuff. A window-shade job. Spouse B is definitely violating his prenup."

"Is that why you wore the red suit? A client meeting?"

"Specifically to deliver bad news in photographic form, and to present my bill." His expression sobered. "I had Etta do some shagging on this one. She followed the guy to a bar and then to the hookup with the third party. She wasn't happy about tracking down that kind of evidence."

He frowned. "Why?"

"She said it was depressing to help bust up somebody's marriage."

"It sounds like he's busting up his own marriage by screwing around. Can't she see that?"

"The point is, she might be having a crisis of conscience. I think we need to be wary about putting her on that kind of tail."

"Fuck that," Slater said. "Most of the work we do is window-shade jobs. There's not a whole lot of missing kittens and sparkly rainbows."

Max waved a hand. "I don't think she's burning out, exactly. Just noticing that the work has a dark side."

"I've been using her a lot, and she's good at it. If she flakes out on us it's going to be painful."

"I hear you, brother."

In his own office he arranged the TV and the tape deck on his desk, and plugged them into the wall, and connected the cables. It took a minute to figure out how to turn on the TV, and what channel to set it to, and how to insert the tape. But when he finally did, it slid smoothly into the machine and clunked into place. From inside came the high-pitched whir of moving parts. This was definitely the right device to play these tapes.

The TV screen showed snowy static, the same as when he'd turned it on. He knew he'd found the right channel, as the player's interface was superimposed on the static— PLAY in one corner, and LP in another, and a time code at the bottom ticking up the seconds from zero.

Then he realized there was something else—vague outlines of lettering at first, and movement, with bits of color sometimes appearing. Whatever had been recorded on the tape, it was too degraded to make sense of now. He fast-forwarded, working his way through it and watching at normal speed sometimes, but there was nothing legible, and when the time code passed two hours, the tape ended with an audible *clunk* and started to rewind itself.

He heard keys in the door, and Etta's voice called out as she stepped in.

"*Talofa*, gents without sense."

She stuck her head into Slater's office. Etta was curvy, her black hair butched short, today wearing jeans and a blue plaid shirt.

"Is that Samoan?" Slater said.

"The language is called Polynesian. It means howdy." She frowned, looking over the equipment on his desk. "Have you gone retro on us?"

"I need to watch some old videotapes for a case I'm working."

"I'm just here to get paid." She jabbed her thumb over her shoulder. "This guy owes me money."

Rising, Slater followed her over to Max's office. He stepped in and put his hands on his hips, watching her as she dropped into Max's guest chair.

"What's all this about your messed-up morals interfering with the work?" Slater demanded.

Etta frowned at him. "I just thought it was kind of dark that we're giving the guy's wife grounds to divorce him."

"He did that himself," Slater said, raising his voice. "It would be happening whether we were involved or not. If you were the wife, wouldn't you want to have all the information?"

"I'm sure I would." She sighed and then shot Max a look. "Gossip much?"

Max shrugged. "It's about the business. This is the first time I've seen you be anything but enthusiastic about running an op."

"He seemed like a nice guy."

"A nice guy who signed a contract not to fuck other people," Slater said.

"I'm not losing my nerve. This one just struck me as a downer."

"We cannot afford to lose you," Slater said. "You need to snap out of it."

Etta's brow furrowed. "I guess I should be flattered that I'm so valuable."

"You are," Max said. "You know you are, as evidenced by the stack of C-notes I'm about to hand over."

"When you're done with this mook," Slater said, "Come and see me. I have questions that require your expertise." He jabbed a finger at her. "And figure out your bullshit."

Back in his office, he slid the second videotape into the machine, finding only the same kind of vague images and flashes of color, too faint to parse. Eventually he chucked the tapes in the box with Boris's notebooks, and unplugged the TV and the player, and stacked them all on the floor.

Rolling his chair up to the desk, he pulled his keyboard close and searched for info on old videotapes. The guy in the thrift store was right—the consensus was that they degraded with time, and exposure to any strong magnetic field or an electromagnetic pulse would erase them. These tapes had spent a lot of years sitting in that box. It was no surprise that something like that might have happened at some point.

When Etta stepped in, she dropped into the chair in front of his desk. "So what do you need?"

"You used to work for those religious nuts," he said, leaning back.

"More commonly known as the Catholic school system."

"What does it mean when someone is wearing a Virgin Mary necklace?"

"How big was it?"

"Like this." He made a circle with his thumb and finger. "It was silver. The image is Mary showing her palms at her sides."

"Well, the open hands thing means she's inviting you to take her hand and join the fold."

He frowned. "No thanks."

Etta chuckled. "I'd say the person wearing it is devout. Sometimes people wear a picture of Mary if they figure she's helped them out in some way."

"So it probably doesn't mean anything."

"Is this person a target in your case?"

He gestured with his chin to the electronics on the floor. "She's the one who gave me the messed-up videotapes.

They belonged to a guy who went missing in the eighties."

She asked him about it, and he told her a little about Elvaine and the case. Eventually Etta rose.

"See you later, boys," she called as she stepped out.

Slater heard her lock the front door as he lifted Boris's notebooks out of the box. Unlike the content of the video-tapes, these had survived the intervening years. About a third of each book was filled with class notes, and he scanned the pages. It was all about what had been said in the class, with nothing personal or off-topic.

Next he pulled out the stack of essays. The paper was yellowing with age. Flipping through each of them, he didn't bother to read much, until he came to one for Boris's psych class. It was titled "Changing Beliefs: How Our Worldview Shifts with Life Experiences." In the corner of the top page, in red ink with a circle drawn around it, someone had written B-.

He'd seen this in the notebook for that class—something about worldview and life experience. Grabbing the psych notebook, he took a minute to find it again, flipping through the pages. It was a term paper assignment: "Write twelve pages on a personal belief that has changed during the semester." The due date was written below and under-lined twice.

In the essay Boris had written about the meaning of Vivaldi's *Four Seasons,* Slater found, reading through it. It seemed tenuous as a topic for a personal belief. That might explain the B-minus.

Sitting back, he rubbed his eyes, then dug out his phone and called Elvaine.

"I have something for you," Slater said when she picked up. "Are you around today? I can drop it off."

"If it's quick, you can come by my place," she said. "There's a loading zone right in front of the door."

He stacked the electronics on the box again and called good-bye to Max as he carried them out, then down to the street and across to his car. The marine layer had mostly burned off, and the sun felt bright as he drove the few blocks to Spring, and pulled up to the yellow curb in front of Elvaine's building. It was one of the many early-twentieth-century office buildings that had been converted to residential.

When he got out of the car, Elvaine appeared from the lobby doors, briefly shielding her eyes to the sunlight as she called a greeting. Slater opened the trunk as she stepped over.

"Do you need a thirty-year-old TV?" he said.

"What's that for?"

"To watch Boris's videotapes. Unfortunately they're useless." He pulled the top off the box and handed her one of them. "They were with Boris's stuff from college. Bettina had all this."

"She's been holding out on me." Elvaine looked over the videotape, briefly sliding it out of its case. "These were blank?"

"You can tell there was something on them once, but it's too degraded. Apparently they fade with time, and being exposed to a strong magnetic field can erase them. They sat in this box for a lot of years. Stuff happens." He gestured to the stack of paper in the box. "There's an essay that Boris wrote for Cameron in here."

Elvaine leaned into the trunk to rifle through it. "I can't believe you tracked this down." She stood erect again and met his eye. "Sveta knew you were the guy. How did you weasel this out of Bettina?"

"Using my weasel skills," Slater said. "She doesn't want any of it back. I think she was getting tired of talking to me. She said she wants to stop revisiting the story. Her husband said it was traumatic for her."

"You interviewed him too?"

"I talked to him for a hot minute on the sidewalk outside the magnesium den."

"Do you think there's anything of value in this?"

"You'd be a better judge," Slater said. "I scanned the essays and the class notes, but to me it just looks like schoolwork. The computer diskettes are likely degraded too after all this time, especially if they got exposed to the same thing as the tapes. But I didn't check them. You'd need to go to a museum."

Elvaine dug them out of the box. "He wrote 'essays' on the diskettes, so it's probably the same as what he printed on paper."

A guy with a scruffy beard and greasy hair walked up to the curb, standing way too close to them. "Hey, guys. Can I borrow five dollars?"

"No," Slater said sharply. "Keep walking."

"I asked politely," he said, and frowned. "If you can't do five, I'll settle for one."

Stepping up to him, Slater shoved him backward, across the sidewalk. "I said hit the bricks. Do you want me to crack you open?"

He stumbled backward, then straightened up, and puffed out his chest. "You can't just push people around."

Slater took a step closer and slapped him hard, left and then right, a firm kovac. "Why do you make me do this? It's like you want me to crack you." He shoved him again, hard, with both hands. "Why do you do it?"

"Stop it," he shouted, raising his arms over his face.

He balled his fists. "If you don't beat it, I'll break your fucking nose."

"Asshole," he shouted, but turned and walked away.

After he'd watched him for a few seconds to make sure

he wasn't going to double back, Slater went to the trunk of the Continental.

"That's one way to deal with the homelessness crisis," Elvaine said.

"Aren't you sick of it?" He absently wiped his palms on his jeans. "You live right in the epicenter of it here."

"Don't get me started." She lifted the box out of the trunk. "I'm still waiting to hear back from Jeff. I'll let you know."

Interesting that she didn't seem perturbed by the altercation, he thought, watching her lugging the box into the building. It meant she wasn't sheltered from reality. She'd seen interactions like that before.

NINE

ON THE STREETS THE shadows were growing long as Slater drove to his house and nosed into his garage. Upstairs he found Pike at the dining table with his laptop. He sat back as Slater walked in.

"You're not using your desk?"

"That's for work," Pike said. "On the weekend I don't want to feel like I'm working. I'm just messing around."

"How was softball?"

"A lot of fun."

Approaching him, Slater lifted his leg over Pike's knees, squeezing in between him and the table, and sat on his lap, facing him. He cradled his head in his hands and kissed him, getting lost in his mouth. Eventually he pulled back.

Pike caressed his back, a grin on his face. "You're no featherweight. Aren't you worried about breaking my legs?"

"You can handle it."

He squeezed Slater's thighs. "You're a handful, Ibáñez. Literally."

"Elvaine says I'm a weasel."

"Because of your silky fur and sharp teeth?"

"More like I work fast and I'm sneaky."

"Sneaky definitely fits," Pike said. "Like that twenty grand stashed under the bathroom sink."

"I need that lettuce. I've got a mortgage to pay. And that stash might just save your neck someday."

"It's pretty nervy of her to call you a weasel."

"I've heard worse."

"It reminds me of the song that ice cream truck plays," Pike said. "About the monkey and the weasel. It was out there on patrol today."

"Lots of my informants in this case definitely qualify as monkeys."

"I can totally imagine you chasing a monkey around a mulberry bush."

Slater got up. "Do you want to eat soon? I have a cooking class after."

Pike laughed. "You could just eat there."

"It's magnesium-based, so my working assumption is that it'll be inedible."

"Is it at your target's magnesium store?"

"It's somewhere near there, but she's teaching it. I need to get a bead on what she's up to."

"There's stuff to make quesadillas," Pike said, and got to his feet.

In the kitchen Pike pulled on the apron he kept in the broom closet, and set to work, and soon they had a couple of golden half-moons. They carried them out onto the deck to eat in the fading daylight.

Once he'd finished, Pike wiped his hands on a napkin. "Considering this stuff never saw a dairy barn, it's pretty cheesy."

"I'm sure it's better for you too." Slater stacked their plates, then sat back in his chair. "I should go."

"It sounds like you don't want to."

"I want to stay here with you, and read, and skull-fuck you."

He raised his eyebrows. "Such an elegant impulse, petal."

"I'm also questioning the utility of going to this class when it's so far. It's in fricking Venice."

"Traffic's not as bad on Saturday."

"Max says 'You are the traffic.'" Slater heaved himself out of the chair.

"That sounds like a Zen koan. If you think about it, it's actually true." He rose and picked up the plates. "Maybe I'll smash you later. Make you scream my name."

"Right on." Slater nodded. "At least there's something to look forward to."

Backing the Continental into the street, he waited for the garage door to roll down, then headed to the freeway. Despite Pike's optimism, even on Saturday there was congestion, and it was almost an hour later when he pulled up at the address for the class. He found street parking farther down the block. When he walked back to it, the place looked industrial, with no windows or signage, just the street number. When he tried the door, it was unlocked.

Inside was a foyer with a guy sitting behind a desk, his dreads piled behind his head, clad in a blue shirt with epaulets and a security guard badge on his chest. He was a little curvy, and basically fuckable.

He looked up from his phone screen as Slater stepped in. "Are you here for Life-Changing Vegan Cooking with Magnesium?"

"Do they pay you to say that?" Slater said.

He chuckled. "It's at the end of the hall. The studio on the left."

The space looked like an oversize kitchen, he saw as he strode in, but with familiar consumer appliances, not commercial gear like in a restaurant. The guard implied it was a sound stage, but there was no video equipment in sight. Then he saw the back wall, where he'd walked in, was lined with bleachers, the benches and the railings all painted matte black. Nobody was sitting there, but it was definitely set up for a studio audience.

At the far wall were two big Frigidaires, like in a kosher kitchen, and deep sinks, and a double-size stovetop in the middle of a big island. On the counter nearby was some kitchen equipment, tongs and a lifter and a stack of small plates, and next to them an array of little product packages, the same as the ones he'd seen in Bettina's shop, bottles and tubes and jars of magnesium supplements, all branded Mondo Mg.

Half a dozen other people were already here, standing around the island, all of them the white Westside wellness crowd. In their thirties and forties, they were all uniformly dressed sporty, like they were headed to a yoga class or a hike later.

Slater could feel many eyes on him as he walked in. He was dressed like the guy who'd fix the plumbing, not like a magnesium-curious white-collar type. Stepping up to the island, he stood with his feet planted apart and folded his arms. Across the island he met the gaze of one of the men, and raised his eyebrows, and glared at him. The guy quickly looked away.

Some of them were jabbering, like people usually did, and he tried to tune it out. A couple of other people wandered in, and stood near the island, and eventually Bettina appeared. She was still dressed in her white work outfit, wearing a headset now with a mike in front of her mouth. It didn't seem like there were enough people here to need amplification.

Flashing a big smile, Bettina introduced herself and

looked around at the crowd. Her brow furrowed fleetingly at the sight of Slater.

"It's so great to see all of you here," she said, her voice booming through the speakers mounted high on the wall. "I'm glad so many people are motivated to make their lives better. Let's dive right in."

Her body language was polished, rehearsed, and she gestured widely, making eye contact with everyone in the room.

"Magnesium is a miracle supplement that people have used for millennia to improve our health and live well," Bettina went on. "Your body needs it to function properly, especially your muscles and your digestion. It can help you sleep better, and give you clear skin, and build muscle. It can even help you lose weight."

She stepped over to one of the iceboxes, and pulled out a metal tray, and set it on the island next to the stovetop. It bore neatly trimmed celery stalks. Reaching below the counter, she produced a bottle of yellowy-brown liquid.

"The first dish we're going to create is braised celery with a magnesium reduction."

Bettina talked through the entire preparation process, partly explaining the technique and partly promoting the products in her store. She cut the celery into long sections, then pulled out a wok and cranked the flame up high. Once it was hot she dropped in the celery, without any oil, and it sizzled a little. Lifting the wok, she tossed the contents around every few seconds. Eventually she reached for a little white jar among the products lined up on the island.

"There are many forms of magnesium," Bettina said. "You can see them at my shop, Mondo Mg, right up the street. This is magnesium glycinate. In compound form the mineral is more accessible to your system. Mixed with apple cider vinegar, another miracle food, it can cure gall-stones, and give you more energy."

She sprinkled powder from the little container into the wok, and gave the contents another toss, then poured from the brown bottle. The hot wok roared as the liquid boiled off, a cloud of steam rising into the vent hood above. He could smell the tang of hot vinegar.

Bettina killed the burner and plated the celery, tipping the contents of the wok onto a white platter, and then set a pair of tongs on it. She tapped the stack of little plates.

"I encourage everyone to take a taste. I'll be back in a minute."

She folded the mike away from her face and walked to the side of the room, over by a tall rack of cooking equipment. The saps who'd paid for this were crowding around the celery, ignoring her now. She eyed Slater and gestured with her head. When he stepped over to her, Bettina spoke intently, her voice low.

"You stick out like a thistle in the petunia bed."

"You really shouldn't plant petunias," Slater said. "It's better to put in natives. And I can't be the only brown guy on the Westside."

"That's not what I mean. Why are you here?"

"I know you're holding out on me, toots. You need to come across."

She scowled. "What are you talking about?"

"What do you know about Boris's disappearance?"

"Settle down." She glanced toward the island and the crowd munching on celery. "Everything I know is in the police record. Elvaine asked me all the same questions again, and again, and again, and now you."

"Bullshit. Your nebbishy husband said you know more than you've told anyone."

Bettina raised her eyebrows. "He said I know exactly

what killed Boris, is that what you're talking about? Is that what Mark told you?"

"You know for certain that he died?"

"I never saw his body, but I'm certain of it." She held his gaze. "It was his diet."

"He was dieting? Like he was anorexic?"

"No—he ate hamburger sandwiches, and french-fried potatoes, and ketchup sauce. Little blobs of ground chicken deep-fried in industrial oil. Boris loved that trash. He ate so much of it."

"The guy wasn't overweight," Slater said. "Not in the photos I've seen. He was still a teenager—junk is kind of what teenagers eat."

"It's so toxic," she said intently. "That amount of poison would kill anybody."

"So if he'd eaten celery with hipster vinegar and magnesium sprinkled on it, he'd still be alive."

"I'm sure of it."

Closing his eyes, he rubbed his forehead. "What am I doing here?"

"My question exactly," Bettina said. "If you paid for the class, you can stay for the magnesium-crusted free-range chicken breast, but not if you disrupt things."

"Like I disrupted the celery?" Slater demanded. "Wait—actual chicken? I thought you said you were vegan. It's in the name of the class."

"I am, but you need to feed your blood once in a while. It's just the one dish." She waved a hand. "It's not like it's red meat."

He scoffed and flashed his palms. "I'm out."

Striding out to the street, he walked up the block and climbed into the Continental. It was dark out now, and he flicked on the headlights. The freeway was moving, at least, on the trek back to civilization. He could still smell boiling vinegar on his clothes, so he rolled open the window to get some air moving and blow it away.

Upstairs the bedroom was dark, and he climbed up to the kitchen. Only the low lights under the cabinets were on. A bottle of scotch was sitting out on the counter. He walked into the big empty room. The lights were off. Pike's rig was parked on the street—had he walked somewhere, or was he outside on the deck? He started toward the French doors, then heard a soft "Hey."

He could just make out the silhouette of Pike's form, sitting in one of the lounge chairs. As he sat up, he heard the tinkle of ice—he had a tumbler in his hand.

Slater stood facing him. "Are you mad at me?"

"Why would I be mad at you?"

"You're sitting in the dark drinking scotch. It makes me think you're going to pack up your stuff and drive back to Albuquerque. Toss your house keys in the dirt at my feet and shout, 'So long, sucker,' then punch it and peel out, the gravel from your tires pelting me all over. And I'm left tits-up in the gutter."

"You really think our relationship is teetering on a knife edge like that? Why, Slater? I'm here, and I'm with you. My career is here."

"So why are you sitting in the dark? Did something happen at softball?"

Pike sighed. "I'm just having a drink and thinking about things. My life. You can sit with me if you want."

Dropping onto the faux turf in front of him, Slater leaned back against his shin. Pike put a hand on the back of his neck.

"You're so tense. Like you're anticipating a catastrophe." He massaged his neck muscles. "You can relax, forty-niner. I'm not going anywhere. You're the best thing that's ever happened to me."

"So why are you sitting in the dark?"

Pike grabbed his arm and pulled him up to his knees. He turned to face him, and Pike drew him in, and met his mouth. Eventually he pulled back.

"I'll be down in a while," Pike said. "We can do that stuff we talked about."

Getting to his feet, Slater walked back through the kitchen. He briefly considered assaulting that beautiful amber bottle, just sitting there on the counter, and taking it down a finger or two, but he wanted to be functional for the next event, so he kept walking. Downstairs he got undressed, and climbed into bed, and read stuff on his phone.

He couldn't figure Pike out sometimes. Mostly the guy was buoyant, and optimistic, and didn't let things keep him down. But it was impossible to understand everything—he couldn't climb inside his head. In her shrinky meddling yenta talk Doris had told him that the infatuation they had would eventually get familiar, and they would have to acknowledge that they were different people, connected but independent. He thought he'd been doing that by not worrying about Pike's gun-range excursions or his poker nights or freaking softball. Maybe that's what was happening for Pike—the infatuation was wearing off, and he was seeing Slater for the fraud that he really was. Maybe that's why he was sitting in the dark.

When Pike came downstairs, he stripped off his clothes and climbed in beside him, running his hands over his belly, squeezing his cock. "I'm going to fuck you."

He could smell scotch on his breath. "Let's see what you've got."

Grabbing the lube from the bedside table, Pike shifted close, on his side, and mouthed his neck as he pressed into him, his arm around his waist. Moving slowly at first, he built up to pounding him, and eventually grunted as he climaxed, pulling himself tight against him, his chin on Slater's shoulder. Once he'd caught his breath, he started to pull away.

Slater reached back and grabbed his butt. "Don't move."

Pressing into him again, Pike grabbed his cock, and stroked it, building up speed until Slater came, his body spasming. They clung together for a minute. He could feel Pike's heartbeat gradually slow. Eventually Pike rolled onto his back.

"There's no gravel."

Slater shifted to look at him. "What?"

"There's no gravel in front of the house," Pike said. "I couldn't spray you with gravel when I peeled out. The most I could do is a cloud of tire smoke on the asphalt."

TEN

SLATER WOKE TO THE buzzing of his phone, and scrabbled for it on the night table. It was Elvaine.

"Jeff can meet you today," she said when he picked up. "I'll text you his address."

"The roommate," Slater said, struggling to focus. "Excellent. I definitely need to have a word with that guy."

"That makes it sound like you're planning to bust his kneecaps."

"If he doesn't come at me, nobody will get hurt."

"Jeff is a civilian," Elvaine said. "Go easy."

Forcing himself out of bed, he got dressed and went upstairs. Pike was out on the deck in the morning gray, so he poured himself a coffee, and grabbed an apple, and went out to join him at the patio table.

"What have you got lined up for the day?" Pike said.

"Work. I'm interviewing a witness."

"Well, I'm going to take Grace furniture shopping."

Slater frowned. "She asked you to do that?"

Grace was the elderly woman who lived in the ADU behind the garage. She'd been his neighbor in Westlake, and he'd moved her over here when he bought this place.

"I dropped in to check on her," Pike said, "and she mentioned that she needed a sideboard. I offered."

"It feels like something I should be doing. Checking in on her, and driving her places."

"I can shoulder some of the work. You don't have to do it all yourself."

"I know you know how to do this stuff," Slater said. "Tune in to people, groove with them, help them out. I just figure if she needs something, she'll text me."

"It'll be fun. We're going to that big warehouse place in La Mirada."

"You're such a good person. Like with Doris. You ask all the right questions, and you make her laugh. You fill in the empty places that I've neglected."

"That means we have complimentary skills. We make a good team."

"I just don't see anything that I do that improves your life," Slater said. "It's like I'm on the take. You're the only one functional enough to give anything, and I just take from you. Like a goddamn grifter."

Pike held his gaze. "You bring plenty. It doesn't have to be actual labor or mileage on your car. You make my life good."

After he'd munched on the apple, and the java started to kick in, Slater went down to the garage and backed the Continental into the street. The address Elvaine had sent was in hilly and affluent Ladera Heights. The neighborhood was closer to the coast, so the sky felt more heavily overcast than on his side of town. He navigated the winding streets until he found the place. The driveway sloped upward, and he nosed in. A black Mercedes sedan was parked in front of the garage, and he pulled in on the opposite side, leaving room for the Benz to leave if it needed to.

The house was low-slung ranch style, and the plantings out front were well established. A plumeria was already starting to bloom in white, and a neatly groomed hedge lined the driveway. Slater paused to look it over. This was an island mahogany. Squatting for a second, he checked the soil underneath, spotting an irrigation line half buried in the earth.

A guy stepped out the front door of the house. He was tall, with his Black hair graying and trimmed short, built thick but not chubby. Based on his age, this was Jeff. Wearing dark chinos and a collared shirt, his look was a little square, but he was basically fuckable.

"Is there something wrong with the hedge?" Jeff called to him.

Slater rose. "Not at all. I'm impressed that you planted a native species."

"I'm told it's a mountain mahogany."

"Technically it's a variety called island mahogany." Slater stepped over to him. "They grow on the Channel Islands. It seems happy here."

"We get the sea air. It's cooler and wetter than downtown."

"You can turn down the water on it. It doesn't need it."

"Elvaine said you were a researcher, not a gardener."

"You must be Jeff."

He cracked a smile. "Come on in."

The place was a mid-century classic, with an open ceiling held up by dark wood beams. At the far end was an angular fireplace, and at one side a wall of big windows and a sliding door looked out on a patio, with a placid swimming pool beyond. At the side of the yard a bougainvillea hedge was trimmed up tight and rife with bright magenta bracts.

"This is a great house," Slater said.

"We've tried to stay authentic to the original."

"I can see that."

The furniture was mid-century too—not the ubiquitous familiar designer pieces, but chairs in bright colors, a couple of tables in simple styles.

A woman stepped out of the back of the house, lanky and dressed formally in a dark suit. He knew Black women spent a lot on their hair, and her do looked expensive, styled straight and close to her head.

"My wife, Diane," Jeff said. "This is Slater."

Diane raised her eyebrows. "We usually have coffee after we get back from church. Can I get you a cup?"

"If you're already making it, sure. Just black." He put his hands on his hips. "Are you Catholic? I've run into a lot of them this week."

She smiled. "No, sweetie. We're AME."

As she stepped out, Jeff waved at the furniture. "I'd say we could sit outside, but it's a little chilly."

He took a club chair, and Slater sat in the adjacent one.

Jeff folded his hands over his belly, and spoke in an affable tone. "Elvaine said you were helping her with new research on Boris's disappearance."

"I'm going over some things. Looking for details that might have been missed. You knew Boris well?"

"We were good friends. It was terrible when he disappeared. I kept thinking he'd turn up. Or his body would. It made me question everything."

"Someone I talked to called you Natasha," Slater said. "Did you do drag back then?"

Jeff laughed. "That wouldn't be a very clever drag name. Natasha was my nickname. I'm not sure who gave that to me. Someone on our floor in the dorm. It was because of Boris. They called him Boris Badenov, and I was always with him, so they called me Natasha. Do you know the reference?"

"Enlighten me."

"It's from an old cartoon. Boris and Natasha were partners. Soviet spies. I was in the Russian studies program, so it fit."

"And Boris's name was already Boris."

"Teenagers are not always very creative."

"*Dobre den,*" Slater said.

"You mean *Dobre utro*. You say *Dobre den* in the afternoon. Why do you know Russian greetings?"

"One of my vendors is Russian. She got me interested. I only know a few phrases." He shifted in the chair. "So Russian studies means Russian language?"

"Politics and culture and language. I only took one year and then got into engineering. The only jobs for someone in Russian studies were with the government." Jeff threw up a hand. "Who wants to work for them? Engineering is a lot better paid."

"Hence this beautiful house."

"You know it." He sat up as Diane walked in.

She set a mug for each of them on the table. "Let me know if you want a refill."

"Were you around when Jeff was at Live Oak?" Slater said, reaching for the mug.

Diane raised her eyebrows. "I've heard the stories, but that was well before my time. When Jeff was in college I was still a schoolgirl back in Illinois."

As she walked out, Jeff shook his head and lowered his voice. "I'm not that much older than her. It's not like she was a child then."

Slater slurped at the mug. "That's good joe."

"Boris disappearing really threw me for a loop. I made a lot of changes that summer. Not just my major."

"The night he disappeared, someone put a fish in Boris's bed. What did that mean?"

Jeff scoffed and set his mug down. "That guy. It was just a prank. It wasn't meant to be mean-spirited. We did a lot of that. Dorm life was pretty hectic—loud music, drinking, horseplay."

"Did Boris drink? What about drugs?"

"He didn't drink to excess, at least not more than once or twice that I saw. And nobody did drugs. It was less tolerated back then."

"Not even weed?"

"There were stoners, and some rasta guys, but they kept it quiet. The ones I knew would go smoke in the parking lot."

"So Boris didn't have any real enemies in the dorm."

"Not at all." Jeff waved a hand. "It was like a big party most nights. Young people expressing themselves for the first time, growing into their adult personalities."

"And you two were the Russian spies."

He laughed. "We played it up. In the dorm we both used to say 'Raskolnikov' as a cuss word." He raised a fist and repeated it, deepening his voice. "It was kind of like 'Damn it.' It fit with our brand, and we loved that nobody knew what it meant."

"I never heard that one either."

"It's not really a cuss word. Boris and Natasha used to say it in the cartoon. It's actually the name of a character from Dostoevsky."

"Which book?"

"*Crime and Punishment.* Raskolnikov is the main character. He gets shipped off to Siberia for eight hundred pages."

Slater watched him for a moment as he sipped at the java. That was the second time that book had come up in this case. "Do you keep up with Heather from those days?"

"I remember who she was. I haven't even thought about her since first year."

"She makes B movies in Culver these days."

Jeff nodded. "Good for her."

"Boris played violin," Slater said. "What was that like?"

"I think he was pretty good at it, the few times I heard him practice. I know the police asked a lot of questions about why he'd left the instrument in his car. They thought that must be significant for some reason. But Boris didn't treat it like it was all that valuable. He'd leave it out in the room. It probably wasn't an expensive model."

"You two had a TV in your room."

"We were quite proud of that." He raised his eyebrows. "It seems silly now. The thing took up so much space, and there was a TV right down the hall in the common room."

"What was it for?"

"We'd watch sitcoms and other stuff. Movies sometimes." He waved a hand. "Why does anyone have a TV?"

"You said Boris didn't do drugs. Did he smoke?"

"I don't think he did, but he carried a pack with him. I remember people would bum them off him outside."

"Why would he carry them if he didn't smoke?"

"Maybe to be sociable." Jeff shrugged. "I'm not really sure."

"He didn't sleep in the dorm the Saturday before he disappeared," Slater said. "Where was he?"

"Nobody ever figured that out, as far as I know. I'd gone home to my parents that weekend. I didn't see him until that Monday."

"Was Boris gay?"

His eyebrows shot up. "Not that I know of. He never came out to me. Never hit on me either. He never dated any boys that I heard about."

"Or girls, though, right?"

"That one you mentioned, Heather. She was sweet on him. She hung around a little." He gestured helplessly.

"When you put it that way, yeah, maybe he was gay. But if he was, he was definitely hiding it. Or maybe he didn't even know it himself."

"What do you think happened to him?"

Jeff sighed and looked toward the windows onto the backyard. "Well, he left without his ID or his keys. He didn't even take his wheels." He met Slater's gaze and lowered his voice. "I think he went downstairs to talk to someone who called up. Somebody he had some kind of relationship with. Somebody he owed money to. Then he got abducted and murdered. His bones are out there in the ground somewhere."

Draining his mug, Slater rose. "I appreciate your time. Thank Diane for the java."

Jeff rose with him and walked him to the door. "I can't believe you're actually going to uncover anything new after all these years."

"I hear you, Jeff. I have to admit I'm dubious myself."

He walked out to his car and climbed in, then headed toward the freeway. It was warm out but there was no sign of the sun through the marine layer, even back in his own neighborhood.

Something was off about Jeff, but he couldn't quite put his finger on it. Slater hadn't wanted to punch him in the face even once. That stood out as unusual. Maybe it was Slater that was off—was he getting soft, letting his guard down?

There was no sign of Pike's ride on the street, he saw, as he pulled into the garage. He was still out with Grace furniture shopping. How did he even know she needed help with stuff like that? It was like he spoke a language Slater couldn't even understand.

Upstairs he grabbed his laptop and sat on the sofa, then pulled his boots off, enjoying the feel of the fake grass under his feet. Leaning back on the arm of the sofa, he swung his feet up and read online about Boris and Natasha, the television cartoon characters from the middle of the last century. They were archetypical Cold War villains, it seemed, and like Jeff said, they used Raskolnikov as a cuss word.

On the coffee table his phone rang, with the most grating ring tone of all: *No wire hangers! I buy you three-hundred-dollar dresses and you treat them like they were some dishrag!*

"Damn it," he muttered, and picked up. "What do you need, Doris?"

"You asked me for a favor, remember? Hugo."

"Right. Will he talk to me?"

"He invited you to his house. He lives by the Brewery, on the other side of the freeway. I'll send you the address. He's home today."

"Great."

"Hugo actually remembers you from when we worked together," Doris said. "You would have been in fifth grade."

"I don't remember him."

"You might when you meet him. Go easy on the man. He's quite sensitive. He lost his husband less than a year ago."

"You think I'm going to assault the guy?" Slater demanded.

"It wouldn't be the first time."

"I am not a hooligan." He huffed. "I appreciate you setting this up," he said, and ended the call.

That was the second time today he'd been profiled as heavy-handed. What was wrong with people? From downstairs he heard the front door, and then the sound of footsteps on the stairs. A minute later Pike dropped onto the sofa and pulled Slater's feet into his lap, and Slater folded his laptop closed.

"How was the furniture store?"

"Grace bought a sideboard," Pike said. "It's very tasteful."

"Do you need help moving it inside?"

"It's being delivered later this week. The guys on the truck will bring it in for her." He raised his eyebrows. "My work is done."

ELEVEN

"HAVE YOU EVER HEARD of Boris and Natasha?" Slater said. "From a 1960s cartoon."

"That sounds a little familiar." Pike squeezed his toes.

"They got arrested for throwing rocks at girl scouts."

Pike laughed, in that deep rich tone he had. "That's just cold. Like, really cold."

"There's two sides to every story. What was the scouts' role in it? Maybe they were price-gouging on those cookies. They aren't cheap."

"It's conscientious of you to consider all the possibilities. Like schoolchildren committing financial crimes. Why are you reading about old cartoons?"

"It's part of my case."

"What the hell does cartoons have to do with the missing college kid?" Pike said.

He told him about interviewing Jeff, and the nicknames, and Raskolnikov. "Jeff and Diane are AME. Do you know that religion?"

"I went to a funeral at an AME church. They're actually

not crazy compared to lots of the evangelicals."

"No brandishing snakes and convulsing on the floor?" Slater said.

"With lots of evangelicals," Pike said, "the message is, you're a piece of trash, you should be very afraid of god, so come on board or else you're in for a world of hurt. At AME it was more like, we've got something good here, you're missing out, you should get on board because you'll really enjoy it."

"So it's more positive. How do you know all that?"

"The small towns we work in. It's guns and ammo and church."

Slater swung his feet onto the floor and sat up. "I have to go. I've got another interview."

Leaning in to embrace him, Pike mouthed his neck, and his jaw. "Do you love me?" he murmured.

"More than girl scout cookies." Slater inhaled the heady scent of his hair. "More than guns and ammo. More than life itself."

Once he'd trotted down to the garage, and backed into the street, he plugged the address Doris had sent into his navigation app. Hugo's place wasn't far, in Lincoln Heights, on the other side of Chinatown and that stupid stadium.

The street was lined with compact old bungalows spaced tight together. Some had been renovated, but lots of them still looked rough, in need of paint and shingles. Every single yard had a fence up tight to the sidewalk. Backing into a street space in front of Hugo's address, he saw that the gate across the driveway was open, with a ten-year-old Subaru wagon parked farther up, in front of the garage.

The marine layer had finally retreated, and as he climbed out of the car, Slater stretched and turned his face to the sun. As he walked up the driveway he checked out Hugo's plantings. There were a couple of lush cycads, and some stripy agaves, and a small tree with warped and twisted bark. Stepping closer, he looked at the leaves, running his hand among them. This was a pomegranate. By fall these little buds would be fruit.

At the house, the steel-mesh screen door swung open, and a guy called to him. "You like pomegranates?"

Slater walked toward him. "It's hardy when there's drought, so it's not inappropriate here." He gestured at the other greenery. "Neither are the cycads."

He furrowed his brow. "I'm so glad you can tolerate them."

Hugo had dark Latin hair with some gray in it, and he was built slender, with solid cheekbones.

"Doris said I might remember you," Slater said, "but I don't."

"I probably haven't seen you since you were in middle school. You had a lot going on as a teenager."

"True." It wasn't really surprising—there were lots of blank spots from back then. He'd seen photos of himself at events and in situations that he had no memory of.

"You turned out to be quite the looker," Hugo said, giving him the once-over. "I guess it's not surprising. Your father was handsome."

"You knew him?"

"Not well. Doris and my husband and I were all work-ing at the same school when he died. I know that was hard on you both. How old were you?"

"Thirteen," Slater said. "It definitely messed me up."

"I remember when you were younger than that, maybe around ten, Doris had some people over. Maybe it was a housewarming. You were sitting on his lap with your arms around his neck. The pair of you were talking, all quiet, sharing secrets. It was adorable, the connection you had with him. Some neighbor who was at the party thought you were too old to be daddy's boy, but Doris set her straight. She told her you two had important things to discuss."

"I'm sure we did. Doris said your man died recently."

"It's strange to be single again at this age."

Slater put his hands on his hips. "Well, guys are still willing to put out these days, Hugo, and you're hot. You can get all the dick you want." He waved an arm. "I'd do you myself if you weren't a friend of my mother's."

His eyes narrowed. "Thanks for the encouragement. Why don't you come inside?"

The interior was dark, the front room compact and a little cluttered, with overstuffed furniture. One wall was lined with shelves of books. Hugo walked through to the kitchen.

"We'll sit outside," he said. "Do you want some lemonade?"

From a pitcher in the icebox he poured into a couple of glasses, then handed one to Slater and stepped out the back door. These lots were narrow but long, and he had a decent amount of space back here. Fences on both sides were overgrown with gnarly English ivy, and a mosaic-topped patio table and chairs sat on a patch of scrubby grass. Over by the garage was a citrus tree.

"Is that a lemon?" Slater said as they sat at the table.

"Grapefruit. Unfortunately they're no good. Too bitter. The peel is an inch thick."

He sipped his lemonade. It was tasty—strong and not too sweet. "You can improve that by putting some potassium and magnesium in the soil. If the fruit is bad, you have to graft on branches of something that tastes better."

Hugo grinned. "I'm no gardener. My neighbor gives me lemons, hence the lemonade."

"So you taught Boris Brooks in high school."

"I did. I recognized his photo in the paper when he disappeared."

"You must have taught hundreds of kids every year. What made Boris memorable?"

"I taught music," Hugo said. "Not many kids take up violin. His outbursts were also memorable."

"He got violent?"

Hugo lifted his glass and sipped from it. "More like he got emotional. Lots of tears. I don't think he ever struck anyone."

"What was his damage?"

"I couldn't tell you that. Nowadays they'd check him for autism spectrum. Back then it was just considered teen drama. Usually that stuff was about bullying or romantic crushes. It's so long ago. I don't remember the specifics."

"Was Boris gay?"

He raised his eyebrows. "That's totally possible. He was that kind of kid."

"The fuck does that mean?" Slater demanded.

"He was musical, and academic. Not into football or smashing stuff."

"Gay guys smash stuff too."

"I remember that well," Hugo said. "It's fortunate your mother got you on the wrestling team. At least that gave you an outlet. I think things got better for her after that."

He remembered lots about wrestling, but he didn't remember Doris's life shifting. "Unfortunately I remain a source of perpetual heartache for Doris."

Hugo set his glass down on the table. "Think about the parallels. You're looking into Boris. Boris had trouble containing his emotions. You got into wrestling for the same reason."

He narrowed his eyes. "I wouldn't say I had trouble with my emotions. I had trouble digesting other people's unlimited capacity for stupidity. The breathtaking bottomless well of it. And why is that similarity in any way significant?"

"Reality is not what you think it is. You have to look beyond the surface."

"That sounds like a religious thing," Slater said. "Are you Catholic?"

"It's actually closer to science. If you look beyond the superficial appearance, you can see things differently, and get an alternate perspective on reality. I remember you went missing up in the Sierra for a few days in your youth. Just like Boris, you disappeared."

He sipped at his lemonade. "I didn't actually go missing. I knew exactly where I was."

"Doris had the rangers out looking for you."

"It started snowing, and I couldn't get back to camp, so I headed downhill. Eventually I found my way to a road, and met a ranger parked in the middle of it. He gave me a ride. Doris makes it sound so dramatic. Like the Passover story about wandering in the desert for forty years on the way to the promised land." Slater waved an arm. "It's not like I wandered into a snowstorm wearing flip-flops and a Speedo. I had snacks with me, and boots, and a warm jacket. There was no drama except in her mind."

His eyes bright, Hugo held his gaze. "Think of it in another way. Boris disappeared, like you did, only he didn't come back."

"And Boris is still missing. It's really not about me."

"The synchronicity is something to listen to, though. The overlap in your story and Boris's is like a text that you can read."

"You've lost me, professor."

"It's called hermeneutics," Hugo said. "Named for the god Hermes."

"I know that guy. The messenger. He moved fast. Wore winged sandals and that cool hat."

"He was also the god of crossroads, and liminal places,

where meanings can shift. Hermeneutics means any event can be like a book that you can read. There's the literal meaning, like Boris disappeared, and then there's the wider subjective meaning—what does Boris's disappearance mean symbolically? What does it mean in the big picture?"

"It sounds like you've done a lot of acid," Slater said.

Hugo laughed. "I did, back in my salad days. Recently people have looked at synchronicities with hermeneutics. They call it synchromysticism. You can find some interesting patterns if you pay attention, consider the meaning, and glean information in those patterns."

"Explain synchronicities."

"A synchronicity is like a coincidence," Hugo said, "but with meaning. You and Boris both disappeared, and there's no causal connection. It's just a coincidence. But now you're looking for him. That makes it meaningful. It's a synchronicity."

"How is comparing my experience to Boris's going to tell me anything about his whereabouts?"

"You'll only know that once you start considering the synchronicities that come up."

Slater looked away and sipped his lemonade. "The boyfriend and I have been reading the classics."

"That's why you know who Hermes is."

"You know the character Cassandra?"

"She was given the gift of prophecy," Hugo said, "but was destined never to be believed."

"That's what I'm picking up from you here." He swirled his palm toward him. "It sounds valuable, but it's awfully hard to swallow. I can't believe synchronicities are going to lead me to Boris."

"I get that. Just keep it in mind." He sat up. "You implied that you think Boris is still alive. Why?"

"We had a séance. Nobody in the spirit world has seen

him. That means he's still on this side."

Hugo scoffed. "You're skeptical about hermeneutics, but you're totally down with data gathered at a séance."

"I don't believe any of it, man. It's all mystical bullshit. I'm knee-deep in the stream, trying to pan out a few flecks of truth among all the muck."

"And yet you're still open to it." He slapped the table with his palm. "You have to come ghost hunting."

"Are you fucking kidding me?" he demanded.

"It's kind of a hobby. I have a crew. We make videos."

"You're on television?"

"We're amateurs," Hugo said, "but we have a following online. Lots of people watch our content. We're doing an abandoned hotel tonight. Ghosts have been reported there, so we're going in to assess the weirdness."

"You know what's weird, Hugo? I don't choose this stuff, but it seems to follow me around. Sasquatch and flying saucers and séances. And now a damn ghost hunt."

"I'd say there's a message there for you. The question is, are you listening?"

"I'll tell you what I think is going on," Slater said. "Our species is devolving, and fracturing, and getting stupider. The truth is malleable now. People believe whatever sparkly thing catches their attention."

Hugo threw up his hands. "So what's the harm? Maybe you'll see a ghost."

He pursed his lips and watched him for a moment. "Can I bring the boyfriend? He loves all this stuff."

"I'd like to meet him. Doris says he's a honey dripper."

"Doris needs to stop gossiping about me." He sighed. "Pike definitely knows how to talk to people. It's actually odd."

Hugo told him about the plan, and then answered a few more questions about Boris. There was nothing new or even worthwhile in his vague memories, Slater decided, except maybe the assertion that Boris had teen drama going on. Eventually Slater rose and carried the glasses into the kitchen, and Hugo followed him to the front door.

"I hope you find the answers you're looking for."

"We'll see what happens," Slater said, and walked out to the street.

Once he was behind the wheel of the Continental he started the engine and pulled into the street. Talking to Hugo was like watching a movie with subtitles and not paying attention. He quickly lost track of what the hell was going on.

Hugo had used the same words as the psychic: *pay attention.* Could that mean anything? It was so damn vague, and people said things like that every fricking day. It carried about as much weight as *be good* or *take care.* But there was an overlap in this case. Not about him and Boris both going missing—that was just bogus, Hugo's burned-out synapses misfiring. The thing about *Crime and Punishment* was harder to explain away.

Heather had brandished a hardback copy of the book for her movie reboot, and Boris and Jeff used to say "Raskolnikov." It was definitely a coincidence, but was it one of Hugo's synchronicities? Jeff said he had no contact with Heather, so it couldn't be connected, not in the way he understood reality to work, where people caused carnage when they did stupid things to get money or sex or power. He just had to figure out those specifics, he decided. In the tangible version of reality. Raskolnikov couldn't tell him anything. Focusing on it would be wasting time chasing links that didn't really exist.

TWELVE

UPSTAIRS AT THE HOUSE Slater found Pike on the deck, stretched out in a lounger with his sunglasses on, reading a hardback. Straddling the chair, he leaned in to maul him, mouthing his neck and his jaw. The book splayed on the deck as it fell from Pike's hand, and he ran his fingers into Slater's hair. Eventually he pulled back.

"You smell amazing." Slater picked up the book and read the spine. "Jackson, *The Lost Weekend*. It looks old."

"World War II era. It's about an alcoholic on his way to rock bottom. He gets tossed in the jug."

Slater frowned and handed it to him. "Don't be getting any ideas. I'm just relieved you're not reading *Crime and Punishment*. It came up twice in my case for no reason. If you were reading it too, I'd toss myself in the jug."

"I was thinking we could walk down to that burger joint on Sunset," Pike said, "then later go to the floor show at that hotcha place in Los Feliz. There aren't going to be many more opportunities to see Danny and Frances perform before they move on to their ultimate reward."

"That place is definitely where the hep cats go to groove.

But I've got a counter for you." He massaged Pike's forearms. "We walk down to that burger joint on Sunset, then go on a ghost hunt with one of Doris's old teacher henchmen."

"Seriously? That sounds like way more fun than those flashy octogenarians."

"Danny actually turned ninety a while ago. Doris sent me a story from the paper about his birthday. He's still at the nightclub pounding the eighty-eights."

"Tell me about the ghost hunt."

"Doris's confederate is an *alte kaker* named Hugo. He has a squad—him and another ghost hunter and a camera operator. They film it for their online fans. We'd be assisting them."

"So I'm not going to wind up on late-night TV."

"He says they're hobbyists."

"Maybe I'll use a pseudonym anyway," Pike said.

"Great idea. Somehow they got access to an old hotel downtown. It's been shuttered since the nineties."

"Is there a dress code?"

"Hugo said wear whatever makes you comfortable."

"So booty shorts and a crop top for me," Pike said.

He leaned in to massage his pecs. "If you dress all hoochie, I won't be able to focus on anything else. I'll just stand there drooling all night with a giant stiffy in my pants."

"You're very sex-oriented."

"And you love it. I'm also very Pike-oriented. You love that too."

Pike pulled him close, and mashed their mouths together. When Slater pulled back, he stood up.

"My stomach is growling."

Downstairs in the bedroom, Pike pulled on a pair of jeans and a plaid shirt with short sleeves, and they walked down to Sunset. After they'd ordered at the counter they sat at a table on the sidewalk to eat.

"These taste like actual burgers," Pike said. "They're getting more realistic all the time."

"Have you heard of hermeneutics? The guy I interviewed today talked about interpreting synchronicities with hermeneutics, so you can see bigger meanings in coincidences."

"That's part of the whole New Age extravaganza."

"Hugo said it's about science."

Pike set his burger down. "It's about beliefs. Religion or spirituality. You can't use science to figure out synchronicities."

"Explain it to me."

"In the *Odyssey* and *Theogony* the gods are like people. They do petty human things. Get angry and then get revenge, and beat the crap out of people."

"Like Uranus getting his dick chopped off."

"The Jewish god was originally a natural force. Thunder and rain to help you out or mess you up. Then the Europeans turned their god into a king. They were supposed to adore him and fear him at the same time. But New Age thinking strikes me as more modern. You're responsible for what happens to you, and you can change it yourself. Hippie hermeneutics is like that—you can see whatever you want in things, and personalize it. Random coincidences start to have meaning. The idea lines up with American optimism. That idea that you can achieve whatever you want to if you just work at it."

"You're American optimism." Slater jabbed a finger at him and raised his eyebrows. "You."

Pike grinned. "It is kind of the way I'm wired."

"I love that you read so much, and think about this kind of stuff. It makes me feel dumb in comparison."

"You're a lot of things, forty-niner, but dumb isn't one of them."

As they walked back to the house, dusk was setting in, and Pike put his arm around his waist. It felt comfortable and familiar, part of his reality now. Slater bumped him with his shoulder as they walked.

In the garage they climbed into the Continental, and Slater drove downtown. The hotel was in the Historic Core, and when they pulled up on the building, the street was lined with a row of steel shutters and no signage. He parked at a meter and they climbed out.

"I've driven by here a thousand times," Slater said. "I had no idea it used to be a hotel."

Pike pointed up to the ornate stonework. "It doesn't get elegant until you're above the ground floor. Nobody's looking at that when they're driving."

"I was told the service entrance is in back."

They walked toward the alley at the end of the building and found a steel gate across it, topped with coils of razor wire. The pedestrian door built into the gate had a keypad on it.

"Hugo gave me the code," he said, stepping up to it and digging out his phone to find the number.

The door swung open, and they stepped inside, letting it slam shut again on its spring. The gritty and potholed alley was lined with dumpsters parked outside the back entrances to the shops and offices. Unlike most secluded places, there were no tents, no shopping carts full of stuff, no stench of stale urine. The razor wire had kept the homeless out.

On the hotel side of the alley was a set of heavy double doors. One of them was ajar, and Slater pulled it open. The lights were on inside, and it looked like a storage room, with a concrete floor and heavy pipes running overhead. The walls were scuffed and grubby, the dull green paint job peeling in places. A rotund guy wearing a guard's uniform stepped into the room. Wearing a black jacket, he had a sidearm on his hip.

"Gentlemen."

"We're with Hugo," Slater said.

"They're in the lobby." He gestured through the doorway he'd just come from. "Through there and to the left. You're the last of the five."

"Have you seen ghosts in the building?" Pike said.

He cackled as he slammed the big door. "That would be no."

They walked into the hallway, painted the same utilitarian flat green, then into a broad space with a high ceiling. A coffered ceiling with intricate decorated plasterwork marked this as a public space—the lobby. It would have had lounge furniture when it was functioning, but now there was just wide empty floor. Worn pathways and dark blotches stained the carpet, and sections of it had been torn up at one side, revealing the concrete below. Water stains marred the walls, bubbling the paint.

Running along most of one side of the room was a counter fronted in dark wood, likely mahogany, and standing in front of it were Hugo and another guy. A third man was over by the doors to the street, filming something with a video camera, even though there was no view to the street, obscured as it was by the heavy steel shutters on the exterior.

Hugo called a greeting, and they walked over. Wearing black pants and a black shirt, his graying hair looked darker now, slicked back and neatly styled.

"This fool is Fermín," Hugo said. "He's our lead ghost hunter. Over there is our camera operator, Michael."

Fermín was about Hugo's age, and had gray roots in his dark hair, with a bit of a gut bulging over his belt. His face was lined from sun exposure or maybe just age. He was also clad in black and wore a bulky black backpack. The straps on his shoulders made his pecs stick out. Basically fuckable, Slater decided.

Michael walked over, the video camera dangling at his side. He was a lot younger than Hugo or Fermín, still in his twenties, and built lanky. His longish black hair was tucked under a ball cap, and he was wearing a red T-shirt, and cargo pants, and scuffed construction boots.

From the hallway, the security guard called, "Hey, boss."

Hugo strode over to the guard, and Pike introduced himself and Slater to the others. As he gave them the once-over, Fermín's gaze rested on Slater's waist.

"You see something you like down there, chief?" Slater briefly grabbed his crotch.

"What? No."

"You don't have to be shy."

"I was thinking the jeans are a little casual," Fermín said. "We tend to go with black."

"You can film me from the waist up, but your viewers will be missing out on the money shot." He gestured to Michael. "How come you get to dress like a hobo?"

Michael frowned at him. "I'm not on camera."

Walking back to them, Hugo said, "We're on our own—the guard left. He'll be back later to let us out."

"How long has this place been empty?" Pike said.

"The hotel closed in the 1990s." Hugo looked around the lobby. "I know it looks neglected. The last renovation was sometime in the 1980s."

"I can see that in the decor."

Fermín eyed him. "You're a decorator?"

"It's the paint colors." Pike gestured to the walls. "Those pastels are typical eighties."

"If you say so. Listen, you two need to sign likeness permission forms. So we can use the video of you." Fermín slid off his backpack and started to zip it open.

Pike put his hands on his hips. "Yeah, I'm not doing that. Isn't this just going up online? I'll give you verbal permission to use my image. You can record me saying it."

"There's a chance the series will get picked up by a network." Fermín stood erect. "I need a signature."

Hugo held up a palm. "We can revisit that if the series gets distribution. Verbal permission is fine for now."

"We're also using pseudonyms," Slater said. "If you need to use my name on camera, it's John Slade."

"Likewise, I'm Seth Pine," Pike said.

Fermín closed his eyes for a moment. "Fine," he said flatly. "Let's get started."

"Don't you need to tell us what to do?" Pike said.

"Fermín has some equipment," Hugo said, briefly resting a hand on Pike's shoulder. "Basically they're ghost detectors. We'll set them up in various places, but really it's all about your experiences. Just let it flow. If you feel a chill or a presence, definitely say something."

"I'll give you stuff to do," Fermín said. "Reposition a sensor, or switch it on or off. You can talk freely about what's happening. The banter makes good video. If you remember, try to use each other's names when you talk. It helps the viewers connect with us."

Pike nodded. "That works."

Raising the camera, Michael took a few steps back. "Let me frame you with all the little letterboxes behind you. They totally say 'abandoned hotel.' You guys can stay where you are. I'm rolling."

As he aimed the camera at him, Fermín cleared his throat and turned to face the lens. He pulled the backpack on again, and posed with his thumbs hooked in the straps. When he spoke, his demeanor shifted, and he suddenly sounded bright and upbeat.

First, Fermín introduced himself, then gestured to the

room. "Tonight we're at the Hotel Luran in downtown Los Angeles. The structure has been abandoned for decades. Gaining access to this Gilded Age gem took a lot of negotiating by our chief of operations, Hugo Rodríguez."

Michael panned to Hugo, who beamed and nodded, then moved the camera back to focus on Fermín.

"Hugo got permission for us to spend some time here before the renovations start," Fermín said. "Also helping us out tonight are John Slade and Seth Pine."

It was actually impressive that the guy remembered both those names, Slater thought, as Michael panned toward them. He raised his eyebrows at the camera, and Pike grinned and lifted a palm in greeting.

"Behind the camera as always is the highly skilled cinematographer Michael Tran," Fermín said, once the lens was on him again. "Tonight we're going to do some research on the retail floor. It's just upstairs from the lobby. There's been a lot of reports of paranormal activity in that area." He cracked a smile. "So let's go poke around."

Michael panned toward the big staircase that led upward, lingering on it for a moment, and then lowered the camera. "Got it."

"Do we need a second take?" Fermín said.

"You were golden, man."

Fermín nodded and walked toward the stairs. Wide at the bottom, they tapered to a landing, with more steps leading up at a right angle.

As they followed the trio, Slater walked next to Pike. "Seth Pine was awfully close to the top of your mind."

"I use it for work sometimes."

"I get it. Seth sounds like Zeb, and Pine sounds like Pike. It's hard to miss."

THIRTEEN

T HE RETAIL FLOOR LOOKED like a small-scale shopping mall, a single wide hallway lined by abandoned storefronts. They still had glass display windows but all the doors had been removed. One of the shops near the head of the stairs had MENSWEAR painted on the glass. Slater stepped over to look inside. Grimy linoleum stretched back into the gloom, and at one side sat a lone rolling rack with a few empty hangers dangling from it.

Fermín stopped in the middle of the broad hallway, and pulled off his backpack, and set it on the floor.

"Can we get some of this neon turned on?" Michael said. "It'll make for good video."

"Let me check." Hugo strode over into one of the shops. "There's juice," he called, and a moment later a green sign in the front window flickered to life. It said MILLIE'S in cursive lettering.

The dull electric buzz of the sign was audible now, and Slater stepped over to look inside. There was nothing but the grubby bare floor. It was hard to say what Millie had sold back in the day.

Across the hall, Hugo went into another shop, and soon an orange sign with GOLD and below it DIAMONDS in blocky letters flicked on. Farther down he switched on another, a soft pink LIDO with a big curly capital *L*.

"I can't believe nobody took these signs when they moved out," Pike said.

"If you were shutting down your business, you'd have no use for it," Hugo said. "You can't really resell them."

Once Hugo returned, Fermín eyed Slater and Pike. "From now on we're going to film everything. For the camera I'm going to instruct you two to set up some sensors."

From his backpack he pulled out a device that looked like a handheld level meter that electricians used. He stepped close to them and held it out to demonstrate.

"This is the power switch, so you turn it on, then pull out the stand. Then just set it on the floor."

Taking it from him, Slater looked it over. It had a numerical readout and an array of LED lamps studding the front. "What does it measure?"

"Electromagnetic anomalies. For some reason the spirits find it easy to manipulate electronics." He waggled his fingers to take it back, then eyed Michael. "Are we ready?"

"I'm rolling." He had the camera trained on Fermín.

Suddenly sounding warm again, Fermín handed Slater the device, along with a second identical one. "John, let's set up these sensors at the end of the hall. One on either side."

"I'm on it." Slater took them and strode toward the dimly lit far end. He heard Fermín instruct Pike to put more of them near the top of the stairs.

Michael was following him now, he saw, with the camera trained on him. Ignoring it, Slater dropped to one knee to click on the power switch and pull out the little stand. Once he'd set up the sensor, he crossed the hall to do the other one.

As he started back toward Fermín, Michael turned and walked ahead of him, the camera now aimed at Pike. Eyeing one of the shops, Slater paused to look over a hand-painted sign mounted next to the doorway. It was a laundry list of electronics: RADIOS • STEREOS • PORTABLE VCRS. Inside he could see bare shelves and an empty glass display case.

Hugo stepped closer and spoke in a low voice, even though Michael and the camera were at the other end of the long hallway.

"Are you feeling ghostly energy?"

"It's actually one of your synchronicities." Slater pointed to the sign. "VCRs. That specific defunct technology keeps coming up in my work on Boris. I actually bought a VCR machine at a thrift store yesterday to watch Boris's old tapes."

Hugo clapped him on the shoulder. "You see? You're doing it. That mind-set is going to shed a lot of light on your quest."

Fermín was eyeing them, Slater realized, a scowl on his face. What was his damage? The camera was on Pike right now, nowhere near them.

A loud squeal pierced the air, and Hugo started. It was the sensor he'd just set up. The one on the opposite side sounded next, repeating the shrill tone. The LED lamps on the front of it were lit up in orange and red.

"We've got one." Fermín hustled toward the sensors, and Michael trotted after him, the camera trained on the action. The rest of them followed, and when Pike caught up, Fermín eyed Michael. "Let's get footage of John here examining the readings."

"How do I do that?" Slater said.

"Pick it up and hit the button marked PEAK. That shows the strongest signal it detected. The background level is under forty. Just say all that."

Stepping over to the sensor, Slater scooped it up, and planted his feet apart, and pressed the Peak button. "Fuck me—the peak signal is sixty-three. That's well above the normal background level. It should be under forty."

"Knock it off with the cursing," Fermín said, scowling at him. "When you do that, we have to bleep the video."

Standing next to him, Pike briefly stroked his jaw. He was stifling a laugh.

"Go do the other one." Fermín gestured to it.

As he picked it up, Slater could feel the camera on him. "That burst hit eighty-three. Are you seeing this, Hugo? The background level shouldn't be above forty."

Hugo stepped next to him and took the device, and peered at it, his brow furrowing. "A spike like that can only mean one thing, John." He paused and looked at Fermín. "There's a strong presence here."

Michael shifted the camera to Fermín.

"I'm sensing a male entity," Fermín said, his tone hushed. "I feel it flitting around this hallway." He raised his voice. "I'm addressing the entity in this space. Did you work here?"

Michael slowly stepped closer to him as he spoke. The sensor that Slater had just replaced squealed again. Fermín flinched and then stood up straighter.

"I'll take that as a yes. We mean you no harm. And you need to be nice."

The sensor squealed, for longer this time, followed by the same noise from one that Pike had set up at the opposite end of the hall.

"Seth, can you check on that?" Hugo said.

Striding over to the device, Pike dropped to one knee to examine it. He waited for Michael to get closer before he spoke. "Three spikes in the low nineties." He held up the device and gestured helplessly. "I've never seen anything like this."

Slater had to suppress a scoff. He'd never seen anything like it because he'd never been on a ghost hunt before.

Pursing his lips, Fermín looked around at the ceiling. Michael was focused on him now, and stepped toward him, so close that his face would fill the video frame. "He doesn't want us invading his space."

Once Pike had replaced the sensor, he stood up, and Hugo put a hand on his arm.

"You're a natural. You should be a regular on our team."

Pike just laughed and squeezed him around the shoulder. The camera wasn't aimed at Fermín, and Slater could see his face contort as he watched them talk. The guy might be psychic, but he wasn't very good at masking his emotions. Was he jealous of Hugo?

Both nearby detectors squealed again, and Pike stepped over to check the other one.

"That one maxed out the sensor. Take a look at this, Fermín." He held it out toward the camera. The number readout said 99.

"The entity is restless," Fermín said.

"What's he doing here?" Hugo spoke in a hushed tone and looked around at the ceiling. He raised his voice. "Why are you fixated on this place? Why are you in the retail area? Were you a shopkeeper?"

"I sense that this is a thin place," Fermín said.

Hugo eyed him. "You mean that ghosts are attracted here?"

"A thin place is where the veil between this world and the spiritual realm is more permeable," Fermín said. "Spirits from the other side can move in and out of our reality more easily than in the lobby or upstairs in the guest rooms."

He had to be saying that for the benefit of the camera, Slater realized. These guys were on the same squad—Hugo would already know what that meant.

Once Pike had replaced the sensor, he got to his feet. "Just to consider all the possibilities, do you think the neon signs might be setting off the detectors? Those transformers are high voltage. You can hear them buzzing. It makes sense that they'd generate radio interference."

"It's not the neon," Fermín said intently. "Stick with the program."

"Sure." Pike folded his arms. "It's your show."

"Michael, you can edit that out in post." He paused for a moment, then raised his voice. "We want to help you move on. There's no need for you to be here. Later this year the whole building is going to be gutted and converted to condos."

All four detectors squealed at once, their shrill alarms filling the air.

"You don't need to get angry at me, sir," Fermín said. "I'm just the messenger." He took a breath. "Take a look around you, sir. You'll see the brightness. Step into the light."

For a while no one spoke, and they stood there in the hall. Michael panned the camera around the space, then briefly focused on each of them as they gazed at the walls and the ceiling.

On his arms and his neck Slater felt cold air, and he inhaled sharply. Waving his hands, he found it was cold all around him. It felt like a flash of winter. "Whoa—does anyone else feel that?"

"It got cold," Hugo said. "All of a sudden."

"Really cold," Pike said. "It's like I stepped into a Frigidaire."

Moving next to Pike, Fermín put a hand on his shoulder. "You're right, Seth. I feel it too. But it's more like the Frigidaire stepped into you."

Pike furrowed his brow. "Can you explain that, Fermín?"

"We call it the funnel effect. The entity is creating a

vortex and draining it of energy. It's able to remove the heat." He spoke louder and glanced around at the walls. "Look around you, sir. Look for the light. Move toward it. That's your next step."

The nearby devices squealed again.

"This is one stubborn ghost," Hugo said.

The sound of clanking metal came from one of the shops. It was the empty menswear store by the stairs, Slater realized. Fermín and Hugo sprinted toward the noise, followed by Michael, trotting after them and holding the camera level.

Slater and Pike followed as they hustled into the empty store. Fermín and Hugo were standing next to the rolling rack, lying on its side now, wheels up, the hangers scattered across the grubby linoleum.

"Did this just fall?" Hugo said.

"I looked in here earlier," Slater said. "When we first came up. It was upright then, and all the hangers were on the rail. I remember wondering if those had been dangling there since the place shut down."

"It's a class 1," Fermín said.

Hugo furrowed his brow. "What's a class 1?"

He had to know that already, Slater knew, just like he had to know what a thin place was. This was all for the viewers.

"It means a spiritual entity that can manipulate physical objects," Fermín said. "Those are the most dangerous of all." Looking around the room, he raised his voice. "Sir, we mean you no harm."

It went on that way for a while, Fermín talking to the air, the detectors squealing intermittently, but nothing else fell over or made noise. Eventually Michael lowered the camera.

"I think we have enough footage for the episode. The guard should be back by now."

"Let me do a closing bit." Fermín gestured to Millie's bright green sign. "Get me with the neon." Once he was posed in front of it, and the camera was on him, he shifted into his aimable persona. "The Hotel Luran definitely has some spectral residents. We can't say they're malevolent, exactly, but like many ghosts, they seem restive, and not content with their situation. My hope for tonight is that we've been able to encourage them to move on and find peace."

"Perfect," Michael said. "That's a wrap."

Hugo walked into Millie's, and a moment later the sign went dark. Once he'd turned off the others, they followed Fermín down the stairs to the lobby.

The security guard was leaning against the front counter, and once they'd descended, he led them to the door into the alley. "How did the ghost hunt go?"

"You've definitely got an infestation on the retail floor," Fermín said.

"Good to know." His expression deadpan, he pushed open the door.

Once they were out through the gate at the end of the alley, Fermín and Michael walked up the street, but Hugo hung back.

"I'm glad you came. Maybe we'll pull you in on another case. You're both great on camera."

"I'm not sure Fermín would agree with you," Slater said.

"I can handle him." He raised his eyebrows. "Just keep paying attention. You'll be amazed at what you find."

Raising his palm, Hugo turned and walked up the block.

"Keep paying attention?" Pike said as they walked to the Continental.

"It's the synchronicities thing. Hugo's brain is burned out from too much psychedelics. He's seeing faces in the clouds. It doesn't mean there's people up there."

"The psychic told you the same thing at that séance."

Slater stepped into the street and unlocked the driver's door. "Yeah, there's that."

Once they'd climbed in, he started the engine and pulled into the street.

"So are you convinced there's a ghost in that hotel?"

"I'm convinced some electromagnetic energy set off those sensors," Pike said.

"The transformers for the neon."

"But then there was that cold flash. I felt it too."

"I suppose it could have been an air-conditioner malfunction."

"I'm glad we went," Pike said, gazing out at the dark city rolling by. "Now I can say I've been on a ghost hunt."

FOURTEEN

P IKE HAD ALREADY LEFT for work when Slater woke to the gray daylight outside the windows. He thought about the ghost hunt, and the painted sign for VCRs. That damn VCR machine and the deadweight little television set were still cluttering up his trunk. A stop at the thrift store would fix that. Thinking about it, Heather said Boris and Jeff had a high-end TV set in their dorm, and those videotapes had been among Boris's college stuff. Grabbing his phone, he texted Jeff:

Did you and Boris have a VCR in your dorm room?

Jeff's reply came a moment later:

Affirmative. Why?

Slater sent a terse response:

We need to talk.

Rising, he got dressed, and upstairs found java that Pike had left in the pot, at room temperature now. Once he'd filled a mug, he took it and half a bagel out onto the deck. He was still waiting to hear back from Jeff when he finished the joe. The guy had responded quickly to the first text. Was he suddenly afraid of him now? Why couldn't people just keep it together?

"Idiot," he muttered, and took his mug back to the kitchen.

From below he heard the doorbell ring, and he headed down the stairs. At this hour it was likely a package. Pike got stuff sent to the house sometimes.

When he pulled open the front door, no one was there, and he stepped outside to look around for the delivery. Sometimes they just dumped the boxes in front of the garage, but it was so close to the sidewalk that it made easy pickings for anyone walking by. In front of the garage he found a guy in jeans and a dark T-shirt, wearing a black-and-white keffiyeh around his head, leaving only his eyes visible.

"You must have taken a wrong turn," Slater said. "There's no Palestinian blockade around here."

He should have anticipated trouble, but the guy had the advantage of surprise, and came at him fast, and punched him in the mouth. Slater struck back and managed a glancing blow to his face under the keffiyeh. In the same moment the guy landed a left hook to his eye, and then kicked him hard in the balls.

"Fuck," Slater roared, and crumpled around his crotch.

"You need to let it go," the guy growled. "Just stay away."

With that he turned and strode off.

The searing pain went well beyond his groin, radiating into his abdomen. It felt like it was piercing his lungs and cutting off his breath. Forcing himself to inhale, he managed to stand partly erect, then hobbled down the block after his assailant.

A few doors down the guy climbed into a matte-black

sedan. Slater stopped to watch, breathing hard. It looked like a Charger. The engine revved loud when he started it—it had a Hellcat engine. Within seconds he roared off down the street. But Slater had been close enough to read the plate.

Wincing with the effort, he forced himself to straighten up enough to pull his phone out of his jeans, then typed a note with the tag number. It was totally stupid of the guy to let his target see the vehicle. More likely it didn't matter what he saw—it was a stolen car.

Slater stretched his back and walked to his house, moving slowly and massaging his belly. Gradually he was able to breathe more deeply, and that helped to dispel the pain. He knew it would subside eventually.

What the fuck did that knucklehead mean by 'stay away'? People needed to be more specific. Thinking about it, somebody had tried to intimidate Elvaine when she'd made a FOIA request. Was this about Boris going to work for the feds? But if some shadowy agency wanted to scare him off, they would have sent someone with more finesse, like Elvaine's men in black. This guy seemed more like a hack.

Upstairs in the bathroom mirror he saw that his eye looked red, the first stage of a shiner, and he already had a fat lip. In the kitchen he took a bag of frozen peas from the freezer, and went out to the deck, and stretched out on a lounger with the bag on his face. The dull cold made his skin ache, but it might make the damage less dramatic.

In his pants his phone buzzed, and he pulled it out and peered at it with his uninjured eye. It was a text from Jeff:

I'm home all day.

"Finally," he muttered, and set the phone on the ground.

Once he was over the pain in his nards, and had caught his breath, he forced himself up. Tossing the peas back in the freezer, he went down to his car and headed toward the freeway.

When he pulled into the driveway at Jeff and Diane's, Slater parked along the side and climbed out. The plumeria looked to have even more of the crisp white blossoms than just yesterday.

When he rang the bell, Jeff pulled open the door and frowned. "What happened to your face?"

"I walked into a door."

"OK," he said evenly. "Come in. I've got a pot of coffee on."

Slater stood waiting in the living room until Jeff returned with a mug in each hand, and gave him one, then sat on one of the mod lounge chairs. Taking the adjacent one, he sipped at the java.

"This is the good stuff."

"You asked about a VCR," Jeff said. "We definitely had one. It was plugged into the Trinitron."

"What was the VCR for?"

"To record things and watch them later. Back then you could also rent movies on tape from video stores. When you asked about it, I got to thinking. I remember once I found a tape that was left in the machine. I played it to see what it was." Jeff raised his eyebrows. "It turned out to be an explicit video of some men together."

"Gay porn? It was Boris's?"

"It had to be. It wasn't mine. I only watched a minute of it."

"Didn't that make you think Boris was gay?"

"It didn't register." He gestured helplessly. "I guess it was too far from my reality."

"Even though you called each other by couple nick-names?" Slater said.

Jeff laughed. "Have you ever watched those cartoons?

I'm not sure Boris and Natasha were a couple. More like partners in crime." He shifted in his chair. "We used to rent movies at a video store off campus. My card got confiscated because I racked up too many late fees."

"That seems irresponsible for an engineering student. The engineers I've met are kind of methodical and myopic."

"I didn't start out as an engineer. I had to learn it. Anyway, we both started using Boris's card. I had it when Boris disappeared. When the search started, I put the card in a plastic bag. I thought the police might want it. I told them about it, but they never took it from me. I still have it."

"You just remembered this?" Slater demanded.

"Today. When you asked about the VCR."

"Why did you put it in a bag?"

"I thought they might want to get his fingerprints. When I brought it up, they told me they already had a full set. Boris had been fingerprinted in elementary school."

"Did he knock over a gas station before he even hit puberty?"

Jeff raised his eyebrows. "It was some program to keep track of kids in case they got kidnapped. I think they still do it if you want your kid fingerprinted."

"Can I look at the card?"

"You can have it." He pushed himself up out of his chair. "Come with. It's up in the attic."

Slater followed him into the hallway, and watched as Jeff pulled on a rope handle at the ceiling. A set of unfinished pine stairs folded down, and they both went up, stooping in the low space under the rafters. The attic was hot but it was clean, and smelled like pinewood, with corrugated boxes and plastic tubs neatly stacked on the board floor on either side of the stairs.

"Even your attic is mid-century modern chic," Slater said.

"Authentic to the era, at least." Jeff knelt and pulled out a cardboard box from the middle of a stack. In thick black marker it was neatly labeled LIVE OAK. When he folded open the flaps, the box was only half full, and he pulled out the stuff on top—plastic sheets with brown strips in them.

As Jeff set them aside, Slater squatted next to him and picked one up. The sheets had a series of long pockets, and the strips tucked into them had the distinctive sprocket holes of photo negatives. Peering at them, he could read the words and numbers along the margins, but he couldn't parse anything in the blotches of orange and brown that formed the images.

"Is there any chance Boris might be in some of these?"

"You've probably already seen them," Jeff said. "A while back Elvaine scanned all the negatives I had and printed any that were of him. They were in this same box, but I never even thought about the video store card when I let her borrow them. She'd only asked about photos." He met Slater's eye. "I guess that's the myopic engineer in me."

That fit, Slater decided, setting down the sheet. He'd seen several photos of Boris in the dorm.

Jeff pulled out some stacks of loose paper, and spiral-bound notebooks like in the box Bettina had kept, and some stapled typed pages. Chuckling, he handed Slater a single sheet of wrinkled pink paper. It was a photocopy of a hand-lettered flyer:

Boris and Natasha
invite you to
Slime & Sleaze '88
Saturday, March 26

A grainy cutout of the familiar cartoon characters appeared in one corner, angular Natasha in a sleeveless dress and heels, towering over squat Boris in his black fedora.

"Was it a party?"

"Slime and sleaze was like a trashy version of a wine and cheese," Jeff said. "The guys were supposed to dress like slimeballs, and the girls were supposed to dress sleazy. I'm sure it sounds thoroughly sexist today."

"I bet it was fun."

"I think it was. I remember turnout was low because it was spring break. Lots of people had left campus." He lifted out more paper, then pulled out a flat plastic sandwich bag and handed it to him. "This is it."

A little bigger than a bank card, it was laminated cardstock, he saw. It had a red logo with SNAPPY VIDEO at the top, and in the white space below, BORIS BROOKS had been typewritten, along with an account number.

"Do you think your prints will be on it too?" Slater said.

"I'd say that's likely. I've done work at secure government facilities, so I've been printed multiple times. If the police find any prints on the card, they'll be able to eliminate mine by checking those databases."

"I'm not even sure I need this, but I'll take it." As Jeff started to load stuff back into the box, he said, "Nothing else in the box is Boris's?"

"It's all mine. I should probably just dump it." He folded the flaps together and lifted the box back into its place.

Slater descended the stairs and waited for Jeff to push them up.

"Let me get you something to carry that in," Jeff said, and came back a minute later with a brown document envelope.

Dropping the plastic bag with the card into it, Slater folded the flap closed. "*Spasiba.*"

"Nice." He laughed. "You have good pronunciation."

"I'm glad you remembered this."

Jeff shrugged. "Maybe it'll be useful."

He walked out to the driveway, and climbed into the Continental, and headed toward his office. Once he'd parked in the surface lot, he took the envelope and hustled across the street.

The lights were on when he walked into the office. Etta wasn't here, he knew, because the bony statue of Rey Pascual was still facing the door. When she was around she always turned him to watch her work at the front desk. Slater double-clicked his tongue to greet the little guy, then looked into Max's office. He was behind his desk, focused on his computer screen, today wearing his gray suit with a yellow tie.

Max looked up, and frowned, and sat back in his chair. "Ouch. Did you run into somebody's fist?"

"Some knucklehead jumped me this morning." He dropped into one of the guest chairs. "Right in front of my own damn house."

"It doesn't look too bad." Max sat up to peer at him. "It might turn into a shiner, but it might not bruise much. I'd say it's borderline. The fat lip will subside tomorrow or the next day."

"The fact that you know all that, man." Slater threw up a hand. "We really are in the cesspool. What the hell are we doing?"

"I'm trying not to get too mucky. And slogging in the cesspool pays for all this." He waved at the office. "Besides, what else are you going to do? Fix computers, or sell greeting cards? If you only did landscaping, you'd get bored out of your mind in a hot minute. You need the dustups to balance all that quiet stuff."

Slater stared at him. "I hate that you know me that well."

"Maybe what we do provides some drainage now and then. We can lower the level of the cesspool."

"Can you run a plate? The moron was wearing a face

covering, but I watched him climb into a vehicle after he clobbered me."

Max pulled his keyboard over and clicked around. "Why would you hide your face but not your license plates? Did he steal it, or is he just not very bright?"

"I don't think he was a birthright lowlife. More like a tyro. Although he did get the drop on me." Pulling out his phone, he recited the plate number.

Max pecked at the keyboard with his pudgy fingers and then stared at the screen. "It's registered to Linda Tran," he said finally. "She lives in Westminster. I'll text you the address."

Tran was the surname of the camera guy from Hugo's ghost hunt. Michael Tran. That was no mystical coincidence—he wouldn't be needing Hugo's hermeneutics to figure this one out.

"Linda is eighty-two years old." Max met his eye. "Did somebody jack her car, or did you get beat up by a senior citizen?"

"She wasn't the one driving it today. I think I know who it was. It wasn't stolen." He tucked his phone away. "I'll pay you whatever that just cost you."

Max scoffed. "It's a business expense. I'll take it from the cash supply in the safe."

In his own office, Slater swung his feet up on the desk. His head was throbbing now, and he massaged his temples. Michael Tran had some explaining to do. But things were piling up, and he needed to triage.

First was Boris's fingerprints. The cops told Jeff they already had his prints. He hadn't seen an actual print card in the police file. There had been something about fingerprints in Elvaine's box of paperwork. Some form or document. It hadn't seemed important, so he'd only briefly scanned it, and right now he couldn't remember what it was about.

Heaving himself out of his chair, he went down to the parking lot and retrieved the banker's box from the trunk of the Continental. Back in his office, he set it on his desk and pulled the lid off. There were definitely no prints in the police file, he found, paging through it. Digging deeper, he found the document he'd seen before: "Request for Information: Fingerprint Records." Elvaine had submitted this to the FBI. He scanned the contents. She had requested a copy of Boris's prints, and there was a response letter, but the prints weren't attached. Why would she need to do this if the local cops already had a set?

He set the document on top of the pile in the box, and pulled out his phone, and dropped into his chair. Tapping Elvaine's name in his contact list, he listened to it ring until she picked up.

"Why did you request Boris's prints from the feds?" Slater said.

"Because the cops misplaced them. The police file is a collection of different documents, right, and it has an inventory list at the front. It's like a table of contents. On about the fifth page of that, it says a copy of Boris's print card was included in the file. But it wasn't there."

"The cops had no explanation for why that specific page was missing?"

"They told me that things get misplaced all the time, it wasn't that important, they were still in the federal database, blah, blah. But you can see that my Freedom of Information request came back from the FBI as having no responsive records. That means the feds don't actually have a copy of Boris's prints—or they won't admit that they do."

"Jeff told me the feds had them from when Boris was a child."

"They did," she said intently. "I have proof that they did. In the years after he disappeared, the prints from several unidentified bodies were compared to Boris's prints. The local cops got them from the feds, and did the comparisons, and kept records of the negative results."

"Why did you want Boris's prints?"

Elvaine raised her voice. "Because they're supposed to be in there. It's like the men-in-black thing. Nobody has Boris's prints anymore. That seems extremely suspicious, don't you think? It's hard to believe the FBI is so incompetent that they misplaced them. For some reason they're being suppressed."

"You think it's more evidence of the Professor Cameron and MKUltra scenario," Slater said.

"Why are you looking for his prints?"

"I might have a lead. I'll let you know if it pans out."

Slater ended the call and then pulled the plastic bag out of the envelope, peering at the video store card inside. He couldn't tell if it had prints on it or not. If it did, and the official copies really were lost, these might be the only ones for Boris that existed.

FIFTEEN

ICKING UP HIS PHONE, Slater dialed Conrad, his idiot ex-boyfriend. The guy was grating, and annoying, and had trampled Slater like street trash when he'd thrown him out, but he worked as a cop and had cop resources.

"Hey, Slater," he said when he picked up. "What do you need?"

"What do you mean, what do I need? You can drop the attitude. I need your full attention. So put your dick away and zip up your pants."

"The question stands."

"How difficult is it to pull prints off a piece of plastic?" Slater said. "It's a laminated card."

"The technicians usually do that."

"But you can do it."

Conrad groaned. "Why would I? I see no benefit to me. No upside."

"It'll help you keep yourself in practice. In case it comes up in the field."

"That never happens. You just want me to help you."

"It won't take you long," Slater said, "and it's in your own best interest."

"You know, in a way, I think you're right. If I don't jump when you say jump, you'll just keep bugging me, or show up at my station and make a scene, or slash my tires."

"See? You're not nearly as dumb as you look."

"Fuck you, Slater." He sighed. "I'm not going to do it at my station. I'm headed downtown now anyway. I can grab a kit and come by your office."

"Wise choice. I'll be here."

Once he'd ended the call, he texted Pike:

Are you at your office today? Got lunch plans later?

His response came soon after:

I can do that. Text me when you're downstairs.

Pushing himself up out of his chair, Slater went out to the front desk and looked in the drawers. Among the pens and office supplies was a bottle of ibuprofen. Of course Etta would have this stashed here. She dealt with middle-schoolers all day, so she was prepared for anything. He shook a couple into his mouth and dropped the bottle back in the drawer.

In his office again, he put his feet up on the desk and closed his eyes. He was half dozing when Max stuck his head in the doorway.

"You look like you need some sleep."

"I'm waiting for the painkillers to kick in."

"Are you going after Linda Tran? I'd hate for her to get the drop on you again. Maybe wait until she's taken her evening pills. She'll be groggy."

"The ass that needs to be kicked is probably her grandson's."

Max chuckled. "Feel better."

He closed his eyes again and heard the sound of the front door closing, and Max twisting his key to lock the bolt. Before long came a knock, and Slater got up to unlock it.

Conrad stood there, a dumb smile on his face, with his thick dark hair and his barrel chest. He was wearing a sharp gray suit without a necktie and had a briefcase in hand. Such a beautiful man.

"Nice suit, for a change," Slater said. "Did you pilfer that from the evidence room?"

His brow furrowed as he stepped in. "Who came at you?"

"I don't even know." He absently touched his swollen lip as he closed the door. "I'm dealing with it."

"Just don't grease anybody."

"That's not what you said when I was demolishing you with my dick."

Conrad followed him into his office. "We had some fun, didn't we?"

"Sit down." Slater shifted the banker's box onto the floor, then slid the video card in the plastic bag across the desk as Conrad took the guest chair.

"That's it, huh. It's not very big, so it won't take long." He lifted his briefcase onto the desktop and snapped it open. "Who's Boris Brooks?"

"A college kid who went missing from his dorm room in 1988."

He met Slater's gaze. "Did anyone mention that to the cops?"

"They looked for him, but they never got anywhere. Then they lost his fingerprints."

"It happens. The longer stuff sits on the shelf, the more likely that kind of issue is." Conrad pulled out what looked like a makeup brush and a plastic jar with a black label, then slid the plastic sleeve off the brush. "You're hoping to lift a new set from this."

"You could almost be a detective."

"Fuck you, Slater." He said it so often that it sounded perfunctory, devoid of gravity or emotion. He wriggled his hands into a pair of blue latex gloves. "Hard plastic is a good medium for latent prints. I'm sure we'll find something."

"Did you bring that gear from your station, or from your makeup kit?"

Conrad clicked his tongue. "You don't want to be putting this stuff on your face." He wiped the top of the desk with a piece of cloth, then shook the video card out of the plastic bag onto the surface. Once he'd screwed the lid off the jar, he gently twirled the brush in the black powder, then twirled it on the video store card. "Oh, that's nice."

"There's prints?" Slater said.

"Lots of them. Give me your phone."

"When a cop says something like that, it makes me nervous."

He waggled his fingers. "Just open the camera."

Slater handed it over and watched as he photographed the card at close range, then took another from a different angle. Eventually he set the phone aside.

"I'll transfer these, but sometimes they're cleaner before you do that."

From his briefcase he took out a half-size sheet of what looked like shiny white plastic, and peeled a layer of clear film away from the white, and gently pressed it onto the video card. Pulling it off again, he sealed the film onto the thicker white side and then studied it.

"Look at that. A couple are smudged but they're mostly perfect." He handed Slater the sheet. "You should photograph that too. As close up as you can get."

He spent a minute with his phone taking close-ups of

the sheet, checking to make sure the images weren't blurry. While he did that, Conrad turned the video store card over and dusted the back, and photographed it, and transferred the prints to another white sheet. Slater took photos of it while Conrad peeled off his latex gloves.

Leaning toward him, Conrad pointed to some of the prints on the transfer sheet. "That's probably a thumb, and on the other side those are the index and middle fingers of the right hand."

"How do you know which hand it is?"

"It's not a hundred percent, but see the loops on the fingers? Usually those open toward the thumb, so it's likely a right hand."

Slater peered at the faint black lines against the white. He could see the loops he was talking about.

"So what are you going to do with those?"

He met Conrad's eye. "See if I can track the guy down."

"It's interesting that you haven't asked me to run them."

"I don't want to overwhelm you with too much at once, and cut into your time staring into space and drooling."

"More like you have another route to access the federal databases," Conrad said. "Like your G-man main man."

Slater raised his eyebrows. "Loose lips sink ships."

"I'm not actually worried about your stuff." He rolled the brush into a piece of cloth, and tucked it and the jar of powder into his briefcase, then snapped it shut as he got up. "How's it going with Pike?"

Slater stood up with him and stretched his back. "I'd say our narrative complex has stabilized. It's operating in multiple dimensions, but it doesn't feel like a head rush quite as often anymore." He threw up his hands. "I can't quite figure out what he's doing with me. I'm afraid he'll wake up one day, and realize I'm trash, and head for the hills."

"That guy is a catch," Conrad said. "You should be

grateful for whatever deep flaw it is that makes him attracted to you."

He frowned. "Such sage advice."

Lifting his briefcase, he grinned. "Later, Slater."

As he walked out, Slater tucked the white sheets with the prints and the envelope with the video card into the top of the banker's box, then locked up the office and carried it down to the parking lot. In the trunk of the Continental he moved the print sheets into his satchel, and slung it across his shoulder, and slammed the trunk.

There was nowhere to street-park in the Civic Center, but Pike's office was right near the metro, and it wasn't far to walk to a station from here. Striding out of the lot, he headed toward the nearest one.

This neighborhood was hopping, with fashion retailers and food vendors, the clothes and accessories displayed on a jumble of racks along the sidewalk and lining the gutter. It felt like chaos, but it was the good kind—people were hustling, and scraping by, but they weren't mired in the cesspool.

On the platform waiting for the train were blue-collar clothing industry types and students from the nearby tech college. When the train pulled in, he stepped into the car to find a gaggle of homeless people sprawled on the seats at this end, a cart stuffed with bulky black trash bags parked blocking the aisle. The tang of overripe bodies and weed smoke hung in the air. Along with the others who'd just boarded, he walked to the opposite end of the car.

The homeless thing only seemed to be getting worse, and he saw more of them every day. The metro was like an all-day homeless shelter. They used to keep them east of Main Street, on Skid Row proper, but now they were camped all over. Retail Broadway and the white-collar Financial District were as piss-stained as everywhere else.

He rode the few stops to the Civic Center and texted Pike as he was walking up on the building. A minute later Pike stepped out into the gray daylight, dressed in dark pants and a blue dress shirt, his ID on a lanyard around his neck. He flashed that easy smile. The sight of him made Slater's heart soar, and he embraced him as he stepped up.

After a sloppy kiss, Pike pulled back, his brow furrowing. "Somebody punched you in the face."

"A guy jumped me. I'm dealing with it. Max says it might not even bruise."

"Who jumped you?"

"I'm not quite sure yet. He warned me to stay away. I don't even know what he was talking about specifically." Slater waved a hand. "I've got a lot on my plate."

Pike studied his face. "You're a lot of man, forty-niner."

"I'm not compartmentalizing. I honestly haven't tracked him down yet. I plan to."

"Let's go eat."

They walked to a pizza place over by the police station, crowded and noisy at this time of day. They ordered at the counter and found a table by the window. Once they'd eaten, Slater sat back.

"So the feds have better access to fingerprint records than the local police do, correct?"

Pike raised his eyebrows. "Why do you ask?"

"I might have a set of Boris's prints from 1988." He explained how the print card had gone missing from the police file, and how the FBI said they didn't even have a set, but he left out Elvaine's conspiracy theory.

"That's odd." Pike frowned. "The feds should still have them on file if the missing persons case was never resolved."

"They wrote back to Elvaine's FOIA request and said they didn't have them. No way am I going to give these to the cops. They already messed it up once." He raised his eyebrows. "But you could run a search for them. In case Boris is still alive and using a different name."

Pike groaned. "There's so many reasons doing that is just wrong."

"I get that." Slater took a breath. "I really don't want to fuck this up. I mean us. I always feel like I'm one unreasonable demand or one stupid decision away from totally blowing it. Driving you away. I'll get back to the house one day and open the closet to find all your clothes gone."

"I'm not going to leave you in the middle of the night." Pike sat back. "Remember that twelve-step book? There's a whole section on catastrophizing. You think if you make one wrong move you're going to inadvertently blow us up. I know you—you're not making unreasonable demands on me. If you do, we'll talk about it." He waved a hand. "Let me be a stable presence in your life."

"So you'll do it."

He chuckled. "We should go. People are waiting for tables."

Slater slung on his satchel, and followed him out to the street, and they walked back toward Pike's building.

"I can't make it a habit," Pike said finally. "Helping you with your research."

"It's not really about me. It's about the greater good. We all deserve to know what happened to Boris."

He eyed him sidelong. "When you put it that way, it sounds like I'll be doing the whole world a favor."

"There you go. It's also an unusual situation. I doubt it'll come up again."

Pike stopped in front of his building. "Do you have the prints with you?"

"I've got them on those white transfer cards. I took close-ups of those too."

"Show me the pictures."

He dug out his phone, and pulled one up, and handed it over. Pike spread his fingers on the screen to zoom in.

"These are pretty clear. You can just send me the photos."

He handed the phone back, and Slater tapped at it.

"There's probably two people's prints. Boris's roommate said he used the video card too."

"We'll figure it out."

Tucking his phone away, he grasped Pike's biceps and pulled him close. "You know what happens later, right? I'm going to eat your dick, then fuck you until you scream."

"Stop that." He kissed Slater's neck. "I can't go back inside with a tentpole in my pants." Meeting his mouth, he lingered in it, then pulled back.

"While you're up there, I want you to focus on this." Slater grabbed his own crotch. "Think about what's waiting for you."

A woman walked up and greeted them, a wry grin on her face. He'd met her before—Pike's colleague Brewster. About as tall as Pike was, and wearing plaid trousers and a sport coat, she had her long hair tied back.

"Did you drop by just to manhandle this guy?"

"You saw that, huh," Slater said.

"I wish somebody would come over at lunchtime and paw me like that."

"I can't help myself. I think he has a pheromone imbalance." He frowned at Pike. "You should probably see a doctor."

Brewster laughed. "You're addicted, Slater."

"Guilty."

"I'll ride up with you," Pike said. His face looked a little red.

Brewster pointed a finger at Slater. "Let's hang out sometime."

"Sure."

Pike met his gaze, his eyes bright. "Later, forty-niner."

He stood watching them as they walked inside, and tried to swallow the lump in his throat. It didn't make sense why that happened. It served no purpose.

SIXTEEN

꿰꿰꿰꿰꿰꿰꿰꿰꿰꿰꿰

TURNING TO WALK TO the metro, Slater rode the train back to the Fashion District, and got in the Continental to drive to his house. Upstairs he grabbed his laptop and went out on the deck. It finally felt warm since the sun had burned through the marine layer. At the patio table he sat facing it to keep his screen in the shade.

Tran was a way more common name than he'd assumed it would be, and even with Linda Tran's home address he couldn't find a lot about her. She had her name on a couple of DBA records, but it was hard to say what kind of businesses they were, as the names were in Vietnamese.

There were too many Michael Trans to single out which one was the camera guy. He could ask Hugo about him, but then he'd have to explain why he was asking, and Hugo might tip the guy off that Slater was coming for him.

Sometime later he heard the door downstairs. He folded the laptop closed and went inside. In the bedroom Pike was stepping out of his work trousers.

"I love those skivvies," Slater said. "Red like a fire truck. They set off my fire alarms."

"You love what's in them."

"That's technically correct. You're back early."

"I've got an electrician coming over to quote me on putting in an EV charger," Pike said, pulling on a pair of gray chinos.

"So that's really happening."

"There's no immediate cause for alarm." He pulled a henley over his head, pushing his arms into the sleeves and pulling it down over his torso. "I haven't been car shopping yet. I just want to get the pieces lined up."

"I'm sure I'll get used to the idea of a new car hogging up the garage and crowding the Continental. At least it'll boost real estate values on the whole block if you stop parking your janky flivver out front."

Pike raised his eyebrows. "I plan to hang on to that too."

Stepping in front of him, Pike put his hands on his neck and kissed him. Slater leaned in, his hands on Pike's belt, and pulled him close.

"Slow down, Seabiscuit," Pike murmured. "The juice man will be here any minute."

Slater mouthed his neck, then stepped back when the doorbell sounded.

"You should talk to this guy too," Pike said. "It is your house."

Adjusting his crotch, he followed Pike down to the front door, and into the garage, where he hit the button to roll up the door. A white work truck with a lightning bolt logo on the door was parked in front of it. A guy with his black hair in a natty cut stepped over. He was wearing dark-blue work clothes with a patch on his shirt embroidered with GORDO. It was a nickname, Slater knew, and it meant chunky, but this guy was the opposite, built like a runner, and totally fuckable.

Pike greeted the guy and waved him into the garage. "Let me show you the panel."

"I love your whip," Gordo said, looking over the Continental as they walked past it. "I hope you're not going to replace it with an EV."

"This one's my ride," Slater said.

At the back of the garage, by the laundry machines, Gordo pulled open the little door on the panel.

"There's room for an EV circuit," he said, "so the work will be straightforward. Where do you want the charger?"

"Up front, by the Continental," Pike said.

"I could run the wires there." Gordo pointed to the wall.

"I have a tenant on the other side of that," Slater said. "I'd rather you put the wiring on this side."

They talked about it, and Gordo quoted a price for the work and the equipment, and eventually they agreed that he'd start on it the following week.

Gordo closed the door on the panel. "So you two are a couple, I take it."

"Stuck together like glue," Pike said.

"Is that a closed system?"

Pike put his hands on his hips. "Are you suggesting a hookup?"

"This is my last job for the day, and I'm going to have to set something up anyway." He waved a hand. "We're all right here already."

Pike eyed Slater. "Are you two related?"

"I'd be down for that," Slater said.

"I know you are. I wasn't asking." He looked to Gordo. "Will I get a discount on the labor to install the charger?"

Gordo laughed. "It depends on your performance."

"No pressure, though." Pike gestured. "Come on up."

Slater hit the button to roll the garage door down, then

headed up the stairs after Gordo.

"Do you hit on all your clients?"

Gordo glanced back. "Only the hot ones." Stepping into the bedroom, he looked at the ceiling. "Those are good fixtures. Energy efficient." He squatted to untie his boots.

Pike was grinning, he saw, as he pulled off his shirt, and he unbuttoned his own.

"How did you get the name Gordo? You're not."

"I was chunky as a kid. Mexican families are not subtle." He jutted his chin at him. "You must know the drill."

Slater pulled off his boots. "So what's your sex thing, Gordo?"

"I want to fuck you," he said, and then pointed to Pike. "While that's happening, I want this one to fuck me."

"That works," Pike said. "The man knows what he wants."

Slater started to unbuckle his belt, and Gordo, shirtless now, said, "Hold up." He stepped over and grabbed Slater's belt, and held his gaze while he popped the buttons of his fly. Moving closer, he reached behind him, resting his chin on his shoulder, and ran his fingers down the small of his back, onto his butt, and slid his jeans down.

Naked now, Pike stepped behind Gordo, and reached for his belt, and unbuckled it. Once he'd stepped out of his heavy work pants, Gordo turned and squeezed Pike's swelling cock.

"It looks like you're ready."

Leaning in, Pike kissed him, his hands on his neck. Watching them made Slater's heart pound. He wasn't jealous, exactly, but it felt weird, seeing Pike with someone else. Stepping closer, he put a hand on each of their necks, and pressed his face into theirs, his tongue exploring their mouths. They spent a minute absorbed in it, the intensity of it, until Gordo pulled back.

"Let's do this."

Slater followed Gordo to the bed and grabbed a condom and lube from the bedside drawer. The guy was rock hard, and he squeezed his cock, then rolled the condom on him. Pike climbed up next to him as Gordo maneuvered Slater onto his side, and started to press into him, wrapping an arm around his chest. He was moving faster than Pike would have, but Slater could handle it, and he screwed his eyes shut, taking a deep breath.

Groaning, Gordo paused for a moment. Pike was into him now, and he could feel his thrusts telegraphing through Gordo. Eventually Gordo started moving himself. He felt Pike's hand on his arm, drawing him close.

He heard Pike grunt and whimper as he came, and then Gordo did, straining into him and squeezing him tight with his arm. Once he'd pulled away, Gordo shifted him onto his back, and sat up, and took him into his mouth. Moving closer, Pike ran a hand into Slater's hair, and kneaded his chest, mouthing his neck and his jaw.

The guy was skilled at giving head, and Slater quickly climaxed, his mouth locked on Pike's. Afterward he stretched out, limbs intertwined with both of them, feeling sweaty and sated. Before long Gordo got up.

"I'm all hungry now."

"You can forage in the kitchen," Pike said.

"I'm sure my mom has supper waiting for me." He stepped into his work pants, then pulled on his shirt, and squatted to tie his boots. "That was fun, fellas."

He walked out, and they heard footfalls on the stairs, and then the front door closed.

"Gordo is all business," Pike said.

"It definitely simplifies things. No yapping, or airing of grievances, or processing emotions."

"It hardly feels like addictive behavior at all."

"He doesn't seem like an addict," Slater said. "And

you're getting pretty comfortable with the old three-way. You set it up yourself."

"I learned from the maestro." Pike sat up. "Should we order Thai?"

"I'll do it." Slater reached for his jeans, and dug out his phone, and tapped in an order.

He pulled on a pair of shorts and a T-shirt, and before long the doorbell sounded, and they took the food outside to the patio table. The sun was still out and casting long shadows. After he'd eaten, Pike pushed his plate away.

"I've got some dirt for you. Brewster has great timing. On the way upstairs she asked why you'd dropped by."

"She's such a cop."

"I guess it's instinctive. I asked her to check those prints. She can do it without getting flagged since she's running a bunch of evidence from a case she's working."

"Did she find anything?"

"It hasn't happened yet," Pike said. "She's doing her print runs tomorrow. But I did a bit of digging myself. I wondered why the FBI didn't have Boris's prints on file. I thought it must have been a mistake. The record shows they were purged from the FBI collection eight years ago."

"Why the fuck did they do that? The guy could still be alive."

"I asked around. Apparently they routinely purge those records. The rules are that it's done ninety-nine years after a person dies, or when they get a court order to destroy them."

"It can't be the ninety-nine-year reason," Slater said. "It hasn't been that long since Boris disappeared. Can you tell if there's a court order?"

"If it had come from a regular court decision, there'd be a document cited. The fact that there's no mention of it means it was an order from a national security court. They're extremely secretive, and they don't issue any records. Even requesting it would jeopardize my job."

"Fuck me." Slater threw up a hand. "What does that mean?"

"I can only guess, but I'd say for some reason, Boris was important to national security."

"Do you know the date the prints were purged?"

"I wrote it down. I'll send it to you." Pike dug out his phone and tapped at it.

"Did you tell Brewster all this?"

He glanced up at him. "Hell, no. Unlike our personal lives, this is a situation where you have to compartmentalize. She's going to see if the prints match any existing records. Nothing more. She doesn't need to know anything else." Pike sighed and set his phone on the table. "It makes me wonder what you've stumbled into."

"I don't stumble, son." Slater lowered his voice. "I know you're taking a risk for me."

"I wouldn't do it if I couldn't handle it."

"I've got some work to do. Can you entertain yourself for a few hours?"

"I actually did that for my entire life before I met you. I should be able to manage."

They gathered up the food containers and took them in to the kitchen, then Slater went down to the garage to retrieve the banker's box from the trunk of the Continental, and carried it up to the dining table.

Pulling off the lid, he dug out Elvaine's FOIA request for Boris's prints. Every part of it had a date filled in, and he compared those to what Pike had texted. Boris's print record had been purged not long after Elvaine had asked for them. No way was that a coincidence. He flipped through the sheaf of paper. Their "no responsive records" answer was dated almost a year after the purge.

"Raskolnikov," Slater muttered.

Pulling out his phone, he called Elvaine, glad that she answered.

"So Boris's prints were purged from the federal database six weeks after you made that FOIA request for them," Slater said.

Her voice was loud. "Are you kidding me? How did you find that out?"

"I can't reveal my source, but the dope is solid."

"Damn it. Doesn't that imply they're hiding something?"

"Absolutely. And if they trashed his print records, I'd bet cash money that they got somebody in the local PD to disappear that copy of the print card too."

"That tracks." She huffed. "It really pisses me off."

"I get it. It's frustrating when the cops are the ones running bunco. But if you take a step back from it, it's also great news."

"How is this in any way great news?" she demanded.

"It bolsters your theory that Boris went to work for the feds," Slater said. "Somebody is trying to obscure any record of him—and nobody could make the feds do that except other feds."

"Can you send me the details you have?"

After he'd ended the call, he typed a brief message to her with the details that Pike had given him, then packed up the banker's box and carried it down to the trunk of the Continental.

Upstairs he found Pike on the sofa, barefoot, his shoes discarded on the faux grass. He was reading his hardback and had music on the radio. Slater sat with him and grabbed his hand, kissing the back of it.

"How's *The Lost Weekend*?"

"It's getting good. He steals a woman's purse in a bar to buy booze."

"These days it's a lot easier," Slater said. "Tweakers can just shoplift in the big-box stores and sell the stuff to get high."

Pike chuckled and set the book aside. "The later it gets, the better the music on this station is."

"You're the music." Slater squeezed his hand. "You get better when it gets later." He raised his voice. "It's all you."

Pulling him close, Pike met his mouth, then leaned back. They lay that way for a while, bodies together, warm and perfect. Eventually Pike stirred, waking him, and they both went down to climb into bed.

"I have to go out for a minute later," Slater said. "I'm going to set an alarm for late."

"What for?"

"It's work. I won't be long."

Pike frowned. "I want to say that sounds awfully suspicious."

"Svetlana says 'Not my circus, not my monkeys.'"

"Pithy, but the Russian isn't someone I'd normally look to for wisdom or advice."

Slater killed the light and shifted close. "Let me worry about the monkeys."

———◆———

LATER, WHEN THE ALARM buzzed, Slater quickly grabbed his phone to kill it. Pike's breathing was still in the even rhythm of sleep. He got dressed in the dark, then hustled down to the garage and opened his gear storage. It was designed to look like a standard office-supply cabinet, but it was really an armored gun safe, thickly reinforced and bolted to the floor, hiding in plain sight. He didn't have any firearms but he kept his illicit tech inside, all the black-market gear he got from Svetlana. It wasn't foolproof, as Pike knew what it was, and one of his colleagues who'd visited had pegged it as a safe at a glance. But any junkie who broke in here to steal copper and tools wouldn't waste time on it.

In the cabinet he pulled a vehicle tracker from its charger. A black plastic box about the size of a thick cell phone, it had magnetic ribs studding one side. Backing the Continental into the street, he flicked on the headlights and headed for the freeway.

The navigation sent him on the 5 and then the 605. It went fast, as there was almost nobody on the road at this hour. He'd timed it for the sweet spot—long enough after the bars closed, but before most people needed to head to work.

The street was lined with suburban bungalows, he saw as he turned onto it, with neatly manicured lawns and no fences in front. He parked near the corner and killed his headlights. The house was farther down on the opposite side, and he watched it for a few minutes, but there were no signs of life.

Looking at his phone, he checked the plate number of Linda Tran's car. The three letters in the middle were PGX. It took a second to come up with a mnemonic to remember it: *pedestrian ghost experience.*

From the glovebox he pulled out his stealthy eyeglasses, and found the power switch, and clicked it on. Another of Svetlana's tools, the frames were studded with little UV and IR lamps that messed with surveillance cameras to obscure his face, even though the glare was invisible to the naked eye.

He put on the blue ball cap he kept in the backseat, pulling it low over his brow, then wriggled his hands into a pair of black latex gloves from the box on the floor. Grabbing the tracker, he wiped it on his shirt to remove his prints, then climbed out and walked toward Linda Tran's house.

It had a wide driveway, with a couple of young trees on the lawn that had been carefully limbed up. A low *Westringia* shrub grew along part of the curb, and he could smell its peppery medicinal scent, drawn out by the early morning humidity. Two vehicles sat in the driveway, a gray Prius and a matte-black Charger. The plate matched the pedestrian ghost experience. This was the car the moron in the keffiyeh had climbed into.

As he strode up the driveway, a floodlight on the eaves of the house flicked on, and Slater winced at its glare. It had to be motion activated. He looked up at it, but he couldn't see a camera with it. Even if there was one, hopefully the stealthy glasses would obscure his face.

Crouching next to the Charger, at the rear tire on the driver's side, he reached up into the wheel well. It took a minute for the magnets to find a chunk of steel to adhere to, but eventually he felt the satisfying tug.

He stood erect and walked back out to the street. There were no lights or sound from inside the house—he hadn't woken anyone. Those motion lights went off all the time, from wind moving the foliage or a feral cat strolling by.

Once he was behind the wheel of the Continental, he pulled off the latex gloves, and stowed the glasses, and headed for the freeway.

It was still dark when he got to his house. Upstairs in the kitchen he grabbed the bourbon bottle from the cupboard and took a long pull. He'd missed out on it earlier, knowing he had to get up again.

Down in the bedroom he stripped off his clothes and climbed into bed. Pike was still out cold, and he rolled next to him, notching his knees behind Pike's, draping an arm around his torso. The warmth of his body and the amber elixir suffusing from his belly quickly sent him into sleep.

SEVENTEEN

When Slater woke, Pike had already gone to his office. In the bathroom mirror he saw that Max was right—his eye was still a little messed up, but it wasn't going to bruise. It might take another day for the swelling in his lip to go down, but overall he didn't look too bad.

Once he'd showered and dressed, in yesterday's jeans and a clean shirt, he trudged upstairs to the kitchen and poured tepid coffee into a mug. Grabbing a flat muffin-looking thing that Pike had bought, he went out to the deck, even though it was gray and chilly out.

Slurping at the java, he looked at his phone and opened Svetlana's app. The tracker on the Charger was working. Early this morning the car had moved from Westminster to Pasadena. He zoomed in on its location. The device used Wi-Fi and cell signals to estimate its location, so it was far less precise than GPS, but it also didn't need a view of the sky, and it used way less battery power. The green circle for the estimated location covered most of a large building. It was a parking structure, he saw, and it was on the campus of Pasadena City College.

He tucked his phone away and munched on the bread. Michael Tran could be a student, he decided. The guy was definitely in his twenties, like lots of students were.

Once he'd eaten he went down to his car, and backed into the street, and navigated to the 110. When he pulled up to the parking structure at the college, it was signed as student parking. He drove in and started prowling the floors. Eventually he found the Charger, and spotted the PGX on the tag. He took a parking spot in the next row, facing it, far enough away that he wouldn't be spotted but with a clear view of the driver's door.

He needed to make sure it was Michael Tran driving the Charger, but sitting here now, he realized he should have thought it through, and picked another stop, later in the day, where the car would spend less time separated from its driver. If the guy had more than a class or two, he could be here all day.

After half an hour or so he was considering bailing, but then someone walked up on the vehicle. Slater instinctively slid lower in his seat. That was definitely the Michael Tran from the ghost hunt—lanky, with the long hair, today wearing a dress shirt and dark trousers.

Michael climbed in and started the engine, then revved it obnoxiously loud before he backed out and headed toward the exit. Slater didn't need to follow the guy—he'd learned what he needed.

He waited a few minutes to minimize any chance of running into Michael, then started the engine and drove out of the lot. As he was merging onto the freeway, his phone buzzed. The caller ID said REDDY KILOWATT.

"Are you anywhere near downtown?" Pike said when he picked up.

"I can be. I'm a few minutes away. Are you hungry

already?"

"I've got lunch plans later, but we should meet for coffee."

"Are you going for lunch with Davis?" Slater demanded. "That fricking guy. You know he's trying to get into your pants. He'll use some messed-up psychology to try to brainwash you into sleeping with him."

"Once you disembark from the crazy train," Pike said, "I'll be here in consensus reality, at that coffee joint near my office. Text me when you're close."

When he got downtown he left his wheels in the garage under Grand Park, and texted Pike as he walked the block or so to the coffee joint. As he walked in, he saw Pike at a table with two cups on it, his back to the wall, absorbed in his phone.

Pike looked up and cracked a smile when he walked over. "I got you an oat-milk latte."

"*Mi vida*." He leaned in to kiss him, then sat opposite.

"Brewster found two people's prints in those images," Pike said, leaning toward him, his voice low, even though no one was nearby. "One set belonged to a guy named Jeffrey Watkins. He's registered as a government contractor."

"That's Boris's college roommate. He's the one who had the video store card."

"I figured. The other set were several fingers and a thumb. There's no records on the fingers, but the thumbprint got a hit. A guy named Charles Martin."

"Fuck me. That could be Boris."

"Or somebody who worked as a video store clerk back then, or somebody from the dorm who borrowed the card." Pike raised his eyebrows. "Brewster said there was a name but no other details about the person. Not even a date of birth."

"Is that typical for fingerprint records?"

"The hit wasn't from the print database. It was recorded by a bank when Charles Martin cashed a check twenty years ago. It's a private database. Legally the banks have to make all those available to the feds, but it's handled by a completely different office from the FBI's records on criminals and missing persons."

Slater sipped his latte. "But it still came up in a search."

"The federal government is byzantine." Pike waved a hand. "Brewster knew there were separate databases."

He thought it through. Whoever purged the prints in the main database after Elvaine's FOIA request likely either forgot to check the banking one, or didn't bother because it wasn't linked to Boris's name.

"Do you know what bank it was?" Slater said.

"I had to look it up. It went bust in the crash of 2008. The record didn't specify what branch, but it was a savings and loan that only had outlets in Southern California."

"This is potentially huge. Tell Brewster she's the boss."

"I'm not going to tell her anything about it," Pike said. "Compartmentalized, remember?"

"And we're not doing that in our personal narrative complex."

"Ideally."

"So even though we're building trust and openness," Slater said, "it's really none of my business who you're having lunch with."

"Have you been reading that twelve-step book? That sounds like a direct quote."

He raised his eyebrows. "Is it Davis? You know he has ulterior motives."

"You are so damn crazy."

Slater sat back and rubbed his eyes. "I know."

"You look tired," Pike said. "Are you still hurting from the beatdown?"

"It feels like there's a lot happening all at once. This Boris stuff, plus I have to go after that knucklehead."

"Have you figured out who it was?"

"Remember the camera operator on the ghost hunt? Long hair, and he was wearing those fuck-me boots."

"Michael?" Pike frowned. "Are you kidding me? Why would he come for you?"

"I'll ask him that when I punch him in the face."

Pike pursed his lips for a moment. "Maybe he thinks you're moving in on Fermín. I got the vibe he was like Fermín's apprentice. Michael was definitely tuned in to him, and he always deferred to him. Maybe there's something romantic there."

"I didn't hit on Fermín," Slater said. "I worked hard to tolerate his abrasive attitude, and I struggled to resist the instinct to slap him around. Maybe Michael just doesn't want me on the ghost crew."

"You know, you could probably just ignore it. Focus on Boris. Michael said his piece. He isn't going to take it any farther."

Slater slowly shook his head. "He jumped me. I can't let that go."

"You actually can, but you don't want to."

"If you don't take out the trash, it starts to pile up. That idiot needs to know he can't just use his fists to get what he wants."

Pike's eyes narrowed. "You do that on a daily basis."

"I only throw down when it's justified. Michael had no reason to come at me." Slater stood up. "I need to know why he did."

Rising with him, Pike scooped up his cup. "Just don't get arrested."

———•———

BACK IN THE PARKING garage, Slater climbed into the Continental and checked Svetlana's app on his phone. The tracker on the Charger showed that it was parked again, at a mall not far from here, amid a cluster of office towers. It was right by a metro station in the densest part of the Financial District. He knew that place—it was a huge parking garage, with hundreds of shops and offices within a couple of blocks. What was a college boy from the ass end of Orange County doing there?

Starting the engine, he drove up to the street and cruised along Broadway to Andy's building, nosing the Continental into the surface lot behind it. Andy did research for him, and he was good at finding things, identifying people, parsing out obscure details. He claimed he was just a researcher, not a hacker, but from Slater's perspective that's exactly what it looked like.

Once he'd walked around to the entrance, and up to Andy's floor, he knocked on his door. Andy pulled it open and frowned at him. Wiry, with a perfect mess of brown hair, he had stubble on his face and was wearing his usual boxers and a white tank top. A cute little tuft of hair was visible in his armpit.

"You're supposed to … text me first."

"I did," Slater said. "You must have missed it. Or did you block me?"

"You are such a liar." He went back inside, walking with his uneven gait, and Slater followed, struck by how cool it was. Andy's CP made his metabolism run hot, so he always kept the place cold.

His loft was mostly one big room, with big windows overlooking the square and resin-surfaced board floors that preserved the scuffs and scratches from when the building had been a textile warehouse. Under the windows, not far from the bed, his desk bore an array of monitors.

Parked in a lounge chair in the corner was Kyle, one knee folded over the other, wearing snug trousers and a dress shirt. Slater hated how clothes looked on him, how they flattered his body. He hated that the guy was so hot.

Kyle lowered his phone and frowned at him. "What are you doing here?"

Slater put his hands on his hips. "You married him, sweetheart, but you don't get to decide who he works for. I know work is hard to understand as a concept. It's for people who don't have a trust fund and a life of leisure." He eyed Andy as he dropped into the chair at his desk. "Why are you still letting this gunsel hang around?"

"Till death us do part," Andy said.

He looked at Kyle and narrowed his eyes. "Let me know if you need help with that."

"You seem even more ratty and beat-up than usual, Ibáñez," Kyle said. "Are you high right now, or just hung over?"

"It might be a sugar high from your sweet disposition, cupcake. I can actually feel my teeth starting to ache."

"Slater, focus," Andy said. "What do you … want?"

He huffed and stepped closer to his desk. "I need you to look into a guy. Michael Tran. I'll text you his name and his home address. He lives in Westminster, and I think he's a student at PCC. Today he's hanging around Fig and Seventh. If he's a college student maybe he has a part-time job around there."

"If he's at Fig and Seventh," Kyle said, "maybe he's taking the train somewhere."

"Why would he drive there from the OC sticks? It doesn't make sense. You'd go to a metro station with cheaper parking that was closer to your house."

"He's at his barber, maybe," Andy said, "or his … dry cleaner."

"He'd find those in a less crowded place. In Pasadena near his school, or near his house. Parking in the busiest part of the city is expensive. It has to be about a job with a parking pass."

"You already know where he sleeps," Andy said. "Why not go there?"

"At his home I could give him a tune-up," Slater said, "but if I can find him at work, I can inflict a lot more pain. Maybe even get him canned."

"You sound like a gangster," Kyle said.

"He's actually being stealthy, trying to … sneak up on the guy." Andy eyed Slater and raised his eyebrows. "More like a weasel."

That was the second time someone had called him that on this case. No way did it qualify as one of Hugo's synchronicities—it was no surprise that multiple people had that low an opinion of him.

He looked to Kyle. "If I were a gangster, sweetheart, I would have worked you over by now."

"Because I married a guy you weren't quite into? You need to check yourself, Ibáñez."

"Would a gangster punch you in the face? Because I'm feeling that compelling urge right now."

"Slater," Andy said, raising his voice. "You remember the fourth step?"

He closed his eyes for a second and took a breath. "Twelve-step is your thing, not mine."

"Maybe you haven't been in the rooms, but you … read one of the books. I know you did. Pike insisted on it."

"I read the one for sexual compulsives. It didn't really apply. I don't have that problem."

"Ha," Kyle cackled, and Slater shot him a look.

"Look at me," Andy said. "The fourth step is … taking a fearless moral inventory. It's so you can think about why you have … that kind of resentment, and what your role in it is."

Slater waved a finger in a circle at the room. "In this situation my part in it is zero. You two conspired to freeze me out, cut off my sex supply, chop off my junk with a sickle like Cronus. Case closed."

"You know there are five million other men in this town to have sex with, right?" Kyle said.

He raised his voice. "None of them are you two fools."

"Settle down," Andy said.

"Why would I be resentful anyway? It's simpler than that. Lowlifes and affluent zombies alike say things designed to get me riled." Slater spread his arms. "And lo, I get riled."

"I'm glad that you're so self-aware," Andy said. "It seems like you've … got that one all figured out."

"You are an emotional wreck," Kyle said.

"Am I, Kyle?" he said flatly. "Am I really?"

Andy raised his voice again. "Slater—I'll look into your target today."

"I've got another ask. A guy named Charles Martin. Born in about 1970. He might not be local. I'll text you that name too. I need an address or a job, whatever you can find. But prioritize Michael Tran." Digging out his phone, he texted him the details on both targets.

"A rush job involves a premium upcharge."

"Don't I always pay you what you ask?" he demanded.

"I'm just laying the groundwork so there won't be … any surprises later."

"You're just yanking my chain, more like." He tucked his phone away and jutted his chin at Kyle. "You married a chiseler, son."

As he walked toward the door, Kyle called after him. "Oh, OK, bye, then."

EIGHTEEN

⌘⌘⌘⌘⌘⌘⌘⌘⌘⌘

GNORING KYLE, SLATER WALKED out to the elevator and went down to the street. Once he was behind the wheel of the Continental, he pulled onto Fifth and headed across the chasm of the 110 freeway into Westlake. He had a hankering for pupusas, and the vendor in his old neighborhood made a meatless version. He parked on the street near her stand.

The woman was happy to see him, talking rapid-fire through the little window. He couldn't understand much of what she was saying but he caught part of it, including *mucho tiempo*. She was pointing out that she hadn't seen him in a while.

He ordered a couple of pupusas and tipped hard, then sat at one of the stools outside the shack to eat them. His phone buzzed in his pants, and he pulled it out to see that it was Pike. Swallowing his mouthful of pastry, he picked up.

"I'm going out of town overnight," Pike said. "We've got a couple interviews around Bishop."

"The Eastern Sierra is a nice drive. There's a great diner there."

"I'm sure Brewster will know it. She's been up there before."

"Is Davis going with you?" Slater said.

"Not on this trip."

"At least Brewster isn't hot for you, as far as I can tell. If she is, she hides it well."

"Nobody in my office is trying to get with me," Pike said. "You need to smash that."

"I'd be happy to smash Davis if he lays a finger on you."

"Think again, cave man. He could beat your ass."

"Oh, yeah? Him and what army?"

Pike laughed. "I have to go. We'll talk tonight."

Glancing at the screen, he saw that Andy had texted:

I found one cuff link at the gym in that mall, where you thought it would be. I'm still looking for the other one.

Andy worked fast. He must not have had anything more pressing to do today. As much as he hated to admit it, the guy earned the exorbitant rates he charged. It was smart to use coded language too—his texts didn't reveal anything about the work. He meant that Michael Tran was connected to the gym in the mall at Fig and Seventh, and "where you thought" meant he worked there.

Tossing the wrappers in the trash, he climbed into the Continental and checked the app for the vehicle tracker. The Charger was still parked at the mall—Michael was still at work.

Nosing into the street, he headed back downtown. The traffic was picking up in the late afternoon, but it was mostly in the opposite direction, and he soon pulled into the overpriced parking garage for the mall. It took a minute of walking around to find the gym. When he walked in, he didn't even have to ask for the guy—Michael was standing behind the front counter, wearing a red polo shirt with a name tag on it.

His eyebrows shot up at the sight of Slater, and he stood up straighter. "Hey, Slater. Are you a member here?"

"The only reason you're not lying on the floor bleeding right now is that this didn't bruise." Slater tapped his face under his eye.

Michael looked sideways into the big room with its array of gym equipment. "I'm not sure what you're talking about."

"Cut the crap," he said through his teeth. "Who are you working for? Why did you come after me?"

"Keep your voice down." Michael huffed. "Was the message not clear? Stay away from Hugo."

Slater put his hands on his hips. "It wasn't clear at all. I had no idea what the fuck you were talking about. So this is about jealous boy stuff? If you're into Hugo, go talk to Hugo. Leave me the fuck out of it."

"I'm not into Hugo, you idiot. Fermín is."

"Fermín told you to come after me?"

"Not exactly. But I can read the room. Fermín's taught me everything I know."

Tilting his head back, Slater guffawed. "Here I thought you might actually be dangerous. You're just a deludenoid."

"You were pawing Hugo," he said intently. "I saw it with my own eyes. There's no delusion."

"Does Fermín even know you came at me? You can't act for somebody else without talking to them about it, dumbass." Slater waved an arm. "No matter how much you think you can, you can't read Fermín's mind."

"Listen, Slater, I've got work to do. I really don't want to have to school you again."

He stared at him for a moment. "You really have no idea who you're dealing with, do you." It almost made him think he should walk away. Pounding on this guy would be like roughing up a blind person, or a cornered raccoon, or a child.

"Hugo said your mama was a friend of his," Michael said. "Shouldn't that be a boundary for you? I wouldn't mack on my mother's friends."

"Is your boss around? Let's find him."

He frowned. "You don't need to make trouble for me."

"Are those the locker rooms?" Slater said, jutting his chin. Walking toward them, he raised his voice. "Michael Tran … paging Mr. Michael Tran."

Hustling after him, Michael hissed at him. "Stop that."

There were cameras in the lobby, and probably around all the treadmills and weight racks and stationary bicycles, but there wouldn't be in the changing rooms. A glance around at the ceiling confirmed that. A couple of guys were standing near a bench in front of a wall of sleek redwood locker doors, but the next aisle was empty. Slater stepped into it and turned around.

Michael was on his heels. "You need to get out of here, or I'm calling the cops."

"You started this, sweet cheeks, and I bet I have a lot more experience explaining things to the cops than you do." He threw a fast right that snapped his head.

Michael tried to punch back, but this time Slater had the advantage, and the guy didn't really know how to brawl. Slater twisted sideways to avoid his fist, and it struck a glancing blow to his armpit. Blocking him with his other arm, Slater threw a hard left and hit his nose.

With a sharp yelp, Michael turned away, then sank onto the bench between the lockers, his face in his hands.

"You've got the strength," Slater said, "but you don't know how to use it."

"You broke my nose, you asshole."

There was blood on Michael's fingers, he saw, and he

stepped closer and grabbed his forearms, pulling his hands away from his face as he squatted in front of him. Michael flinched and squinted at him.

"It's not broken, you big baby. You're just bleeding. You earned that." Rising, he jabbed a finger at him. "If you come after me again, I will break your nose, and dislocate your fucking arm."

Walking out, Slater headed toward the parking garage. Why did people have to be so stupid? He could have made a scene, and got the guy fired, but he'd gone easy on him. The idiot was chasing shadows, seeing things that weren't there. Maybe not pushing it farther had been a mistake. Was he getting soft, turning square? In a way, showing restraint was just protecting the stupidity, encouraging it, letting it fester. Stupidity needed to have consequences. But that ship had sailed, and he pushed it out of his mind as he climbed into the Continental.

There was a text from Andy, he saw:

Drop by.

The surface lot behind Andy's building had emptied out, with the office drones vacating the neighborhood for the day, and it was too early for the restaurant and bar crowd to be hogging up the place. Upstairs Andy opened the door when he knocked, and flashed that perfect smile. As he followed him inside, there was no sign of Kyle.

"What happened to spouse B?" Slater said. "Did you finally send him packing? I can help you throw all his stuff into the hall. I know you'll be a lot happier."

"Slater—shut up." Andy dropped into his desk chair. "There are so many people with … that name. Charles Martin. But with that … approximate age, there's a guy here in town that fits. He's listed as a … linguist at the Agency for International Development."

"Who are they?"

"It's the federal government." He raised his eyebrows. "They do disaster relief and ... stuff like that overseas."

"I like that he's a G-man. This might be the right guy."

"It's a little weird that he's got ... no social media presence."

"Maybe he's too old for that."

"He's in his fifties," Andy said. "People usually ... have something online. I'll dig some more, but I do ... have an address for him. From the DMV. He lives near here, on ... Main Street."

"You're on fire today," Slater said. "You found him fast. Michael Tran too."

"I wasn't busy. I feel a little bad for ... Michael Tran. Like I put a target on him."

"I already dealt with that trash bag."

"Is he still breathing?"

"I didn't even have to get him canned. What do I owe you?"

"Let's say eight dollars."

Slater groaned and dug out his wad of cash. "You know that's fricking usury."

"Make it rain, Slater. You know ... you want to."

He peeled off the C-notes, and folded them lengthwise, and handed them over.

"You know what I like," Andy said.

Slater scoffed. "Eight yards for an hour's work. You've got chutzpah, I'll give you that." He watched him for a moment. "Bye, beautiful."

On the sidewalk out front he paused to check the details Andy had sent. The address for Charles Martin really was near here—on the map it was just a couple of blocks. He crossed the street and headed toward it.

Slater knew this building, he realized, as he walked up

on it. He'd hooked up with somebody who lived here, back in the BP era, before Pike. It was one of the conversions of a twentieth-century office block into residential space. They'd turned the courtyard in the middle into a gated private park. That seemed a little elitist, but it made sense to lock it down when you were a block from Skid Row.

Above the entrance, sleek metal lettering said OCHO RIOS. He'd never heard that name. It must be part of the renovation and rebranding. As he strode into the lobby, he went over to the potted palm, across from the front desk and near the elevators. At least nine feet tall, it had grown almost to the ceiling. It was a *Chamaedorea*, but not the ones people used as house plants. He brushed the fronds aside to look at the stems and the trunk.

Turning, he walked toward the desk. The clerk standing behind it was in his twenties, his Black hair in a sharp fade with fluffy twists up top. The guy was totally fuckable. Wearing a navy-blue jacket with a gold name tag, he flashed a standard service-industry smile as Slater approached the counter.

"You like the bush?"

"It's not a bush," Slater said. "It's a tree. And it's weird. Do you know who brought it here?"

His brow furrowed. "I don't. What's weird about it?"

"I can't figure out what it's doing here. It's the highland subspecies. For houseplants it's always the lowland version."

"Are you with the tree police?" he said, his expression deadpan.

"I'm not any kind of police. I have no houseplant enforcement power." Slater glanced at his name tag. "You know, Tommy, you're the best possible advertising for this building."

His eyes narrowed. "Excuse me?"

"You're smoking hot, and you have a sense of humor. People see that when they walk in. Who wouldn't want to live here?"

Tommy chuckled. "What can I help you with?"

"Charles Martin. One of the tenants. Do you know him?"

"I can't disclose any information about Ocho Rios residents."

"Of course not. That's a sensible policy. But there's no cameras in here," Slater said, gesturing vaguely toward the ceiling, "so nobody's watching. I'm thinking they're paying you minimum wage, am I right? They ignore you completely until something goes wrong, and then it's all your fault."

"I can tell you've done this kind of work before. Are you a flat-heel?"

"Something like that." Slater dug out his wad and palmed a fifty, holding it on the counter under his hand so just a corner with the denomination was visible. "Did you know President Grant was a badass? He helped right the ship, and went after the Klan, and put Black folks in government jobs. With that beard he's actually pretty foxy."

"Thank you for the rundown. I actually went to high school too."

Slater lifted his palm. "What can you tell this classic fox about Charles Martin?"

Tommy put a hand on the bill, and it disappeared into his pants pocket. "Mr. Martin is away."

"I'm sure there's more." He spoke louder. "Sing, brother."

"Lower your voice," Tommy said, and frowned. "He's been away for some time. His cleaner comes in once a week. I chatted with her last week. She said she hasn't seen him in months."

"Why would someone rent an apartment and never use it?"

He shrugged. "Straight folks are crazy."

"Do you know he's straight?"

"It's a reasonable assumption. Most people are."

"What does he look like?" Slater said.

"I've never met him. I'm not sure anyone has. The woman on the desk for the morning shift has been here a lot longer. She actually trained me. She called him a ghost resident. We have a couple of those."

"You say resident, but they're renters, aren't they?"

"Correct," Tommy said. "Management prefers the more positive term."

"What shifts do you work?"

"I'm always on swing shift. Management wants the residents to see the same faces every day, so they can make their unreasonable demands of the same people." He waved a hand. "They call it swing shift but it's really afternoons. Noon to eight."

"Ocho Rios isn't a new building," Slater said. "It must have maintenance issues."

"It's endless." He shifted on his feet. "There are internet outages all the time, and plumbing problems are almost perpetual."

"Does his unit have an alarm?"

Tommy's eyebrows shot up. "None of the units do, unless the residents install their own equipment. Why do you ask?"

"Just idle curiosity."

"Now you've got me worried."

"At least you can lean on President Grant to comfort you," Slater said, and turned to walk out.

"Hold on," he called after him. "I'm off soon."

He turned back. "That is interesting."

"You called me hot," Tommy said. "I can't just leave that money on the table."

Slater put his hands on his hips. "I can't go on a dinner date, if that's what you're thinking, or walk on the beach, or drink pinot in some hipster joint, but I'll fuck you, Tommy, if that's what you want."

"I figured as much from that ring on your finger. And I do want. There's a model suite upstairs we can use."

"You're efficient, I'll give you that. Are you a party-and-play guy?"

He frowned. "No drugs. And no thanks if you're a tweaker."

"I'm not. Do I have time to eat?"

"I'll be here when you get back."

Slater turned to leave, and Tommy called after him again.

"Hold up—what's your name?"

"Slater," he said over his shoulder, and walked out.

NINETEEN

⌂⌂⌂⌂⌂⌂⌂⌂⌂⌂⌂⌂

THERE WAS A VIETNAMESE place down the block, and when Slater walked up on it, the place wasn't crowded. He sat at the counter and ordered pho. While he was waiting for his food, he dug out his phone and texted Etta:

> Do you have time for me tomorrow morning? I've got a hands-on job.

Her reply popped up almost instantly:

> Yes! Let's rock.

He texted back:

> Bring your blue coveralls.

The server set a steaming bowl in front of him, and he slurped down the noodles, then walked back to the lobby of the Ocho Rios as the daylight faded. A different guy was behind the counter, scrawny with his streaky blond hair pulled back, wearing the same navy jacket.

Tommy stepped out of the doorway behind him, dressed in civvies now, khaki pants and a T-shirt with a lightweight black jacket. He beamed at him as he stepped out from behind the counter.

"I can show you that suite now if you'd like."

"Lead on," Slater said.

The guy at the desk was ignoring them, and Tommy led the way into a stairwell, then up one flight to a carpeted hallway. He used a key to unlock one of the doors, and Slater followed him in.

They stepped into a small lounge room with a bulky sofa, a table and chairs next to the kitchenette, and windows that looked out on Main. As it was just a few feet above street level, the view was of the buildings across the street, more early-twentieth-century classics with decorated stone facades. Some of the windows were lit up as dusk was setting in.

"It's a one bedroom," Tommy said. "They show it to potential residents. That's why there's furniture."

He led him into the next room, with a bed and a wardrobe.

"Are you the only one with a key to this place?" Slater said.

"Lots of people have keys. The staff actually uses it for meetings."

"And hookups."

Tommy raised his eyebrows. "That's what I meant by meetings."

Stepping out to the main room, he lifted one of the chairs from the little dining table and tucked the back of it under the handle of the front door. It was about the right height. With his boot he stomped on the seat, shoving the legs back a few inches. He tugged on the arms of the chair to test it. It was wedged in tightly.

"I guess we won't be disturbed," Tommy said. "That's so practical. You look like that kind of guy."

"No one's coming through that door without a chainsaw." Stepping close to him, Slater put his hands on his waist. "So what are you into?"

"There was talk of you fucking me."

Sliding his hands inside his jacket, Slater pushed it off, and it fell to the floor. He leaned in and kissed him. His mouth was warm and intent. The guy was good at this.

Eventually Tommy pulled back and peeled off his shirt, revealing his beautiful pecs, then groped Slater's crotch.

"You're getting hard. Come on."

Walking into the bedroom, he stepped out of his pants. The guy was getting wood too. Slater embraced him and ran his hands over his warm skin. Tommy unbuttoned his shirt, then unbuckled his belt, and Slater crouched to untie his boots. As he was pulling off his jeans, Tommy picked up his own pants and fished in the pocket.

"You have to wear a condom."

Slater sat on the bed. "Whoa." It felt like a slab of plywood covered by a thin sheet.

"It's staging furniture," Tommy said. "Not meant to be slept on, just to look pretty."

"Is it going to collapse?"

"It hasn't yet." Pushing him back, he straddled him, running his hands into his hair, then mouthed his neck and his jaw. When he pulled up, he ripped open the condom and rolled it on Slater, then stretched out on his back, and folded his hands behind his head.

Slater moved closer, pushing his knees apart. The guy was so hot. He pressed into him, slowly at first. Tommy closed his eyes as he got into it. He was breathing hard.

Soon Slater was pounding him, leaning over him. Grabbing the back of his neck, Tommy pulled him down into a kiss. With their mouths together, Slater climaxed, straining into him. Eventually he pulled back and squeezed Tommy's cock.

"What are we going to do with this?"

"Want to smoke me?"

Shifting position, he took him into his mouth. The guy was big, and he had to work him using his hand. When he came his whole body shuddered.

Lying on his back, Slater could hear his breathing gradually slow. There was no chance of drifting off—it felt like he was lying on a concrete floor.

Tommy sat up on his elbows. "The shower works if you need it."

"I can do that at my place." He sat up and swung his feet to the floor. "This is a great setup. It's impossible to get too comfortable." He slapped the bed. "That would keep things on schedule. You bring a lot of people here?"

"I don't. It's hard to meet people in this town."

Slater scoffed. "Hot people don't have problems." Rising, he stepped into his jeans.

"It's easy to find hookups, but it's hard to meet quality guys." Tommy rose and started to get dressed.

"You should try twelve-step meetings. There's lots of gay ones. All over town. There's tons of guys."

He frowned. "I'm not a drunk."

"It doesn't matter. There's no admission test. You said you weren't into drugs—twelve-step is a great place to meet sober people." Slater scooped up his shirt. "The meetings cut across social classes too. In this neighborhood you'll meet homeless guys and guys who live in million-dollar condos. Focus on the ones who've been doing the steps for a while. They're less likely to relapse."

"Interesting advice." He adjusted the shiny bed covering so that it looked undisturbed.

Once they were both dressed, they walked out to the main room, and Tommy pulled on his jacket. Slater tugged on the chair under the door, and had to heave on it a couple of times, but eventually it came free. After he'd set it back at the table, he stepped into the hall, and waited for Tommy to pull the door closed.

As they walked into the lobby, the guy behind the desk looked up at them and raised his eyebrows. "How was the apartment? Will you be filling out an application?"

"Not at this time," Slater said.

He eyed Tommy. "Slut."

Tommy cackled. "Bite me, man. Remember that word when you're up there with your girlfriend." Once they were out on the street, he paused on the sidewalk. "That was fun."

Slater jutted his chin. "Back at you."

He felt lighter as he walked toward Broadway and the Continental. It was great to get that out of the way so early, and now he wouldn't need to let some rando into his house. The deal he'd worked out with Pike for the sex rules was that he could fuck other people when Pike was out of town, or if it was for work. That didn't mean Pike was happy about it, and he'd decided he didn't want to hear about it when it happened. Slater knew it was far from equitable. It would drive him insane if Pike slept with someone else.

Back at the house he had just sat on the sofa to pull his boots off when Pike called.

"I miss you," Slater said. "The house feels all empty. Your pheromones are fading by the minute."

"I'm sure you'll think of something to do. Stick your dick in something juicy. Did you eat dinner at least?"

"I'll probably be able to find something at the gas station. They have a whole rack of salty snack treats."

Pike laughed. "I'm not buying it. You can't walk half a block in that neighborhood without hitting a tony vegan restaurant. I'm the one roughing it tonight. In Bishop they roll up the sidewalks at dusk."

They talked for a while longer, and then ended the call. In the kitchen Slater poured his ration into a tumbler, going a little heavy-handed. He needed to be compensated for being left on his own, he reasoned.

Carrying the glass out to the deck, he shivered in the chilly night air, then took a satisfying slurp, relishing the vapor in his nose and coughing a little at the heady burn in his throat. He stood at the low wall surrounding the deck and gazed out at the hillside and the glittering towers of the Financial District in the distance. Soon the warmth would envelop him, the golden elixir suffusing his psyche, softening all the sharp edges.

It was messed up to fuck other people when it made Pike upset. He knew that. And yet he did it anyway, like the piece of trash that he was. It was such a hard habit to break. He took another slurp. In a hot minute it wouldn't even matter.

TWENTY

PIKE WAS GONE WHEN Slater woke. Out of town, he remembered. His head hurt, but maybe it wasn't too bad. He sat up, and swung his feet to the floor, and took a few breaths. It wasn't a full-on katzenjammer, but he must have taken another snort after exhausting his ration. That happened sometimes. In the bathroom mirror he eyed himself. His lip wasn't swollen anymore, but he looked haggard.

"Idiot," he said through his teeth.

He hustled to shower and get dressed, and in the kitchen considered making java, but decided he couldn't be bothered. Pike was better at that. Instead he grabbed an apple and bit into it on the way downstairs.

In the garage he grabbed a pair of coveralls, then unlocked the gear cabinet and pulled out his lock reader. A length of cable with a key-shaped probe at one end and a connector for his phone on the other, it worked with Svetlana's software to come up with a key number, one of the many in little numbered pouches in the thick binder that went with it. The key binder wouldn't fit in a regular toolbox, so he put it with the lock reader into an aluminum case from under the workbench. It was really a briefcase, but it was thick, with reinforced corners, so it could pass for something a plumber might use to carry tools.

He loaded the case into the trunk of the Continental, then finished the apple and tossed the core toward the trash can back by the laundry machines. It struck the lip but cleared it and dropped in.

"Yes," he said under his breath.

Once he'd backed into the street, he waited for the door to roll down, then drove downtown and parked across from his office. Upstairs Etta was already behind the front desk, wearing jeans and a red print shirt.

"Max isn't around?" Slater said.

She spread her arms. "It's just me, baby."

"It's the middle of the week. How can you possibly have time for this gig?"

"I'll go in later. I don't teach this morning, although technically I should be at my desk."

"The life you lead, woman."

"Says the man who's about to break into somebody's place."

"It's not a break-in. We were called in to do maintenance." He frowned. "I never said what we were doing."

"You told me to bring the coveralls. That usually means a maintenance call. So hit me with the details."

Slater outlined the job, and then locked up the office, and they rode the elevator down to the street and climbed into the Continental. It was just a few blocks to Main. He pulled into a structure half a block from the Ocho Rios building, and drove up a few levels, and parked in a quiet corner.

Climbing out, they both stood between the car and the wall to pull on their matching dark-blue coveralls. Slater opened the trunk to lift out the aluminum case.

As they walked toward the elevator, Etta took a deep breath. "I'm ready."

"You look nervous." Slater eyed her as they stepped on. "Just remember you're good at this. I've never seen anyone spin a cover story like you can. Max says you're the best in the business."

Her eyebrows shot up. "If that's the case, I'm going to have to start charging you knuckleheads more. I'm not really nervous. Just getting amped up."

"Think boredom," Slater said. "I'm sure plumbers are usually bored."

"Got it." As the doors rolled open at street level, she adjusted the collar of her coveralls. "Chin up, tits out."

He had to chuckle as he followed her out to the sidewalk. A few yards up the block, they stepped into the lobby of the Ocho Rios building.

The woman on the front desk had her dark Latin hair pinned up. She was wearing the same blue jacket and gold name tag as Tommy and the night clerk.

Stepping up to the counter, Slater affected a Spanish accent. "We're here for Mr. Martin's apartment. Charles Martin."

The clerk frowned. "There's a service entrance in back. The front door is for the residents. Did Manny send you? Nobody told me you were coming."

"Mr. Charles's cleaner called my company. He has a plumbing problem."

"We always use the same provider. Residents don't have their own plumbers."

"You want to leave the water on Mr. Charles floor, that's fine with me. His cleaner said he's out of town. He'll come home to a mess." Slater shrugged. "Whether we work today or not, we're going to get paid. You can decide."

She huffed. "I can't give you the key."

"The cleaner dropped off the key at my office," Slater said. "From you I just need you not to call the police."

"Fine," she said flatly. "Do you know what's wrong? Is it a broken pipe?"

"We won't know until we look at it."

"Let me know if you're able to make the repair."

"Yes, boss," he said, and walked toward the elevators.

"I'm liking the neanthe," Etta said, eyeing the potted palm as she pressed the call button.

"I'm impressed that you know the name of it," Slater said quietly.

"There's lots of them around."

"This one is a little odd. *Chamaedorea elegans* has a couple of subspecies. It's the first time I've seen that one in a pot."

The elevator doors rolled open, and they stepped on. Etta looked around the car.

"No cameras in here," she said, once the doors had closed. "The entrance had a couple mounted overhead, but there were none in the lobby either."

"I'm not sure why. Sometimes rich folks don't want them. These are small apartments. Maybe lawyers and bankers use them to hook up with their side pieces and hookers and drug dealers."

"That's a great reason not to have surveillance. It's the first thing Max asks for when we're on a window-shade job." She lowered her voice to mimic him. "'Where do you keep the security video?'"

Stepping out into the hallway, Slater pointed to the adjacent doorway. "That's the stairs down to the lobby. If we need to make a quick exit."

Farther down the hall they stopped at the door to Charles's apartment. Slater knocked hard on it and called,

"Maintenance." Cocking his head, he listened, then pounded on it with the heel of his fist.

"Crickets," Etta whispered. "Can you get through this lock?"

He dug a pair of latex gloves out of the pocket of his coveralls and started to wriggle his hands into them. "I think so. It's a standard hardware-store model."

As Etta pulled on her own gloves, he flipped open the aluminum case, and retrieved the lock probe, and connected it to his phone. Svetlana's app popped up, and the screen went black and displayed "готов."

"What does that say?" Etta said.

"No idea. I know it means the software is ready for input."

He slipped the probe into the lock, and the screen went red. Easing it out slightly, he adjusted its position, glancing at the screen. The background went green, and a lone number popped up: 032. He tipped the screen toward Etta.

Wordlessly she knelt and flipped through the heavy pages of the key binder, pulling the key from the pouch marked 032, and handed it to him. When he tried it, the key easily slid into the lock, and twisted freely. He heard the bolt retract.

As he pocketed the key, Etta took the lock probe and folded the case closed, lifting it as she got up. He waited until she nodded that she was ready, then twisted the door handle, and pushed it open. No alarm sounded, and they stepped inside.

The lights were off, with daylight from the big windows illuminating the main room. There was no alarm panel in sight. That didn't mean there wasn't an alarm, but with no sound and no panel, it seemed unlikely.

"Maintenance," Slater called, and they stood listening for a second.

Etta pulled the door closed and set the aluminum case in front of it. The layout was similar to the model unit, with windows that looked over the street. These let in more light because they were higher up. Charles had some basic lounge furniture here, and a table next to the kitchenette.

Walking into the short hall, Etta called back: "Powder room, linen closet, bedroom, bathroom."

She'd start back there, like they'd planned. Slater stepped into the kitchen and started opening cupboards. There were dishes and pots and pans, some kitchen linens, and in one cupboard a couple of boxes of cereal and oatmeal. The Frigidaire had a box of milk, and one of orange juice, plus a trio of apples and some oranges in a bowl. An unopened block of cheese was in a drawer, and a six pack of beer sat on the middle shelf. There was nothing green, nothing more perishable than the milk.

Stepping into the main room, Slater stood and looked it over. There was basic bland art on the wall, and a big TV set, but no photographs anywhere—nothing personal, no clutter, no books. Taking it in, he thought about it. It felt unlived in, even though there was food. Maybe that made sense if the guy was on an extended trip or had an unpredictable schedule. He had his cleaner keep food available in case he came back. She'd have to swap it out once a week or so, but it would be waiting for him anytime he showed up.

He walked into the bedroom to find Etta standing at the closet, holding a suit jacket on a hanger.

"It's all men's clothes," she said, glancing at him. "All the same sizes. The shoes are all the same size too."

"So Charles is alone when he's here."

"Every garment has the tags cut out."

"Seriously?" Slater said. "Show me."

She folded open the lapel of the jacket. There was a space where the label had been sewn into the inner surface, but she was right—it hadn't just worn loose. The edge of the label was still there. He rubbed it with a latex-clad finger. It had been cut out in a clean line, with a blade.

"We can go," Slater said.

Etta replaced the suit jacket, and closed the closet, and followed him to the door. In the hallway he pulled it closed and locked it with the ghost key, and they walked to the elevator.

"We should find the service entrance," Slater said, "and leave that way."

Once they'd stepped on, Etta pressed the button marked G. "This is probably the garage. It's below the button for the lobby. I bet the servants come and go down there."

Sure enough, when they stepped into the parking garage, daylight was visible at one side. When they walked over, they found a crash door into the alley, and pushed through it.

"Thoughts?" Slater said as they walked back to the Continental.

"It's set up for one person, but he's not living there. You could drop in and have everything you needed. It's all new, even the toothpaste. It kind of feels like a short-term rental."

"The kitchen had the same vibe."

Etta eyed him sidelong. "Is that useful information?"

"I'm not sure yet. I need to talk to the cleaner."

At the car they both stripped off the coveralls, and Slater put the aluminum case in the trunk, and drove back to the office.

"I'm right by the fence," Etta said as he nosed into the surface lot.

Slater pulled in next to her little red Prius and shifted into Park. "What do I owe you?"

"It wasn't too difficult. A hundo?"

"Done." He dug out his wad, and peeled off a C-note, and handed it over.

"Cha-ching," she said, and climbed out.

Once she was in her own car, he backed out and headed toward the exit. He needed to talk to Hugo. Pulling into the street, he gunned it ahead of the advancing traffic, then headed for Lincoln Heights.

He thought about Charles's sterile apartment. He was missing something—he could feel it. It wasn't just about an affluent person keeping it ready for their unscheduled return.

There was nowhere to park on Hugo's block, but the gate across his driveway was open, and there was room for the Continental behind his Subaru. Nosing in, he pulled up tight to its rear end.

Hugo was in the front yard, wearing a broad-brimmed straw hat, on his knees in the dirt. He waved to him with a trowel as he pulled up. As Slater got out, he saw the guy was actually working on a trio of squat terra-cotta pots, and had a tray of seedlings next to him.

"You've got the right light here for cosmos."

Hugo sat back on his heels. "The guy who sold them to me called them asters."

"They're that too. Cosmos is a species in the aster family." He waved a hand. "I never see seedlings. Most people just plant seed."

"But then how much water would that take?" Hugo said.

"You can keep them blooming all summer if you deadhead them. But you have to keep on it."

"Did you drop by to give me gardening tips?"

Slater put his hands on his hips. "Did you know that Fermín is into you?"

He groaned and got to his feet. "I'm well aware."

"You need to talk to him. His toady came after me to

tell me to stay away from you."

Hugo frowned. "Michael? I can't believe he'd do that. Why would he think you were interested in me?"

"The guy is an idiot. You need to sort that out. Either sleep with Fermín or tell him to shove off."

"I don't think I'm ready to get into that. A relationship or even a casual arrangement." He gestured with the trowel. "And if I tell him no, he'll bust up the ghost crew."

"He's also not twelve years old. He should be able to handle the rejection without getting all petty about it."

"I don't know."

"When did you first get together with your husband?"

"We were young," Hugo said. "In our twenties. We were just starting out in our careers."

"And you were with him your whole life."

"There's been nobody else."

"That explains it," Slater said. "You haven't had to deal with boy-boy stuff in decades. You forgot how."

"I remember Doris sent you to several psychologists when you were a teenager." He raised his eyebrows. "Were you able to obtain your own counseling license?"

"I don't care what you do with Fermín," he said, raising his voice. "But when your squad comes at me, we've got a problem."

"All right, Slater. I get it." He waved dismissively. "Have you been paying attention for synchronicities?"

He took a breath. "Telling me about that has got me thinking differently. I'll admit that. It actually hasn't been completely pointless."

Hugo beamed. "What have you noticed?"

"During the ghost hunt I got an echo of the word VCR. It was on an old sign in that hotel."

"I remember. You pointed it out."

"Focusing on that led me to some useful information."

"Nice." He laughed. "See? It works. What else?"

"This Russian novel keeps coming up in the case for no obvious reason. *Crime and Punishment*. I'm not sure if I need to be looking for meaning in that."

"Have you read it? Maybe you should."

"No thanks," Slater said flatly. "The other one is that I've been called a weasel several times in the last week."

"That's not really a synchronicity, or even a coincidence," Hugo said. "It's like if several people say, 'You're wearing jeans.' There's a clear cause. It's because you are."

He narrowed his eyes. "OK."

"I'm glad you took it seriously. Remember that the more tuned in you are, the more the phenomenon will respond to you."

"You think it's something conscious? Like a person?" Slater frowned. "That makes it sound Jesus-y. I keep running into Catholics on this job. That's probably not a synchronicity either. There's lots of them in this town. Are you Catholic?"

"Not anymore." He gestured with the trowel. "The phenomenon has nothing to do with religion. And it's definitely conscious. Synchronicities aren't just a side effect of the nature of reality." He raised his eyebrows. "There's more going on than you think."

Slater watched him for a moment. "I have to go," he said, then jabbed a finger at him. "Get your squad under control."

Hugo frowned. "Yes, sir."

As he climbed into the Continental, Hugo returned to his work on the cosmos. He knew he probably wouldn't do anything about it, but Michael wouldn't come after him again either.

TWENTY-ONE

C RUISING OUT OF THE neighborhood, Slater followed Main Street to the Ocho Rios building, and spotted a meter, and pulled in. Once he'd plinked in some coins, he walked up the block and bought a coffee at a place on the corner, slurping at it on the walk back to the building. As he strode into the lobby, Tommy grinned in recognition.

"Are you back for more?"

"I wish I had the time," Slater said. "This is a business matter. I need to know the name of Charles Martin's cleaner."

"Unfortunately we're not allowed to divulge information about our residents."

Slater glanced around at the empty lobby and frowned. "You managed to squawk plenty yesterday."

"My memory is somewhat hazy." Tommy raised his eyebrows. "You know, the nutrition in that sweet lettuce you provided last night might sharpen things up."

"Dude—I had your dick down my throat. Doesn't that buy me any credit?"

"That was delightful, Slater, and I'll always cherish the memory. But I'm on minimum wage here."

Slater growled and dug out his wad of cash. Peeling off a fifty, he set it on the countertop. Tommy deftly whisked it away.

"Her name is Teresa. She's actually upstairs in his unit now."

"You're a damn gonif, Tommy." He walked toward the elevators and called back to him. "Sexy as fuck, but a gonif all the same."

The key to Charles's apartment was still in his front pocket, and at the front door he used it to unlock the bolt, and stepped inside. He could hear a vacuum cleaner running in the bedroom. It seemed pointless to vacuum an empty place that nobody used. A paper grocery bag sat on the kitchen counter, and a carry tray of cleaning supplies was on the floor. Slater stood near the door, and left it open, as that would be less likely to alarm her.

"Hello," he called.

The vacuum stopped, and a woman walked in from the bedroom, her eyes wide. In her fifties, maybe, her hair was tied back, and she was wearing sweatpants and sneakers with a floral apron.

Slater forced a smile. "You must be Teresa."

"Who are you? How did you get in?"

"I'm a friend of Charles's."

Her brow furrowed. "I didn't know he had any friends."

"I wanted to ask you a couple of things. How does Charles tell you what he needs, and how does he pay you?"

"That doesn't sound like the kind of questions a friend would ask."

Digging out his wad of cash, Slater peeled off a C-note, letting her see what it was before he palmed it. "I know you're working. I won't take too much of your time."

He extended his hand.

Teresa held his gaze for a moment but then stepped closer. Briefly grasping his hand to retrieve the bill, she tucked it into her pants.

"I've never met Mr. Martin. I work for an agency that tells me what to do. I get paid by the agency."

"What do they tell you to do?"

She hesitated, shifting on her feet.

"That C-note means we have a fiduciary relationship here." He raised his voice. "Sing, sister."

Her eyebrows shot up. "I clean every week and bring food. I change the milk and the fruit once a week, and the juice every other week. Nobody ever drinks it."

"How long have you been doing this?"

"A couple years."

"And nobody ever stays here?"

"Mr. Martin comes once in a while," she said. "Maybe three times since I started. Just a few nights at a time. He leaves some laundry for me. Clothes and towels. And I change the bed. He ate some cereal once, and the fruit."

"Does he travel?" Slater said. "Where is he the rest of the time?"

"New York City."

"How do you know that?"

"Once he left half a sandwich in the fridge. I thought it was strange that it came from so far away. I wouldn't keep a sandwich after a six-hour plane ride."

"It had the shop's name in New York?"

"The bag was printed with the shop's name and address, and it had his name, Martin, and the delivery address written on it in felt pen."

Slater furrowed his brow. "I don't suppose you remember that address."

"It was a while ago. Last year maybe. I don't remember

the house number, but I remember it was on Fifty-Seventh Street, with the direction. East or West Fifty-Seventh. One of those. My grandparents used to live on Fifty-Seventh Street in South LA. Down by Slauson." She grinned. "It stayed in my mind because of that coincidence. I remember wondering how many Fifty-Seventh Streets there are around the country."

There was that word again, *coincidence*. Whether it rose to the level of Hugo's synchronicities or not, it definitely gave him something that might be useful.

"Do you know anything else about Charles Martin?" Slater said. "How old he is, if he brings anyone else here, if he has a car in the garage downstairs?"

"I told you what I know." She waved a hand. "I need to get back to work."

"All right." He jutted his chin. "Lock the door behind me."

"I locked it before you came in."

Walking out, Slater waved to Tommy on the front desk, standing there talking earnestly with a woman in a gray suit. On the street he put more quarters in the meter for the Continental, then walked the few blocks to Andy's building. On the way his phone buzzed in his pocket, and he pulled it out to find a text from Pike:

I'll be back mid-afternoon.

That, he thought, was very good news. Pausing on the sidewalk, he texted him a GIF that they tossed back and forth, an image of a Dachshund nodding its head, superimposed with the word SOON.

When he rapped on the door to his loft, Andy pulled it open, looking perfectly disheveled. Such a beautiful man.

"I'm going to stop answering the door," Andy said. "Then you'll … have no choice but to text me first."

He followed him in. "You'd starve, son. I know your food supply comes in delivery bags."

Andy dropped into his desk chair. "What can I do for you today?"

"That address for Charles Martin was solid."

"Was he there?"

"It's weird—like he doesn't really live there, but he drops in once in a while. I got more dope on him. He has some connection to Fifty-Seventh Street in New York."

"New York City? He works there?"

"I'm asking you to figure that out," Slater said.

"Sure. Let me dig around."

"Where's spouse B?"

"He actually has his own life," Andy said. "I think he went to the … dentist today."

"You can only bleach your teeth so many times before it starts to damage them. Does he know that? Or does he have some kind of sicko dental-pain fetish, drilling into his molars for no reason? That can't be healthy." He put his hands on his hips. "You know you're going to have to deal with that at some point."

"Slater, if there's nothing else, get out … of my place."

"I'm just saying." He looked him over for a moment. "Bye, beautiful."

Walking back to his car, he realized he should probably check in with Elvaine. It had been a while, and stuff was happening. But she was the no-bullshit type—she'd call him when he'd been incommunicado for too long.

Climbing into the Continental, he drove to his house, and took his laptop out onto the deck. The sun was finally shining through the marine layer, and it felt warm out. He was still at the patio table when Pike stepped outside.

Slater pushed the laptop away. "I didn't hear you come in."

Kneeling next to his chair, Pike leaned in to savage him, mouthing his neck and his jaw. Eventually he pulled back.

"How was Bishop?" Slater said.

"Hot, and then after dark, cold." He pulled out the adjacent chair and sat. "Are you done for the day?"

"I don't know what the hell I'm doing." He threw up a hand. "Are you headed back to your office?"

"I'm taking the rest of the day off," Pike said. "The 395 is great, but we took the 15 from Victorville. It's intense. I need to decompress."

"You sound like an Angeleno now. 'The 15.' When you got here, you would have said 'I was on I-15' or 'I took 15 from Victorville.' And then the question that hangs in the air is, you took fifteen what from Victorville? Fifteen rent boys? You'd need a damn bus. Fifteen Vegas showgirls? What were they doing in Victorville? Fifteen kilos of dope? That's illegal, son."

Pike chuckled. "For the sake of clarity it's probably a good thing that I sound like a local."

"The fact that you're talking like that means you are a local. So why would someone cut the tags out of their clothes?"

His eyebrows shot up. "Where did you see that?"

"In Charles Martin's closet."

He closed his eyes and rubbed them. "I'm not going to ask."

"His cleaning person basically let me in," Slater said.

Looking tired now, Pike met his gaze. "You need to stop digging into this guy. Like, right now. No tags means he's working for an intelligence agency."

"How do you know that?"

"Once in a while a dead body turns up with the tags cut out of the clothes. It's usually a clean professional-type hit job. They always stay unidentified no matter what law enforcement does. The consensus is, just file it away. No one is ever going to ID the victim or claim the body, because it's an undercover spy."

"What agency would this guy be working for?" Slater said.

"We have several, but it could be any country's intelligence agency. It's a universal practice. A way to make it much harder to track down the person's origins." Pike pursed his lips, gazing at him for a moment. "Think about his name too. It makes sense for a spy. Even better than Smith, Martin is generic in several languages."

"The cleaner was definitely pronouncing it the Spanish way. Mar-*teen*."

"What else do you know about him?"

"He works for a federal outfit called USAID. He's a linguist."

"Sure he is." Pike scoffed. "Dude is a damn spy. Stop looking for him. These people don't mess around."

Slater frowned. "So I should just tell my client he's probably a spy, that's all I've got, I'm done now, here's my invoice?"

"You don't even know for sure if Charles Martin is Boris."

"It's a hard fact," he said. "Charles's thumbprint matched Boris's."

"Unless the print on the card was from a video store clerk, or some other kid from the dorm who borrowed it." Pike pushed himself out of the chair. "I have to crash for a while. That bus full of rent boys wore me out." He leaned in to briefly kiss his neck, then walked inside.

Pulling his laptop closer, Slater did a search for "unidentified body with tags cut out of the clothes." Pike was right, he soon learned—it was a whole thing, a way to obscure someone's identity, commonly done by people operating undercover. Hotel workers in Oslo found a woman in a locked guest room, shot in the head, but with no weapon present. She'd checked in with a fake ID, and had several wigs in her luggage, and all the labels were missing from her wardrobe. Nobody ever identified her. Early in the Cold War a guy was found dead on the beach in Adelaide. He had no ID on him, and the tags had been cut out of his clothes. All he had in his pockets were smokes and a scrap of paper cut from an obscure book.

He pushed the laptop away. It definitely sounded like spy bullshit. If Charles was part of that world, it increased the risk to him significantly. But he couldn't just drop it. Not now, when it felt like he was so close.

His phone buzzed in his pants, and he pulled it out—Andy. He never made voice calls.

"I found a connection between a Charles Martin and … Fifty-Seventh Street," Andy said. "This guy is really off the radar. He's quite … hard to track."

"What kind of connection?"

"Somebody with that name bought an … apartment in one of those pencil buildings on Fifty-Seventh. It's Charles Martin, but I can't … tell you if it's the same guy I found in LA. It's a … super common name. I'll text you the address."

"The Charles Martin from Main Street spends most of his time away from LA. If he bought the place, I bet he's hanging out there."

"You owe me for this," Andy said. "Separate from the … last payment."

"I know I do. Listen—you need to stop looking into this guy. No more research."

"Why?"

"I think he might work for a spy agency."

"That would explain several things. The lack of … social media, and keeping an apartment that he doesn't use. It's also a … very good reason to drop it. Nobody wants to poke … that hornet's nest."

Slater ended the call and sat thinking about it, gazing at the hillside in the golden light of the end of the day. It was still cool here but in the East it would be full-blown summer. Sitting up, he pulled his laptop close and checked on flights. He could go tonight, and be in New York in the morning. He spent a minute booking a ticket, then folded his laptop closed and took it inside.

He found Pike in the bedroom, stretched out and reading his novel. He'd changed into a pair of fugly cargo shorts and a T-shirt. Slater climbed onto the bed with him and wrapped an arm around his torso.

"You're warm." Pike set the book aside. "It feels good."

Leaning in, he inhaled the heady scent of his hair. "So I'm taking a little trip tonight."

"Where?"

"I found an address for Charles in New York."

"Seriously?" Pike demanded. "What happened to 'You should drop it'?"

"I'm just going to talk to the guy. He's not going to grease me for asking a couple questions."

"If he is Boris, and his new identity is valuable to him, he just might. That secret could be worth more than your life."

"I can't just walk away from this," Slater said.

Pike shifted to face him. "You're like an unstoppable freight train. When is your flight?"

"In a couple hours."

"You'll have to stay over. Do you have a plan for that? Did you book a return?"

"There's dozens of flights every day," Slater said. "I'll just come back when I'm done."

"Are you sure this guy is going to be there? What if he's

at his beach house in Maine for the summer, or flying back to LA tonight? You'll pass him over Kansas City."

"Somebody will have info on him if he's not there. I'm sure it sounds rash, but I need to scope it out in person. You know how that goes."

Pike caressed his cheek with his thumb. "You have to call me."

Meeting his mouth, he lingered in it, and rubbed his belly. "I know you gossip with Doris. Don't tell her I'm in New York. She'll try to set me up with her dud relatives."

"You're afraid they'll try to schnorr off you or something?"

"Worse—they're rich idiots. I don't have time for that."

When he got up, he pulled out his faux-leather jacket, and tucked his laptop and earbuds and a change of clothes into his satchel. Pike was watching him from the bed, his head propped on his arm.

"I'll take you to LAX. Which terminal is it?"

"You don't need to bother. I can leave the Continental there."

"That costs a fortune." He raised his eyebrows. "You know it's OK to ask for help, right? You don't have to do everything yourself. You've taken me to the airport lots of times. It's part of the teamwork. Part of being together."

"But then the Continental won't be there for me when I get back."

"Have some trust that I will."

Upstairs they threw together a meal from leftovers, and Pike put a bagel in a sandwich bag and tucked it into his satchel. Slater pulled on his jacket and slung the bag over his shoulder.

"We should go."

It was dark out when they trooped down the stairs and climbed into Pike's old green SUV.

"This thing is such a hooptie," Slater said.

Pike laughed as he started the engine. "It purrs like a kitten. Hear that? It took me halfway up the Eastern Sierra and back with not one hiccup."

Traffic was flowing at this hour, even the stretch of freeway through downtown that was always congested, and Pike soon pulled in to the curb in front of his terminal. Shifting into Park, he leaned toward Slater. His expression somber, he held his gaze.

"You have to promise me you're going to be safe."

"Always." Slater pulled him into a brief kiss. "I'll be back soon."

Waiting to board the flight, he sat looking at his phone. He still had the link to Elvaine's music that Niles had sent him. He could listen to that on the way, he decided, and downloaded the album.

His seat was against the window, and he got as comfortable as he could, listening to Elvaine's voice. Her tone was simple and pure. It made him think of succulents, and the way they looked. Stark and plain, they were also solid, and present, and inherently beautiful.

TWENTY-TWO

"**G**O EAST." THE PSYCHIC'S words were in Slater's mind when he woke. Groggy at first, he soon remembered where he was. They'd turned up the cabin lights, and he could feel the airplane descending. Go east. He was doing that right now.

On his phone he figured out how to get to the part of the city where Charles's apartment was, and he rode the little train around the airport, then got on the subway. The car was crowded and he had to stand.

People looked different here, partly because it was morning and lots of them were dressed for office jobs. But there was something more, like they were tidier, wearing sharper clothes, had better haircuts. The train was loud too, lurching and banging over the tracks. Everything in LA was comparatively so much newer.

The car doors rolled open, and he stepped aside to let people exit. The walls of the subway station were covered in white ceramic tile, he saw, like in a bathroom. It was all so different from what he was used to. Thinking about it, he had no connections in this city, no way to get anything done. Like Pike said, there was a chance Charles wouldn't even be around. But he was here—it was too late for second thoughts now.

It seemed to take a long time to reach the center, but he knew he was getting close, and briefly crouched to look out the window at the station names. Finally he spotted Fifth Avenue. This was him.

Walking up the gritty stairs out of the ground in Midtown, the sun was out, but it felt cooler than he'd expected. He zipped up his jacket, and took a minute to orient himself, eventually figuring out which direction to go.

Along the verge were boxes of tulips in a riot of colors, yellow and red and pink. He never saw those in Cali. They must need the cold weather. Even more dramatic were the high-rises. There were so many of them in every direction. They made the street feel like a slot canyon. When he found Charles's address, he could see it fit the description Andy had used—it was surreal in how tall and narrow it was, like a pencil. Digging out his phone, he checked the time. It was still mid-morning but not too early to knock on someone's door.

Slater walked into the lobby. It had an absurdly high ceiling and an oversize chandelier, lots of glass and wood, and stone floors. This was definitely designed to awe with its opulence.

As he approached the front desk, a woman with blond hair and a black uniform jacket looked up at him. "Can I help you?"

"I'm here to see Charles Martin."

"Your name?"

"Tell him I'm a friend of Natasha from Live Oak."

Her brow furrowed. "Where's that at?"

Slater jutted his chin. "Just say it."

Reaching for the desk phone, she murmured into it,

and listened, then eyed him as she replaced the receiver. "Go on up. Mr. Martin is in unit 82B."

"What floor is that on?"

She raised her eyebrows. "The eighty-second."

"Got it."

Slater walked toward the elevators. He'd never been in a building with that many floors. When he stepped off, the elevator lobby was small, with just a few doors facing it. The bell for 82B had a camera above the button. Slater scowled at the lens and pressed it.

A guy pulled open the door. Wearing chinos and a brick-red sweater, he had dark hair and a square jaw. His eyes were hard as he gave Slater a pointed once-over.

"You haven't changed," Slater said. "The same eyes, the same jaw line. There's just more mileage on you."

"Who are you, exactly?"

"The name is Slater. Are you going to let me in?"

He stepped aside, and Slater walked past him into the apartment. The space was carpeted, with bulky lounge furniture and a dining table. He stepped across to the floor-to-ceiling windows and felt his heart start to pound from the height and the proximity to the edge. The city stretched away into the haze, the high-rises topping out lower than this vantage, the streets gloomy grooves between them.

"This place is nuts," Slater said. "It's like the view from an airplane. Is that south?"

"How did you find me?"

Slater turned back to him. Charles had closed the door, and was standing there facing him, a boxy black pistol in hand now. It was leveled at him.

"Don't point your gun at me." Slater jutted his chin. "I'm unarmed."

"Talk," Charles snapped.

He put his hands on his hips. "The thing is, you've

already shown your hand. If I just answer your questions, you'll plug me anyway."

"Talk, or I will plug you." He raised his voice. "I'm the one with the weapon."

"I get that. But you're overreacting. I'm happy to talk. I actually came here to talk, not to look down the barrel of your Glock."

A dull buzz sounded, and Charles reached into his pants pocket with his free hand, his aim with the rod not wavering. Pulling out a phone, he glanced at the screen.

"Slater Ibáñez. Los Angeles." He met his gaze. "Known to police."

"Impressive."

"It's not complicated. Facial recognition and a database search."

"I know how you did it," Slater said. "Your stupid doorbell photographed me. What's impressive is your access to resources, and the speed of your access to resources. Who do you work for?"

Charles waggled the heater. "Do you not see this? Most people find handguns intimidating. I'm the one asking the questions."

"Easy, baby." Slater grimaced and rotated his shoulders, then twisted his back. "Can we at least sit down? I've been cramped in a tiny airplane seat all night."

Looking at his phone, Charles held it to his ear. "That's not necessary ... I'll let you know." He tucked it back in his front pocket.

"Was that your staff?" Slater said. "Maybe your corpse disposal crew?"

He sighed and tucked the weapon into the back of his belt. Waving at the lounge furniture, he flashed a fake smile. "Would you like to have a seat?"

Pulling off his satchel, Slater set it on the floor next to

the sofa, then shrugged off his jacket and draped it over the bag. He dropped onto the sofa and sat back.

"You got your teeth fixed too. In college they were a little misaligned."

Charles sat on the adjacent lounge chair and leaned toward him. "Who are you working for?"

"My client's identity is confidential. They're interested in the disappearance of Boris Brooks."

"The journalist," he said. "Elvaine. That woman is relentless."

"Why would you think I'm working for her?"

"She writes about him on a regular basis. Nobody else cares about Boris Brooks. He's long forgotten—except by her."

Slater rubbed his eyes. "You're obviously up to speed. Did you know she does music? Guitar and vocals. She writes her own songs. I listened to some of it on the way here. It's actually not bad. Do you still play violin? Why did you leave your instrument in your car that day, anyway?"

"What led you to me, exactly?"

"Basic research." Slater waved a hand. "I interviewed your sister, and of course I didn't believe anything she said. Then I interviewed Natasha, and I didn't believe anything he said. But one of them had an artifact with Boris's fingerprints on it."

"That would be useless. Boris's fingerprints aren't on record anywhere."

"That's not quite accurate. You have to provide them to the bank when you're not a customer and you want to cash a check. Those are private-sector records. Even the federal government can't erase them."

"Interesting." Charles raised his eyebrows. "You seem to have access to resources too."

"It's my job. I have some connections."

"With your handlers at the Ministry of State Security in Beijing? Or maybe the Revolutionary Guard Corps?"

Slater frowned. "Is that Iran? You already know I'm an Angeleno. The farthest I've been from LA in a long time is Santa Fe."

"So you want me to believe you're just an insurance guy hired to find a missing college student."

"Believe what you want. I don't actually care. Do I look Chinese or Iranian to you?"

Charles was watching him, his gaze even. Slater could see the wheels turning.

"When you're a hammer," Slater said, "everything looks like a nail. Everybody in your world might be trying to mess with you, I get that, but that's not me. When you lie, and make stuff up, and alter police records, it's inevitable that there's going to be loose ends. I just found one of those threads and pulled on it." With his thumb and forefinger he mimed a plucking motion and clicked his tongue.

"What's Elvaine paying you?"

"That's none of your business."

"How much does Elvaine know?"

"See, my problem is, I know you work for some shady people."

Charles raised his eyebrows. "Why would you say that?"

"Aid-agency linguists don't have access to instant facial recognition and federal identity databases. If I tell you Elvaine doesn't know anything, you'll just grease me, and if I say she knows everything I know, you'll grease us both so that we don't squawk."

"So when you said you don't actually care what I think, that's a misrepresentation."

"Let's call it bluster, Chuck."

He laughed and sat back. "Nobody calls me that."

"It kind of fits, though. Charles is too pompous. You

haven't high-hatted me even once. I'm sure you can play fancy when you need to, but in your heart I bet you're not that guy."

He watched him for a moment. "Diplomacy has a template. A set of rules. Black tie and cocktail parties and upscale restaurants. Traditionally it's all done in French. Everyone involved knows how to do it and what to expect. That means you can have meaningful conversations because the environment is already set up."

It fit with the international aid work, Slater decided, when he implied that he was a diplomat. But if he worked for a spy agency, all of that was just a cover story.

Charles's phone buzzed, and he pulled it out to look at the screen. "You've tangled with the feds before. You collected a sizeable reward for taking down a domestic terrorist known as Galliform."

"There you go. Would an Iranian stooge do something like that?"

"It looks like you bagged yourself a boyfriend on that job," he said, scrolling with his thumb.

"Who says so?" Slater frowned. "Big Brother actually keeps track of who I'm sleeping with?"

"Zebulon Pike." Charles glanced at him. "It sounds like he's straight out of the wild West."

"He's from Albuquerque, if that qualifies as wild. I can't really be objective about him. We're embroiled in a multi-dimensional narrative complex, operating on many levels." He traced a random pattern in the air. "Seen and unseen, conscious and transcendent."

"I'm also told you're a small-timer," he said, looking back to his phone. "Not really a threat to anyone."

"That's a little dismissive. I don't have a big job, but I'm not a nickel rat. I caught Galliform with my bare hands when all you idiots and your databases and your black SUVs weren't able to."

Charles set the phone aside. "So you got lucky, and you connected me to a long-ago identity. What do we do now?"

He held his gaze. "First of all, I don't think anybody should get murdertized over it."

"I'm not going to do that. One, you're a civilian, and two, if you helped take down a terrorist, you're on the right side of things."

"So then maybe you could offer me some water, Chuck. I'm all dehydrated from the airplane."

He gestured toward the kitchen. "Help yourself."

Rising, Slater paused to look out the windows. "Isn't it alarming to be this high up? It makes me fricking dizzy." He walked into the kitchen and called back, "What do they pay you, anyway? This place must have cost ten million bucks."

"Eighteen."

"That puts you beyond privileged. More like hyperprivileged." He opened cupboards until he found a glass, then filled it from the tap, and returned to the sofa, and slurped at it as he sat down.

"I really don't want that bit of history dug up," Charles said, "and written about in the media. 'Long-lost student finally tracked down—click to find out what he looks like now.' It would be ugly, and embarrassing, and ultimately expensive."

"I get that."

He raised his eyebrows. "This is the part where you say, 'I'll keep your secrets.'"

"Why would I say that now?" Slater waved a hand. "You're not going to believe me. It's not even worth the breath it would take."

"I know that's an honest answer, at least." He watched Slater drink. "So what's next? You want me to pay you more than Elvaine is paying you?"

Slater scowled. "I don't want your fucking money." He set his glass on the coffee table. "You seem a little tightly wound, Chuck. Maybe we could release some of that tension."

His eyebrows shot up. "You're hitting on me?"

"Elvaine figured you were a man's man, even though Bettina swears up and down you weren't."

"What did Natasha say?"

"Basically he said no, he wasn't, but hmm, yeah, maybe he was. And then Heather said, 'I'm not sure, but OK, probably, yeah.'"

He chuckled. "I haven't thought about her in decades. What is she doing now?"

"She's a degenerate. A film-industry executroid."

"What's degenerate about her?"

"The whole thing," Slater said. "The gray suit and the bougie haircut. Spouting corporate jargon."

"By that standard, there's a lot of degenerates around."

"It's a mad world, Chuck."

"What about Mr. Pike, and that ring on your finger?"

"I can't get sticky with you, obviously, but the rules say I'm allowed to hook up when I'm out of town."

"I love the way those jeans fit, and I'd love to see you out of them." Rising, he walked into the hall.

Slater got up and followed him, into a room with a bed and another big window. It had a different view. There were more skyscrapers on this side, a couple of them as tall as this one, and he could see a corner of green space. Central Park, he realized.

"How do you sleep at night with this going on? It would be like bedding down on the rim of the Grand Canyon."

"I draw the curtains."

Charles pulled off his sweater and started to unbutton

his shirt. "So what are you into, Ibáñez? Top, bottom, vers?"

"I don't really use labels, big guy. I'm up for whatever's going."

"Can I fuck you?"

"Bring it on." Slater pulled off his shirt, and dropped it on the floor, then unbuckled his belt. Once Charles was naked, he reclined on the bed, watching him undress, a grin on his face. When Slater stepped over he pulled him down and mashed their mouths together, hot and firm and intense.

Slater squeezed his cock. He was already hard. Charles shifted on top of him, mouthing his neck and his chest, and gently probed between his legs. He ruffled Slater's hair.

"Is this OK for you?"

"Was that not clear when I dropped trou?" Slater furrowed his brow. "Why would you ask me that when nothing's happened yet?"

He shifted closer and pressed into him as he loomed over him. Gentle at first, he soon started moving faster and thrusting hard. He grabbed Slater's cock and stroked him.

"Are you going to come for me?" Charles said.

"If you keep doing that, yeah."

The guy was intuitive about it, and Slater soon came. Charles pounded him for a minute, then grunted and arched his back. Eventually he pulled away and stretched out next to him.

With his eyes closed, Slater savored the feeling of satiety, but caught himself before he drifted into sleep. He shifted onto his side.

"You kind of remind me of a prostitute," he said.

Charles didn't open his eyes. "I bet you never paid a prostitute in your life," he said flatly.

"It doesn't quite wash. The high-tone job, the good manners, the pricey crib, and then the rent-boy mack."

He shifted up to the pillows, leaning back on them. "It was my job for a long time."

"Sex?" Slater propped his head on his arm.

"I'd call it seduction."

"You were the honey pot for closety Soviet diplomats, and repressed Revolutionary Guards?"

"I wish I'd figured it out earlier, and hadn't let it become work."

"Sex is sex," Slater said.

"The rest of it, though. I wish I hadn't judged myself by someone else's standards. I could have had a normal life."

"Normal is bullshit, Chuck. Free your mind."

"I've wound up alone. I'm an empty man."

"With a lot of freaking dough to insulate that empty space, considering this apartment."

Shifting closer, Charles slowly caressed his side, then his hip. "People in my line of work don't usually live that long. In the early days sex work was scut work. Sex workers were considered expendable. We had a high mortality rate. I got lucky—I've had time to make some side deals, and had some advantageous opportunities."

"At least eighteen million dollars' worth."

TWENTY-THREE

⧉⧉⧉⧉⧉⧉⧉⧉⧉⧉⧉

CHARLES ROLLED ONTO HIS back. "I'm not going to apologize for my lifestyle."

"You shouldn't have to. Hey—smoke 'em if you've got 'em." Slater studied his face, the shape of his jaw, his nose. The guy really was handsome. "So how did you get into it? What happened that night, when the guy put the fish in your bed and you disappeared?"

"I forgot about the fish. That's not what did it. Boris was a vulnerable closeted kid. One of my professors saw that and recruited me."

"Professor Cameron."

Charles looked at him. "How do you know about him?"

"Elvaine put it together. You left the textbook from his class open on your desk. She found out he did a lot of down-low government work, and she guessed that he might be involved. Cameron was pretty tits-out about his research interests—he published articles in psych journals about manipulating people, and he did hypnosis. She never actually got to interview him."

"He's long dead."

227

"Did he come to your room that night?"

"I figured out later he'd done a certain amount of conditioning when I'd had sessions with him. He called them consultations, but it was more than that."

"You mean brainwashing," Slater said.

"I suppose that's what it was. I'd spent the night at his house the previous weekend."

"The Saturday? Nobody ever figured out where you were that night. Just that you weren't in the dorm. Were you sleeping with Cameron?"

Charles frowned. "No—we were just talking. I crashed on his sofa."

"He was programming you to run off and work for his project."

"Probably." He threw up a hand. "He didn't come to the dorm, but he phoned me that night in my room, and said a few key words, and I got up and went to see him. I never looked back."

"You were triggered like a robot to walk out of your life."

"I knew what I was doing," Charles said. "I remember doing it. But I felt compelled to go to his office that night. Somehow he'd exploited my weaknesses."

"It sounds like brainwashing to me. So the job they wanted you for was about sex? Putting the squeeze play on closeted guys?"

"Among other things. It's not just blackmail—sometimes the targets are out but they're not closely following orders, and they're willing to sell information for cash. Sexual intimacy was a way to open that door. Sometimes just getting invited into someone's apartment gave me the opportunity to look through their desk or their computer."

"Why did you let the break with Boris's life become permanent?" Slater said. "Why not check in with your parents, or with Natasha?"

"Cameron convinced me it was better my friends and family thought I was dead than queer."

"Ouch."

"I don't believe that now. But it's been so long. I have no desire to connect to that distant past. I wasn't really happy then."

"It sounds like Cameron really fucked you over."

"Not just him," Charles said. "Before that it was actually my parents. They were hippies, and totally self-involved. They had little interest in their kids. Bettina too. You said you met her. In my last year of high school, she pulled me aside at the mall one night. She said she wanted to have a serious conversation. Basically she told me not to come out. Just bury it, she said. Act normal."

"I can see her doing that," Slater said. "She doesn't seem very bright."

"She showed me this card with a picture of the Sacred Heart."

"I don't know what that is."

"You've seen it. A portrait of Christ with his heart outside his chest, and it's on fire."

Slater frowned. "That sounds painful."

"Bettina's a dupe. Ultimately having no past made me much more effective in my work. The agency became my family and friends."

"And you're OK with being a dick-hound now."

"I've had shrinks who helped a lot. Helped me get comfortable in my own skin."

Slater scoffed. "Helped deplete your bank account, you mean. Those morons wasted a lot of my time in my youth. Years of sitting in their offices, listening to them drone on. The only thing I really learned was what to say to the other shrinks to get them to stop bugging me."

"Maybe they helped you without you realizing it. You

seem pretty functional now."

He scoffed. "I work and I work till I'm half dead, and the gears keep grinding. Wearing me down, rubbing me raw, sucking me dry."

"I think that's what a lot of people experience in this world," Charles said.

"Listen, Chuck, I know it's not even lunchtime, but I got, like, four hours' sleep, and your finely tuned sexual powers took a lot out of me."

"You want to nap."

"I can't keep my eyes open."

"So have a nap." He climbed off the bed.

Moving up to the pillows, Slater folded the covers over himself. He heard the shower running as he drifted off.

———◆———

When he woke, it took a minute to remember where he was. He'd really been zonked out. He looked to the oversize window and the surreal view. That brought it all crashing back into his mind.

He could hear a voice somewhere else in the apartment. Charles. The guy was talking. There was only his voice—he was on the phone.

"He'd be useful," Charles said. "He's exactly the type."

A minute later Charles walked in, dressed again in the chinos and the red sweater.

"You're awake. You like Vietnamese?"

"If it's vegan," Slater said.

His brow furrowed. "You're vegan."

"You sound dubious. Wasn't that in your intel report? Look under my first-grade vaccination records, or my bar mitzvah photos, or the scan of that mole on my butt cheek."

Charles scoffed and pulled out his phone. "Let me order up."

Throwing off the covers, Slater got up and went to shower. Once he'd toweled off, and pulled on his shirt and his jeans, he found Charles in the next room, gazing at a laptop. He was sitting at a desk positioned in the middle of the floor and facing the big windows.

Slater stepped close to the window, his toes against the sill, the view of the hazy metropolis filling his whole field of vision. Folding his hands in the small of his back, he leaned close to the glass, until his nose was almost touching it. He tilted his head until his damp hair brushed the pane.

"Raskolnikov."

"Whoa," Charles said. "I haven't heard that in a while. Natasha used to say that."

"He said you both used to say it. I don't think I'd ever get used to this. It gives me an adrenaline rush." He stepped back and saw that Charles had reclined in his chair, watching him.

On the credenza next to the door was a violin in a stand. Slater lifted it to look it over.

"Do you still play?"

"Careful with that."

Slater set it down again. The credenza was odd, made of rough unfinished wood. He touched it, and it was smoother than it looked, but it was totally fugly. The bookshelves were made of the same material, he saw, and the desk too.

"Who's your interior desecrator?" Slater said.

"You mean decorator?"

"You heard me. All this ratty beat-up wood. It looks like somebody raided a pile of demolition debris. Don't you get splinters?"

"My interior designer assured me this look was recherché."

"You should tell him he's touché, like touched in the

head. I could have pulled all this trash out of a homeless encampment for you for free. I might have charged you for spraying it down with pesticide, but I bet it wouldn't have cost nearly as much as Frank Lloyd Wrong dinged you."

"You are such an ass," he said intently.

Slater put his hands on his hips. "I get that a lot."

Somewhere else in the apartment a bell chimed, and Charles rose, folding his laptop closed. "That's lunch."

He followed him to the main room, and Charles returned from the door with a bag. They sat on the stools at the kitchen counter. The bag had MARTIN and his address written on it. This is what the cleaner had found in the fridge in Charles's LA apartment—a food delivery from the opposite side of the country.

Charles pulled out a couple of bánh mì, and Slater unwrapped his and bit into it. It was perfect, crispy and soft and delicious. Once he'd eaten half, Charles folded the paper wrapper over the rest, and set it aside, then swiveled toward him.

"These days my job isn't really about field work," Charles said. "I run operations."

Slater gestured with his sandwich. "Are you sure you're allowed to tell me that?"

"There's somebody I need to seduce. I'm not his type, but you are. To a T."

"You want me to work for you? I did not see that coming."

"Not long-term. Just this job. Like a contract. You do that anyway, right? Contract work? Freelance gigs?"

"You want me to seduce the guy," Slater said, "and then what?"

"Maneuver him into a situation where we can photograph him with you. You're confident in bed. It'll be easy for you."

232

"I'd be helping you blackmail somebody? No freaking way."

"It's not about blackmail. We're just rearranging some strategic pieces. He's from a homophobic place, and if we can discredit him with the other oligarchs, someone else will step into the void."

"Why would I do that? Make some guy's life miserable, and make him lose his job?"

"It's not about a job." Charles tapped his fingers absently on the countertop. "This is on a different level. It's about contracts his government awards to his array of businesses. We want someone else to get that work."

He set down the remains of his bánh mì. "Like a US patsy."

"More like someone who's less of a threat to democracy and stability in Europe." He folded his arms. "You're mistaken in thinking you should protect this guy. He's bad news. I know you're on the right side of things, Ibáñez."

"You're not going to motivate me with loyalty to the government and your politics." Slater threw up a hand. "This country is a homophobic place too. Lots of the people in it would be thrilled to put me in a concentration camp because I like dick."

"It's not about politics. It's about the big picture. It's about justice."

"I take it you've never been on the receiving end of the justice system. Upholding all that is for you chumps. The privileged and the well-paid. I'm going to do what benefits me."

"You did take down a terrorist."

"Not because of soaring eagles and star-spangled textiles. I'm no eagle, perched up here on the eighty-second floor. I'm down on the ground grubbing in the dirt. More like a weasel." He huffed. "Someone called Galliform a weasel. I'm more like him than like you." Slater looked away, and picked up the bánh mì, and lowered his voice. "That guy was messing with the phone network. I need functioning technology to make my living. He needed to go down. Besides all that, I got paid."

"So we'll pay you."

He gestured with the sandwich. "It's interesting that you're up on the politics of the situation, not just the operational side. That tells me you're fairly high up the ladder. What's your job title, exactly?"

"I'm a linguist."

"Of course you are. And I'm a competitive synchronized swimmer. I'll show you my designer nose clip later." He raised his eyebrows. "What kind of bad news is this target of yours? He's mean to his mama, or he robs banks?"

"More like he facilitated the bombing of civilian targets," Charles said, "including schools and apartment buildings, in Kyiv and Kharkiv. He's personally responsible for the deaths of hundreds of noncombatants. And then he helped broker arms deals that put heavy weapons into the hands of people who would like to set up those concentration camps you mentioned."

"And you want me to fuck him."

"He likes Latin guys. He's not going to be dangerous to you."

"When would this happen," Slater said, "and how long would it take?"

"I can't tell you any more until we make a deal."

"What's your budget on this job?"

He laughed. "What do you want?"

He watched him for a moment. Max once told him that when you're billing Uncle Sam, you add a zero or two, and they won't even flinch.

"I know you have a fat bankroll, renting an empty

apartment in LA, with the food swapped out every week."

"You went inside?" Charles said.

"It was so easy to get in that I started to doubt Elvaine's whole theory about Professor Cameron and covert government work."

"It's easy for a reason. So that anyone who's looking into me can verify that I live there."

"Is that why your pad is on Main Street, and not behind a security hedge over in Beverly, with the bad drivers and the manured lawns?"

"There's also lots of retirees in Beverly Hills, so everyone is in your business. Downtown nobody pays any attention to your comings and goings."

"Everything has a hidden meaning in your world," Slater said. "Unseen motives and machinations. It's so freaking complicated."

"We were talking about your fee."

"You could pay off my mortgage. Shelling out for that every month is a pain in my ass."

"What's left on your mortgage?"

"It's actually almost paid off. There's maybe two left."

"As in two hundred grand?" Charles frowned. "I thought you lived in Echo Park. Did you buy the whole block?"

"When's the last time you were actually in LA? You can't even buy a parking space for under a million bucks right now."

"So you'll do it."

"If you're willing to pay me that much, sure."

Charles slid off his stool. "Let me check with my boss."

"Can I talk to them?"

He scoffed. "No."

"It would go a long way to convincing me to help you."

"You already signed up, my little weasel."

Slater jutted his chin. "Let's see what they have to say about the dough."

Walking over to his office, he went in and closed the door. Slater couldn't hear anything inside, not even the murmur of a voice.

Rising, he stepped over to the big window. Being so high made his heart beat faster. Again he moved so close to the glass that he couldn't see the sill at his feet, and the sides of the frame disappeared from his peripheral vision. Gazing out at the void, he took deep breaths.

The whole thing was way outside his comfort zone. Frenetic New York, and genteel Charles, and sex for money. It was damn good money, if they went for it, but that seemed extremely unlikely. He'd asked for way too much. When you set the fee that high, they wouldn't even bother to counter. Still, even the fact that Slater was considering this meant he was basically a prostitute.

Charles opened his office door. "What are you doing?"

He stepped back from the glass, and Charles waved him in. Once he'd walked into the room, Charles gestured to the desk chair.

On the laptop screen was a video feed of a woman sitting at a desk. She had her Black hair pulled back, and a moon face, and wore a royal-blue jacket. Behind her were office cabinets and bland wall art. Slater took the chair and leaned toward the screen, and she introduced herself as Yvette.

"I understand you're going to do some work for us," she said.

"If you can pay me up front, sure. Where are you, anyway?"

She grinned. "Why would you ask me that? Does it matter?"

"I bet you're in DC," Slater said. "You can't throw a

rock without hitting a fed in that town."

"We can approve your payment request. Your lender says you owe them two hundred and twenty-nine thousand."

"I can't believe you know that already."

"That's more than we'd usually spend on a contract of this type."

"I get it," Slater said. "The whores are small potatoes. Expendable. They make a few C-notes at most, not hundreds of thousands."

Charles was standing at his side, his arms folded. "Nobody said you were a whore."

He glanced at him. "That doesn't make it not true."

"Payment will happen in four to six weeks," Yvette said. "We can't pay you in advance. Unfortunately that's impossible."

"Chuck's doorbell camera pulled up my identity and my boyfriend's name and my dental x-rays in a hot second, but you can't come up with the scratch up front?"

"That's about the bean counters," she said. "I can assure you that the government pays its bills."

"Yeah, I've heard that too. But how do I know you won't just murdertize me after, save yourself some cash, end of story?"

She laughed. "We don't make a habit of killing off our own people. That would be bad for morale."

"That actually rings true. But I'm not trained to do what Chuck does."

"Charles assures me you're well qualified, and you have a solid reputation. All you have to do is get with the target. Charles will take care of the rest." She smiled and leaned forward. "You'll do fine."

The window closed before he could respond. Slater looked to Charles and saw that he was grinning. He swiveled the chair toward him. "What's funny?"

"You're kind of a handful, you know that? I think it's why Yvette wanted to meet you."

Slater threw up his hands. "I actually wanted to meet her. I needed to talk to somebody else involved in this to make sure you're not playing me."

"You really do need to be in charge of things."

"I am in charge, Chuck." He held his gaze. "Of my own stuff, at least."

"Are you convinced now that I'm not trying to scam you?"

"Mostly." He waved a hand. "Give me the dope on the target."

"I will. But first, what are your measurements?" He waved him out of the chair, then sat and rolled close to the laptop.

"You mean my clothes?" Slater recited the numbers and waited while Charles typed.

Eventually he rose. "Let's sit in the front room."

At the dining table, Slater took a chair with its back to the window. That view was too unnerving.

"So where am I meeting this guy?" he said. "What's his name?"

Charles sat opposite. "Let me be in charge, Slater. Just for a minute. I know how to do this. Once I've run through it, you can ask your questions."

"So lay it on me, boss man." He threw up a hand. "I'm sitting right here."

"You can't tell anyone about any of this. Not even Zebulon."

"Nobody calls him that except his mother. It's just Pike. And I actually know how to keep my mouth shut."

Charles raised his eyebrows. "We have to go out of town."

TWENTY-FOUR

Sometime later the doorbell rang, and Charles rose, and came back a second later with a thick padded envelope. Ripping it open, he tipped the contents onto the table, and handed Slater a cell phone and a little blue booklet with PASSPORT and UNITED STATES OF AMERICA emblazoned on it in gold, along with the stylized eagle logo.

Slater flipped it open. "This is the photo from my real passport." He read the name and scowled at Charles. "José María Mateo Martínez. You made me Mexican."

"So what? It's a US passport."

"I don't speak Spanish."

"Lots of Latin Americans don't. Remember your name for the next few days is Mateo."

A yellow sticky note on the back of the phone had MATEO written in Sharpie, and below that CHEEPMINUTES. He peeled it off and set the phone aside. Charles handed him a silver clip with a couple of bank cards in it. When he pulled them out, both were in the name Mateo Martínez. Next Charles handed him a wad of cash.

"That should be about a thousand. You won't need much cash. Use the cards."

"That's easy." Slater leaned back to tuck it in his front pocket.

"You'll have to leave your own phone and all your cards with me."

"First I need to call the boyfriend," Slater said, "and tell him I'm going to be out of touch."

"You can't give him any other details."

"You said that already," he said intently, and stepped toward the kitchen, pulling out his phone. It wasn't out of earshot, but at least he didn't have to look at the guy. Leaning back against the counter, he called Pike, glad that he picked up.

"You made it," Pike said. "How's the weather there?"

"Not as warm as I thought it would be. You sound congested."

"I'm eating my lunch. So Hugo sent a link to the ghost hunt video. They put it up already. It's fun to watch, but I do not love the way I look on camera."

"We'll watch it when I get back," Slater said. "Listen, I'm going to be incommunicado for a few days. I won't be able to call."

"That sounds mysterious. Where are you going? There's cell towers everywhere nowadays."

"I have to turn my phone off for a while."

"Why is that?" Pike said. "What are you up to?"

"I'll tell you about it when I get back."

"I hope you're not doing anything dangerous."

"I'm fine," Slater said. "I love you, Reddy Kilowatt."

"Forever."

Once he'd ended the call, he went back to the dining table, and powered off his phone, and handed it over.

"That was so romantic," Charles said. "It pulls at my

heartstrings."

Slater dropped into the chair. "I got it bad. I can't deny that. It was inevitable—the guy is pure gravy. And then you dig a little deeper, and there's more gravy."

"It sounds like you're not through the initial euphoria yet."

More shrink talk. The guy sounded like Doris. "I actually think we might be. It's getting more routine. I can definitely see what's wrong with him. But all that is still minuscule compared to the good stuff."

Charles's brow furrowed. "What's wrong with him?"

"Lots of things. He dresses like he's in middle school sometimes."

"You dress like it's 1860."

Slater narrowed his eyes. "That's what he said."

"Why do you call him Reddy Kilowatt?"

"When we first met, on the Galliform case, the prick tased me." He jabbed the air with two fingers. "Zap."

"That's a bold opening move."

"It worked, though. I was basically hooked."

"Give me your wallet," Charles said, "and any other personal items. You'll have to leave your satchel too. I'll get it all back to you."

Slater gave him his bank cards and his driver's license and his keys, and dug out the thin stack of business cards he kept in his hip pocket. "Can I keep my cash, at least?"

"Nope." Once he'd taken it, he raised his eyebrows. "Who's your cell phone provider, Mateo?"

Slater met his gaze. "I use one of those virtual ones. It's called CheepMinutes. It has the logo of the little birdie."

He nodded. "Good answer. I knew you could do this."

"It was written on the phone."

Charles pulled out his own phone and glanced at the screen. "The car is here."

He walked into his office, and when he came back, Slater followed him out to the elevators. It felt odd to be going somewhere with only the contents of his pockets, leaving all his stuff behind. The only thing Charles was carrying was a thin leather briefcase—not even a jacket.

Riding down to the lobby, he could feel the air pressure building in his ears, like in an airplane. When they stepped outside it was noticeably darker than up above the city.

Idling out front was a black Navigator, and Charles climbed in the back seat, and slid over. Slater followed him in and pulled the door closed. Looking at his phone, Charles didn't speak to the driver, and the vehicle pulled into the street.

He watched the city roll by, the crowded streets, the vehicles and pedestrians everywhere. Eventually they drove into a tunnel. Like the subway stations it had ceramic tile on the walls.

"Why is everything covered in bathroom tile?"

Charles looked up from his phone. "What is?"

"The subway stations, and this place." He gestured to the window.

"You got me."

When they emerged into daylight at the other end, the vehicle got onto a freeway. Raindrops started to dapple the windows.

"This happens a lot here, I'm thinking."

"What are you talking about?" Charles said, looking up again.

"The rain. It has to rain a lot. Everything's green as fuck."

A few minutes later the Navigator pulled up to a razor wire–topped security gate. Charles rolled down the side window and handed the guard a slender black wallet. Peering inside, the guy met Slater's eye, then handed Charles his ID and stepped back. The gate rolled open, and the guard waved them through.

They were on the actual tarmac, he realized, as the only other vehicle here was a low-slung fuel truck.

"That guy wasn't military," Slater said. "This is a commercial airport."

"Flight data is public record. An aid agency using a military airport would look a little suspicious."

Rolling past a row of small jets, the Navigator pulled up near a white airplane with no markings apart from a number on the tail. Jet engines were mounted on either side of the back end, and up front the door hung open, with a short set of steps on its inner face.

"No TSA agents to x-ray my boots and palpate my genitals?" Slater said.

Charles just laughed as he climbed out and strode toward the aircraft.

On the tarmac near the wing of the plane stood a guy wearing sunglasses, despite the cloudy weather, and a set of can headphones around his neck. He pointed to the ground.

"Please stay outside the red line."

Looking down, Slater stepped sideways, following Charles's path on the other side of it. "What's the red line for?" he said.

Charles paused at the foot of the steps and gestured toward the tail. "So you don't get pulled into the engine. Those produce thirty thousand pounds of thrust."

"They're not even running."

"Sometimes they are. It's called a fast rule. It applies regardless of the circumstances. If you always just follow it, nothing will go wrong."

"Man, the world you live in."

He stepped aboard, and Slater followed, ducking his head to clear the doorway. Standing just inside was a woman wearing a dark jacket, lanky and with short black hair. She beamed at them and spoke to Charles.

"It's a pleasure to meet you, sir. My name is Olive."

"This is Slater," he said.

Olive nodded to him. "If you'd like to get seated, we can get going."

In the cabin were several plush seats, more like lounge chairs, and on one side a little dining table, like in an RV. Charles sat in one of the seats facing backward, and Slater took the one facing him. He watched as Olive pulled up the door and sealed it. Almost immediately the engines started to power up, and a minute later the plane began moving.

Olive leaned in to speak to Charles. "Would you like to dine soon, or closer to arrival?"

"We'll have some snacks now, and a light meal in the morning." He jutted his chin toward Slater. "This one's vegan. What's the flight time?"

"Nine hours. Because of the northerly route it'll be daylight most of the way, with just a few hours of nautical twilight."

"What kind of plane is this?" Slater said.

"It's called a G600."

"Who do you work for, exactly?"

Olive's brow furrowed. "The flight services office."

"Do they pay you well?"

"I speak four languages and have a degree in hospitality. My salary is commensurate with my skills."

"You don't have to answer him," Charles said. "He's a pain in the ass."

"Understood, sir." She smiled and walked toward the front.

Slater studied Charles's face. His demeanor was different with Olive than with him at his apartment. It felt more authoritative.

"She called you sir," Slater said. "That means she knows you're the big dog. She must know your job title. I bet she wouldn't tell me."

Charles leaned toward him. "Do you have your passport handy?"

He pulled it out of his hip pocket and handed it over. Charles tapped the graphic on the front cover, the stylized eagle holding an olive branch in one claw and a bundle of arrows in the other.

"Do you know this image?"

"The eagle with the stars and stripes," Slater said. "You see it a lot."

"I know you're a weasel, not an eagle."

"You're the eagle, Chuck. The way you live." He raised his eyebrows. "Weasels don't have to worry about getting sucked into jet engines."

"This is the Seal of the United States. They put it on all kinds of documents to make them official. It's a symbol of this country. Do you know what the arrows in its talon mean?"

Slater studied it. "It kind of says, back off, sucker, I'm well-armed, and I will mess you up."

"That's definitely one meaning. The power to fight back. But the bundle means there's strength in unity." He held his gaze. "It's easy to snap one arrow in half, but you can't break a whole bundle of them. It's an ancient symbol. The Greeks and Romans used it. It means things work best when we stand together and collaborate. When we're all on the same side. You don't have to be an eagle, but maybe you can be one of the arrows."

"You're telling me to shut up and toe the line," Slater said. "Don't interrogate the flight attendant for information about you that you won't give me yourself."

He shrugged and handed the passport back. "Or maybe

just chill out and go with the flow."

The plane made a couple of turns on the tarmac, and the engines got louder. It started moving fast, and soon he felt the vertical lurch of leaving the ground. For a while clouds whipped by the windows as they ascended, and eventually they broke through into the sunny sky higher up.

Charles had pulled a tablet out of his bag and was engrossed in reading something. Once they'd leveled off, Slater got up and stepped over to the video screen mounted on the bulkhead wall up front. It was outside a little galley, where Olive was working on something, and beyond that was the door to the flight deck. The screen showed the route they'd be taking and their ETA. They were over Long Island now and heading northeast. The arcing blue line implied they'd fly over Halifax, then the tip of Newfoundland, and then the broad North Atlantic.

Olive had them move over to the little table. The food she brought them was more substantial than just the requested snacks. For Slater there was rice and asparagus and some fruit.

After they'd eaten, Charles spoke. "It's not going to get dark, so we have to make our own night."

"I could definitely sleep. Do these seats fold out?"

"They do, but there's a bed too." He rose and walked aft, through a door in the bulkhead, and Slater stepped in behind him. It was a crowded space, but the bed was big enough for both of them.

"Sweet setup," Slater said.

"You don't have to sleep here with me, but you can if you want to."

"This looks a lot more comfortable than that seat. And maybe I can persuade you to put out again."

"Let me talk to Olive."

He stepped out, and Slater peeled off his clothes, and

stretched out on the bed. When Charles returned he closed the door and lowered the lights, then got undressed and lay down next to him. He caressed Slater's chest.

"Is this OK for you?"

"Dude," Slater said. "You can dial it down a notch. I'm not one of your targets."

He frowned. "You make it sound like I'm faking it."

"Aren't you? Where's the real Chuck?" Slater sat up and pushed him back, swinging his knee over to straddle his hips. "What does he like?" Leaning in, Slater massaged his pecs, and squeezed his biceps. He could feel Charles getting hard beneath him. "What does he really want?"

"Just kiss me."

Moving closer, he met his mouth, and got lost in it. Whether it was his age or his experience, Charles was really good at this. He shifted onto his side and squeezed their cocks together. Stroking them gently at first, Slater increased the pace, mouthing his neck and his jaw and his ear.

As he climaxed, Charles grunted, his limbs spasming. Feeling the energy in his body took Slater there soon after. Pulling him close, he relished the heat of his skin. Eventually he stretched out and shoved an arm under Charles's neck.

Charles caressed his belly. "You're a primo specimen, weasel boy. You don't have the six-pack but you're really beautiful."

"Thanks for the assessment. Maybe you could email me your notes."

"We should sleep. Olive seems competent but she might wake us early. Some of them do, some don't. The law says you have to be belted into a seat for descent."

"Why would the law matter in your business?" Slater demanded.

"I'm sworn to uphold the constitution. The rule of law is all we've got."

He scoffed. "Last time I got pulled over I promised to drive the speed limit, but that doesn't mean I'm going to do it. You people have no oversight. You can do whatever you want. Why would you follow any of the rules?"

Charles groaned. "You're relentless, Mateo. How does Pike put up with it?"

"I have no idea why he's with me. The guy might actually have a screw loose somewhere."

"I have to sleep." He rolled onto his side. "Do you want a sedative?"

"I won't need it. But I will need a snort."

"You drink instead of taking a sleeping pill?"

"I need it to make all this tolerable." Slater waved at the room. "Was there no mention of addiction in my files? The usual term is booze hag."

"Well, there's nothing to drink here. You'll have to talk to Olive."

He got up, and pulled on his underpants and his shirt, and went out to the cabin. Olive was stretched out in one of the seats near the galley, and she rose when she spotted him.

"I need a drink," he said.

"Beer or wine?"

"The hard stuff. Bourbon if you've got it. It doesn't have to be fancy. You can hit me with the applejack."

She went to the galley, and returned with a pint, and handed it to him. The bottle was plastic, but he knew the label. It was better quality bourbon that what he bought for himself.

"Thanks."

He cracked the seal and walked back to the bedroom, on the way taking a long satisfying pull, relishing the delicious heady burn. Charles was already crashed out, and he slid off his underpants and climbed in beside him. He could feel his belly warming from the golden nectar, and he soon drifted into contented sleep.

Sometime later Slater woke in darkness. What was that noise, and why was the bed thrumming? Then it came back to him. Charles shifted toward him and spoke in a small voice.

"Hold me."

Wrapping an arm around his torso, Slater pulled him close, and Charles gripped his arm and kneaded it. The guy was shivering, even though it was plenty warm in here. He shifted Charles onto his side, and pulled him close, one arm around his chest, his knees notched into Charles's. Squeezing him tightly with his arm and his chin on his shoulder seemed to help, and he could feel his body gradually start to relax.

The guy was all professional and imperturbable on the outside, and he had the bluster of the boss, but there was more to him, more layers. This was a vestige of his life before, the mixed-up Boris Brooks.

TWENTY-FIVE

W**HEN SLATER WOKE AGAIN**, the lights were on, and Charles was getting dressed. He'd opened the window shades. Slater sat up and looked out. They were high above some rugged verdant mountains and a contorted coastline fronting dark-blue water.

"Where's that?"

"It might be Italy," Charles said. "Do you want some vitamin R?"

"Is that Ritalin? You're a damn wastoid."

"It's work related. It'll keep you alert."

"I'd rather have java."

"I'm sure there's some of that too." He opened the door and stepped out.

Once Slater was dressed, he stepped into the cubicle with the head and a basin to wash up, then went out to the main cabin and sat opposite Charles at the little table. Olive greeted him and served them coffee and bagels and fruit.

"You haven't given me all the dope on my target," Slater said, munching on an apple.

"It's not like I forgot. There's a reason we do things a certain way. You'll retain more of the information if you hear about it closer to the operation." He gestured with half a bagel. "First is your backstory. You're from Los Angeles, you work in the insurance industry as a fraud investigator, and you're here on a short vacation."

"That's easy to remember."

Charles raised his eyebrows. "Why did you pick Chania and not Santorini or Eos?"

"I've never been to Crete before. I found cheap flights, and I got a deal on the hotel. My neighbor Tilly said the food was good. She was here sometime before the pandemic. I think she was actually dating a Greek guy. Plus the internet says there's beaches around Chania like everywhere else."

"Excellent." He grinned as he picked up his tablet and swiped at it. "This is Leonov."

Taking the device, Slater studied the image. It was a headshot of a guy with a flat nose and short dirty-blond hair, styled in a side part. He swiped to the next image, a full-body candid photo of the guy standing on a street corner, wearing a tightly cut linen suit. He was a little paunchy, with broad shoulders.

"He's totally fuckable," Slater said.

"You sound surprised."

"From the build-up I thought he might be a train wreck. I'd tap that even without the financial incentive."

"Leonov does well with the guys, although he's careful. You'll have a hotel room. You should invite Leonov back there. He probably won't go for it the first time—he'll take you to his apartment. But he'll want a second date."

"How can you be sure of that?"

"You're attractive, Slater, and you're a good lay. He'll want more."

Handing him the tablet, he sat back and waited as Olive cleared the plates.

"So how do we get from the airport to the city? Europe's supposed to be all about the old iron horse."

"You mean the train? There's no train, cowboy." His brow furrowed. "You're not nervous about this operation at all."

"This isn't my first barbecue," Slater said. "I've fucked Russian guys before, and I don't even need to use up any brain power to remember my cover story. It's almost exactly the truth."

"We do that to make it easier. So you can talk about things without juggling a bunch of new details. Just don't get complacent."

"I know what I'm doing."

"Chania is small," Charles said. "You could walk from the air terminal to the town center in half an hour."

"So we're walking?"

"You've got a driver, and we're going to split up."

"Where are you going?"

"Onto the base. We'll meet up later."

"Uncle Sam has a military base there?"

"It's a NATO base," Charles said. "Greece is one of our array of NATO allies. I'm sure you know that, being a responsibly well-informed citizen. And you don't need to ask questions like that."

"I bet it's public knowledge online."

"I mean asking about me," Charles said. "You don't need to know what I'm doing. Be the arrow."

"I'm not from your world." Slater swirled a palm at him. "This whole empty void thing. My natural human curiosity is still functioning. It hasn't been cauterized out of me like yours has. I wasn't trained to outsmart Ivan and the rest of those dirty commies in the politburo."

"It's not the Soviets anymore."

"It was when Professor Cameron brainwashed you."

"There are still continual security threats." He folded his arms. "If you're not nervous, why are you acting like a dick?"

"It's nothing personal," Slater said. "I've been told my resting state is dick."

"Moving on. Your driver will get you dressed."

"You don't like the jeans?"

"Personally I adore those jeans, but the vaquero look isn't going to work here. You need to look like you're on vacation. Once you're dressed, you'll go hit on Leonov. He hangs out with a girlfriend at a bar in Chania. Her name is Irina."

"So I'll be competing with a woman?"

Charles shook his head. "Leonov introduces her as his girlfriend, but we think she's just a beard. Irina is under no illusion about her role. She never talks to him like a romantic partner, and she hits on other guys. Our assumption is that she's an employee. I have photos." He tapped at the tablet again and handed it over.

It was a candid shot, a three-quarter image of a woman with sharp cheekbones, and pale blue eyes, her billowy dark hair pulled back. He swiped to the next photo. Here she was walking on a street, carrying a little clutch, wearing red high heels and a white pantsuit. Her waist was tiny and her chest voluminous.

"There's no way nature gave her those breasts," Slater said.

"These people are überwealthy. Plastic surgery is pretty much de rigueur."

"Irina looks like a model. You're sure Leonov isn't sleeping with her?"

"Leonov is a solid 9C," Charles said.

"That sounds like his shoe size."

"It's the scale that measures sexuality. The letter is for sexual attraction. C is strong attraction, and A is asexual. The number is orientation—1 is totally straight and 9 is totally gay. So Leonov has been assessed as very sexual and very gay."

"You are so fucking weird," Slater said. "Does anyone use this system besides you?"

"People in my orbit, doing what I do, assessing ways of connecting with potential assets."

"What do you do if someone is an A on the attraction scale? A total ace?"

"We call that a zero-A. That's not my department." He made a helpless gesture. "Maybe you'd take them bowling."

"Why do you need codes and labels anyway? Why not just let people be themselves and do what they want?"

"Like flying airplanes into office buildings?"

"Call me a hater, Chuck, but I'm not convinced assigning codes to someone's sexuality is going to stop terrorism."

"These are complicated systems with a lot of moving parts. By design you're only seeing a small corner of it."

"That's not exactly reassuring, man." Slater huffed. "So why does Leonov need a beard?"

"Things work differently outside the West. Imagine it's 1952. Where Leonov is from, he'd be physically assaulted if he were perceived as queer. His companies would lose business contracts. He could even go to jail."

"But the Greeks are more civilized."

"That's why Leonov comes to Crete. It feels comfortable for him. We know he feels safe because he never travels with bodyguards, the way he would in Russia or on business trips in other European cities. He's never conducted business here. Only recreation."

"If he's here to mack on guys," Slater said, "he probably

doesn't want any witnesses from home."

"I'm sure that's part of it. Irina answers his phone and sends emails for him. You probably won't have to interact with her, but she'll likely be in the bar. When you go to the place, you should order something Russian. Like a Russian brand of vodka. It might give you the opportunity to start a conversation."

"I actually know how to pick up guys."

He could feel the plane start to descend, and Olive had them move to the seats and belt themselves in. The plane dropped lower, and made a couple of turns, and soon the ground came up to meet them, followed by the reassuring rumble of tires on asphalt.

Out the window he could see mountains in the distance, past the broad flat stretch of land. It looked drier than coastal California but greener than the deserts.

The plane stopped on the tarmac some distance from a long low building, and once the engines powered down, Olive unsealed the door and folded it open. A guy in a navy-blue uniform with a Greek flag patch on the shoulder climbed on board and called a greeting in English.

"Show him your passport," Charles said.

Once he'd checked Olive's passport, the guy took a cursory glance at their documents, and at both of their faces in turn, then handed them back. He spent a minute at the flight deck, checking the pilots, and then left. Charles rose, and Slater followed him toward the front. With the cockpit door open, he could see two guys inside dressed in white shirts with epaulets. Olivia said a polite good-bye, and the pilot in the right seat shot Charles a quick salute as they stepped out.

It felt warm outside considering it was only mid-morning. He could smell dust in the air along with the sickly sweet scent of jet fuel. Slater paused to stretch his back and roll his neck. It felt good to be out of that enclosed space with its low ceiling.

They walked abreast to a door into the building. It had a big number posted over it, and inside it felt like a departure lobby. There was nobody in it. Charles pointed to a double door with crash bars.

"Once you walk through there, you're in the civilian world again. Your driver will be near the baggage belt. She'll have a sign with your name on it. You have to give her a specific phrase. Say, 'I'm Mateo from Bell Gardens.'"

"I know that town. It's over by the river. Bell Gardens is industrial. There aren't a lot of people living there."

Charles closed his eyes for a second and took a breath. "I keep reminding myself that it's because you're not trained. I'm used to working with military people. They do what they're told and don't ask questions."

"No questions," Slater said. "It just seems like an odd thing to say."

"That's the point. It's so specific that nobody else could spoof it and impersonate you. You'll know she's the right person because she'll say, 'Bell Gardens is home to the largest post office in California.'"

"Is that true?"

"I have no idea." Charles raised his voice. "It doesn't matter."

"What if she doesn't say it?"

"Then don't go anywhere with her, and call me. I'm in your contact list as your travel agent." He nodded toward the doors. "On your way."

"You really are the boss, Chuck." Slater held up a palm, and took a step backward, then pointed straight up. "Until we meet again, *patrón*, I'll watch for you soaring overhead with the rest of the eagles."

He turned and walked toward the doors. This was the

commercial part of the airport, with a row of shops and restaurants, and lots of people around. Across from the shops were a couple of numbered gates and rows of seating. Through the windows beyond he could see the nose of a commercial jet. Looking around, he spotted the signs for baggage claim.

Once he was outside the security zone, near the baggage belt, he spotted a woman holding a sign that said MATEO M. Built thick, she had a mass of wavy dark hair and a prominent nose. She was wearing a summery print skirt and a loose white shirt open a few buttons and showing some cleavage.

Slater walked up to her. "I'm Mateo Martínez. From Bell Gardens."

She smiled. "That's where the largest post office in California is."

"So I'm told."

"I'm Alexandra. Call me Alex." She waved for him to follow, and they walked out into the daylight.

Stepping up to a little green hatchback parked at the curb, Alex went around to the driver's side. Slater pulled open the rear door, and she turned to eye him over the seat.

"Are you new? Sit up front. I'm not your damn driver."

He closed the door, and pulled open the front one, and climbed in. "That was exactly the word used to describe your role here."

She twisted the key to start the engine. "I guess that's technically true. But we don't need to display that. In your phone I'm listed as your tour guide."

"You live in Chania?"

"You really are new, Mateo," she said, eyeing the side mirror as she pulled into the roadway. "You don't need to know anything about me. It's better for both of us."

"Understood. There aren't a lot of people in Bell Gardens,

so I haven't had many chances to hone my social skills."

Alex chuckled at that. "Charles said you were a piece of work. I spent some time in LA. I was an Army brat, so we moved around every few years." She braked for a stoplight and glanced over at him. "My mother was Greek, so I speak Greek. That's how I wound up here."

Slater eyed her sidelong. Despite her admonishment, she was telling him lots of personal stuff. He didn't need to point that out, he decided.

The town really was nearby, and a few minutes later they turned onto a street lined with retail shops. Alex pulled up in front of a store with mannequins clad in men's suits in the display window.

"Charles said you were going to dress me," Slater said. "Is that what we're doing?"

"I already got you some clothes. They're in your hotel room. But it's better if you try them on. You need to create a look."

TWENTY-SIX

They climbed out of the car, and as she stepped into the shop, Alex called to the clerk, *"Gya su."*

"What does that mean?" Slater said.

"It's a greeting. You should always say that when you go into a store. Otherwise you come off as frosty and rude."

He paused to flick through some sport coats on a rack. *"Gya su,"* he said to himself, trying to remember it. He only had a vague idea of what the euro was worth, but when he looked at the price tags on the jackets, the numbers seemed high.

He looked to Alex. "This stuff isn't cheap."

"You need to look like money, not like a sex worker. Come here."

When he stepped over, she handed him a pair of strappy brown sandals and pants the color of unbleached cotton.

"These should be your size. Try them on."

Slater held up the pants. They were light, and coarse, maybe linen. "They look too short."

"They're capris."

The clerk came over from the counter. A woman in

her forties with her dark hair pulled back, she had a slight accent. "You can try them on here."

She pulled back the curtain of a little changing booth, and he sat on the bench inside to pull off his boots and socks. Once he'd hung his jeans on a peg, he pulled on the capris, and then the sandals, and stepped out.

"I feel naked."

"The trousers fit you well," the clerk said.

"You think I have the ankles to pull it off?"

She just laughed.

"Those work great." Alex handed him a white shirt. "Try this."

Not bothering to step into the changing booth, he pulled off his shirt and tried it on. It was thin and billowy, with no buttons at the collar or above his sternum—he'd have no choice but to display a swath of his chest. He looked in the mirror next to the curtained booth. Just these few garments gave him a dramatically different vibe. He looked like he was ready for a stroll on the beach.

"A couple of accessories," Alex said, and handed him a thick gold necklace. He pulled it on, and she stepped closer to adjust it. "It goes under the shirt." Next she gave him a smaller thick gold chain.

"What's this for?"

"Your wrist."

"Dude," he said intently, and found the clasp, and snapped it on.

Alex scowled at him. "You don't get to misgender me, you condescending fuck."

He frowned at her. "What are you talking about?"

"I am not a dude."

"That word covers all the genders," Slater said. "It applies to annoying behavior. Not your cha-cha."

"I assumed you'd pegged me as trans."

"Are you trans? I didn't pick up on that." He jutted his chin. "You didn't overdo it on the breasts like people usually do. In LA they say you don't want a passing grade. C is considered modest, and D is pedestrian."

"Why does it matter whether they're real?"

"Because you're making an issue of it," he said, raising his voice.

"Stop shouting at me. Have you even met a trans person before?"

"Sister, I'd bet money I've slept with more trans men than you have. Your jittles don't define your gender. You should know that."

She folded her arms. "You are such a weirdo."

"So I'm told," he said flatly. "I never claimed to be a right guy. You don't get to put that on me." He waved a hand. "It's interesting how you want it both ways—gender doesn't matter, but don't you dare misgender me."

Alex huffed and waggled a pair of sunglasses. They were aviator style with brown lenses. "Try them on."

Pulling on the glasses, he turned back to the mirror.

"That's it," Alex said. "That's the look. A well-heeled tourist."

"I look like Eurotrash," Slater said.

Standing nearby, the clerk spoke, her eyes wide. "You call us that?"

Slater pulled off the glasses and met her gaze. "Not everybody. It's a comment on fashion. A specific look." He shook the bracelet on his wrist. "Men with too much jewelry."

Her eyes narrowed. "I'm not going to tell you what we call Americans."

Looking back to the mirror, he pulled the sunglasses on again. "Whatever it is, I'm sure we've earned it."

Alex handed him a brown paper shopping bag. "Put all

your old stuff in here."

"So I'm wearing this from now on, am I?" He stepped into the changing booth and moved his passport and his cards and cash to the capris.

"Your ring too," Alex called to him. "Ditch that."

"Damn it," he muttered, but pulled it off.

He wasn't just going to throw it in a shopping bag. Pulling the laces of one of his boots out of a couple of eyelets, he threaded the ring onto the cord, then laced it up again and knotted it. He loaded his boots and jeans and shirt into the bag, then stepped out and handed it to Alex.

"You have to pay the woman," she said.

At the register he used one of the cards Charles had given him, tapping it to a little reader. She didn't ask him to sign anything, and handed him a tape receipt.

Alex took the paper, and said something in Greek to the clerk, and walked out. As he stepped onto the street, Slater pulled on the sunglasses.

"The light is really bright here. It feels like the Mojave."

"You're probably jet-lagged too," Alex said as they climbed into the little car. "Your body thinks it should be dark." She started the engine. "I apologize for my reaction in there. I'm just sick of all the bias."

"I get it. We live in fraught times for trans folks."

"It's like living in a pressure cooker."

The streets got narrower and the buildings taller as Alex drove, and soon she pulled into a driveway marked HOTEL ALFRED, and rolled down the ramp into a parking garage.

Alex killed the engine. "Your room is set up, but you have to check in."

They climbed the stairs to the lobby. At the desk was a dark-haired guy wearing a brown suit that looked too warm for the weather.

"Mateo Martínez, checking in," Slater said, and gave

the clerk his passport and one of the credit cards.

Once he'd swiped the card and tapped at his computer, he handed them back. "I believe your tour guide has your room key."

"I do," Alex said, standing behind him.

She led him to another set of stairs and they walked up a flight. In the hallway she handed him a key card and pointed out a doorway. When he tapped it on the lock, it snapped open, and Alex stepped in ahead of him.

It seemed big for a hotel room, with lots of floor space around the bed, and a desk at the wall. Over by the windows was a short sofa and a lounge chair, and a door to a little balcony. The view was over a jumble of bright whitewashed walls and red terra-cotta tile roofs.

Alex pulled open the wardrobe. "There's a suit that should fit you if you need to go clubbing, and a pair of dress shoes." Stepping over to the bureau, she pulled open a drawer. "I got swimwear for the beach, and some other stuff—socks and skivvies. Enough for four days. I put some basic toiletries and a razor in the bathroom."

There was a black roller bag in the bottom of the wardrobe. He wasn't going to need that. It had to be backup for his vacation story, in case anyone rifled his room. Pulling out the lapel of the suit, he saw that the label had been cut out, just like Charles's clothes.

Slater eyed her. "It feels a little weird that you did all this."

"It saves time, don't you think? The captain sent instructions last night before you left the States. I had everything ready by wheels down."

"Charles is a captain? In the military? Which branch?"

Her eyebrows shot up. "What are you talking about?"

"You just said 'the captain.' It explains why one of the pilots saluted him."

"I think you misheard me."

Slater scoffed. "You people are like a black hole. Information goes in, and absolutely nothing comes out. I'm not part of it, Alex. You don't have to be circumspect with me."

"I'm not going to gossip about Charles with a civilian."

He put his hands on his hips. "I bet it's the Navy. This kind of hinky-ass stuff is always the Navy."

Stepping over to the wardrobe, she closed the door. "So those are your clothes."

"What about the ones I'm wearing? Do you need to cut the tags out?"

Her eyes narrowed. "That won't be necessary."

"So where's the cameras?"

"You don't need to worry about any of that. You shouldn't be asking. You shouldn't even verbalize that you know what's going on."

"Even to you?"

"To anyone," she hissed. "The key concept is to compartmentalize."

"I already have that habit. My boyfriend has been lobbying for a long time for me to do exactly the opposite. Openness and honesty and full disclosure."

"None of that works in this business, so zip it." She made a zipper gesture at her mouth. "Christ, where does he find you people?"

"I actually found him, toots, after a transcontinental manhunt." Slater waved his arm. "And somehow I've managed to wind up on the other side of the fricking planet."

Alex flashed her palms. "Just settle down. A few more details. Leonov usually hits the bar after siesta."

"I thought that was a Latin thing."

"They do it here too. Your instructions are to walk around now, explore the town, and memorize the route from the hotel to the bar and back. The bar is marked on the map on your phone. Eat something heavy later, so you'll stay more lucid when you drink. Then go in for a drink around four."

"What are you going to do with my clothes?"

"Stuff them in the trash incinerator, of course."

"Are you fucking kidding me?"

Alex laughed. "Lighten up. You'll get it all back."

He sighed. "If the Russian doesn't grease me."

Once she'd left, he inspected the bathroom, and had a shower, then got dressed again and walked around the town. The streets had definitely been here before the cars. Some of them were barely wide enough for two people to pass. Walking in sandals took some getting used to, and they were only slightly more supportive than a pair of flip-flops, but they were appropriate for the weather. It felt hot in the sun, but it was cooler in the shaded places. He hung the aviators on the front of his shirt. The top button was so low that they hung to his navel.

There were a lot of people around, and most of them looked to be tourists. Some were dressed like him and some were in cargo shorts and fanny packs and floppy canvas hats. He heard snatches of conversation in German and British English and some Slavic language. This central neighborhood was only about tourism, he decided. Hotels and restaurants and shops geared to visitors, with lots of signage in English.

At one point he found a street flanked by a high wall. The blocky irregular stones made it look historical. It had to be a fortress or the walled part of an old city. Pausing on the sidewalk, he searched for it on his phone. The Venetians had built the walls when they controlled the place in the Middle Ages. Slater looked up at the sand-colored stones. It was hard to believe it was that old.

Some of the greenery was familiar, like the bougainvillea

and olive trees and wild-growing oregano, but other stuff was thoroughly foreign, and he could only guess what it was. A specific tree was growing all over the place, and he knew it was a species of oak, but he'd never seen it before. There were citrus trees as well, but they didn't look much like the California versions.

Eventually he found the harbor, with an open pedestrian space along the water. He sat for a minute on a park bench, at the other end from a young couple dressed the same way he was, and looked out at the water. It was a mild shade of blue, and there were hardly any waves. He could see a breakwater with a lighthouse, but even beyond it the sea looked innocuous.

This was the Mediterranean, he knew, but it was acting much calmer than when Odysseus had to sail around in it. Back then he'd described it as dark and violent. That guy had spent time in Crete on his decade-long schlep home from the war. He'd also told people he was from Crete, but that was a lie—part of his cover story when he snuck back into his own palace disguised as a bum.

He'd read all that with Pike. Sweet sexy Pike. He missed him, he realized. Pike would love all this—Odysseus's sea, medieval walls, the dense weight of history oozing out of every brick and paving stone.

Checking the map on his phone, he stood up again. He felt a little spacey, and it wasn't just from the jarring shift in scenery and these weird-ass airy clothes. Like Alex had said, he was jet-lagged. He closed his eyes and turned his face to the bright sun. It felt good on his skin, and he relished it for a minute, then walked the route between the bar and the Hotel Alfred. It was easy to remember, with just a couple of turns, and he only had to check the map once more as he navigated it.

When it was pushing four o'clock, he walked back to

the bar, sited at the corner of two pedestrian-only streets. A row of tables sat outside on the paving bricks, and inside it was tiny, with just six stools at the bar. It was early for drinking, but the place was open. A straight couple sat at one of the tables on the street, and at the bar a lone patron sat at the far end. He recognized her when she glanced at him as he stepped in. Irina. He nodded to her as he sat at the opposite end.

TWENTY-SEVEN

T HE PHOTOS CHARLES HAD shown him implied that
Irina was attractive, but in person she was more
than that. She had an air of glamour, her hair light
and windblown even in the heat. Slater had never seen
anything like the flowing white thing she was wearing. It
hung to her knees but had gaps in it, showing a lot of skin
at her thigh and her back and her midriff. She had multiple
silver bangles on her wrists and heavy makeup. It was hard
to believe that stuff didn't melt and run in this weather.

As the bartender stepped up, Slater said, *"Gya su."*

He grinned at that. "What can I get you?"

"Can you do a Greek coffee?"

"Of course I can do Greek coffee."

As he turned away, Irina rose and stepped over. She
swiveled the chair next to him and sat facing the street, her
elbows behind her on the bar. The pose emphasized her
breasts.

"Why are you drinking coffee? The day is almost over."
Her accent was like Svetlana's, but softer.

"If I get some caffeine first," Slater said, "I'll be able to drink more alcohol later."

Irina laughed, tossing her head back. "I like your logic." Running a hand into her hair and pushing it back, she met his eye. "Are you staying in town?"

"Over at the Hotel Alfred."

"I'm a visitor too." She dropped her chin. "Are you traveling alone?"

"You're so beautiful," Slater said. "I don't want to be disingenuous. I can't flirt back—I only date men."

She made pouty lips. "This is unfortunate. Perhaps you can buy me a drink anyway."

"Of course. What are you drinking?"

Sitting up, she swiveled to face the bar. "Gin and tonic."

The bartender set his coffee in front of him, in a little white cup on a saucer.

"Gin is perfect for this weather." Slater eyed the bartender. "Bring us two of those."

He nodded and stepped away.

"Where are you from?" Irina said.

"Los Angeles. I'm here on vacation."

"Everyone is here on vacation. I'm from Moldova."

He knew that was a lie—she was Russian. But she must have a reason for saying it.

"I've never been there," Slater said.

"I've never been to Los Angeles. Are there many film stars?"

"Probably, but not in my orbit. I never see them."

The bartender set down two highball glasses, a lime wedge perched on the rim of each. Irina picked up one and clinked it on his.

"Cheers." She took a sip. "Here we say *Eviva* for cheers."

"*Eviva.*" He slurped at his drink, then picked up the little demitasse cup and sipped at the java. It was strong and sweet and delicious.

"What's your name?" Irina said.

He almost blew it, and started to say "*Sluh—,*" but then coughed. "It's Mateo."

"Irina." She extended a hand, palm down, and he gave it a delicate squeeze.

"I have a friend who would like you," she said. "A man. We work together. He's here on holiday too."

"What does he look like?"

"Blond. Older than you. He'll be here later. You say you can't flirt with me, but you should definitely flirt with him."

"I'll do that." Slater gestured with the little cup. "When he gets here, point him out to me."

"Oh, you won't miss him. He's quite handsome, and you're his type." Her brow furrowed. "Also, he likes assertive men, and kissing on the mouth, and oral sex."

Slater laughed. "You sound like his pimp."

"I'm just a friend. I know what he likes." She sipped at the highball. "Do you know about the Minotaur?"

"I've heard of the Minotaur. He terrorized Crete before somebody went and killed him."

"That's the one. It's why he was kept in the Labyrinth, so that he couldn't easily get out and eat people."

"There was a lot of that happening in classical Greece," Slater said. "That one-eyed giant ate a bunch of Odysseus's sailors too."

"The ruins of the Labyrinth are here on the island. Near Heraklion. You can walk around them."

"Can you still feel the vibes of the Minotaur?"

She made her eyes wide. "Yes, you can, Mateo. You really must go see the Labyrinth. You will know you're in the home of the Minotaur. Can you imagine such a creature? The body of a man but the power of a bull. It would be so terrifying."

"I hear you."

He drained his coffee, then picked up the highball glass, and listened to her talk about the Labyrinth, and Knossos, and other places she'd been on the island.

A while later a guy walked in from the street, and Irina waved to him. Leonov. The guy was taller than he expected, and wearing that same white linen suit. A smirk on his lips, he nodded to Irina. It clicked then—she was working for him right now, scoping out guys before he showed up, chatting with him to keep him here until Leonov arrived.

Irina said something to him in Russian, a sentence or two, and Leonov gave her a two-syllable answer. She turned to Slater.

"I was telling Leo that we were talking about Greek history."

Slater swiveled toward him. "Classical mythology more than history. A lot of it happened on this island. Irina says the Minotaur lived right down the road."

Leonov's eyes flicked over him, then held his gaze. "You remind me of a man from this history. Heracles. The shape of your jaw, and your hair."

He laughed. "I know that guy. Odysseus met him in Hades. You know he wasn't a real person, right?"

"He was a demigod. The son of Zeus." Leonov slid his hands into his pants pockets. "At the other end of the island there's a whole city named for him. Heraklion."

"I guess that makes him pretty real," Slater said.

"The historian Plutarch said Heracles had more male lovers than anyone could count."

"Sweet." Slater nodded. "He sounds like a lucky demigod."

The bartender greeted him, and Leonov gestured to the highball glasses. "The same as what they're drinking."

Sliding off her stool, Irina said something in Russian,

then took the next stool over.

"Irina says I should sit next to you," Leonov said.

He swiveled back to the bar. "Fine by me."

Once he'd perched on the stool, he exchanged a few words with Irina, then turned to Slater. "You're American, I think. Not South American. Where do you come from?"

"Los Angeles."

"I don't know it."

Slater waited while the bartender set down Leonov's drink.

"It's a pretty big place." He picked up his glass and clinked it on Leonov's. "Right on the Pacific. It has the entertainment industry, and a big sea port for all the dreck we import from Asia."

Gesturing with his glass, Leonov scoffed. "You think I've never heard of Los Angeles? You take me for a fool."

Slater scowled at him and raised his voice. "Dude—I don't know you. I don't know what you know, apart from all that dope on Heracles."

"Hot-blooded. I like that." With a smirk, his eyes softened, and he swiveled toward him. He reached for the back of Slater's neck.

When his hand was close, Slater grabbed his wrist and stopped him. Leonov's eyebrows shot up. Pulling him closer, Slater leaned in, and met his mouth, and explored it. When he released his grip, Leonov pulled back, his eyes bright, and took a breath.

Irina got to her feet and said something in Russian. Eyeing Slater, she added, "It was lovely to meet you. I'm sure I'll see you on the island. We must have lunch." With a wave, she walked out to the street.

"No way does she eat lunch," Slater said. "Not with a waistline like that."

Leonov picked up his drink. "In Russia to be beautiful

is like currency. Irina's beauty is the equivalent of a million dollars."

"She called you Leo. Is that a nickname?"

"You can call me Leo. You are?"

"Mateo." Slater extended his hand.

He grinned and gave it a quick shake.

"Are you Moldovan too?"

"I'm Russian. I work in many places, but I love Crete."

"It's my first time. I'm loving the heat."

"You're so beautiful," Leonov said.

Slater met his gaze. "I don't hear that very often."

"It's the truth." He jutted his chin toward the street. "We should go somewhere."

"I have a room at the Hotel Alfred. It's not far."

"We'll go to my flat." Leonov rose and dug out a wad of colorful cash, then plucked out a yellow one and set it on the bar. It was emblazoned 200.

Slater dug out his own cash, but Leonov waved his hand. "I've paid for our drinks."

Rising, he put a hand on Slater's shoulder, and steered him out to the street.

"Thank you, *afendiko*," the bartender called after them.

Leonov didn't acknowledge that, and gestured up the block. The guy was flashy—two hundred euros was a lot more than the few drinks they'd ordered.

Outside it was still broad daylight, and as they walked up the pedestrian street, Slater spotted Charles, sitting at a table outside a café just a few paces from the bar. He was wearing a seersucker jacket and gazing at his phone, a cup of java in front of him. He didn't look up as they passed.

Leonov turned into a smaller street, just a few yards wide, and stopped to face him. He ran his fingers into Slater's hair. Grabbing his waist with both hands, Slater pushed him back against the stone wall, and leaned into him with the weight of his body, mashing their mouths together. He ran his tongue along his jaw, and mouthed his neck and his ear.

Craning his neck, Leonov put his hands on his back, running them down to grasp his butt. Eventually Slater pulled back and adjusted his crotch.

"Where's your place?"

"This way." Leonov had that smirk on his face again.

He led the way farther down the alley, and into a doorway, and up three flights of stairs. The apartment had high ceilings, with a kitchen at one side and oversize lounge furniture. A balcony ran the length of the room, and the big windows and glass doors looked out on the medieval wall. From this height he could see what was on the other side of it—more whitewashed tile-roofed buildings, and beyond that, the water.

"Nice place," Slater said.

"Let me show you my bed."

He followed him into a bedroom where the drapes were closed. Leonov pulled off his jacket and started to unbutton his shirt. Pulling his own shirt over his head, Slater tossed it on a chair.

"So what are you into?"

"I like that you're firm with me," Leonov said.

"You want it a little rough?"

"I'd like that very much."

Leonov kicked off his shoes and ditched his trousers. He hadn't trimmed his pubes. Maybe that was a Euro thing. They were the same muddy blond shade as the hair on his head. The guy was already getting chubby.

Once he was out of the capris, Slater stepped closer, and slapped him hard enough to turn his head.

Leonov gasped. "How dare you do this? No one does that to me."

"You'll take it and you'll like it," Slater said through his teeth, and slapped his other cheek.

Breathing hard, Leonov glared at him, his eyes bright. Slater grabbed his wrist and twisted it behind him, up his back, and pushed him down onto the bed. Climbing up to straddle him, he massaged his back and his shoulder blades. He was already hard.

Leaning in, he growled in his ear. "I'm going to fuck you."

"You must wear a condom." Leonov gestured to the nightstand.

Slater climbed off him, and found one, and ripped it open. Once he'd rolled it on, he straddled him again and started to press into him. Leonov whimpered, and he took his time, gradually pushing deeper. Eventually he worked up to pounding him, his hands grasping his waist. As he came he sank down on top of him.

"Please," Leonov said. "Let me go."

"No," he growled, and shoved his arms under Leonov's.

Pulling him up, he mouthed his neck and his ear, inhaling the scent of his sweaty hair. When he finally let go of him, Leonov shifted onto his side. His cock was rock hard, and Slater squeezed it.

"What do you want me to do with this?"

"You have all the power. It's your decision."

Sitting up, Slater shifted behind his back and wrapped an arm around his torso. With his other hand he took hold of his cock and stroked it as he mouthed his neck. Leonov leaned back into him, breathing hard. When he reached for his own cock, Slater slapped his hand away. He could feel the guy getting closer, and then Leonov groaned, his body vibrating as he came.

Slater released his grip and lay on his back, folding his arm over his eyes as he caught his breath. He could hear

Leonov breathing, and then his hand on his belly.

"I'm going to shower."

Slater heard him get up, and the sound of his bare feet on the tile floor, then water running in another room. He started awake when Leonov returned and tossed a hand towel on him as he sat on the edge of the bed.

"Will you have dinner with me?"

Slater sat up and wiped himself off. "Sure. Do you know a place nearby?"

"We'll eat later. You can meet me back at the taverna at ten."

He frowned. "That's hours from now. You eat that late?"

"It's the Mediterranean way."

"I might have to do some light snacking between now and then," Slater said, "but I guess I can handle that."

Leonov scoffed. "Americans and their snacks. Whenever I have meetings with Americans, they always bring food to eat. Little bags and bottles, sweets, a little plastic package with crackers that they dip into the attached pocket of foie gras. And they eat right in the meeting."

"I know those things. I don't think it's foie gras. More like cat food. Sometimes they have peanut butter in them." Stepping off the bed, Slater pulled on his capris. "What kind of business are you in?"

"Manufacturing." He waved dismissively. "That's not important." Stepping closer, he put his hands on Slater's waist and kissed his bare shoulder. "I had a very nice time."

"Me too. Great sex."

"So you will definitely come for dinner?" Leonov said. "You won't fill up on crackers and cat food?"

He ran a hand into Leonov's damp hair. "I wouldn't miss it. You're the most interesting thing in this whole city right now."

Once he'd pulled on his shirt and his sandals, Leonov

walked him to the door. He seemed impatient now. Maybe he had something else to do before dinner.

Out on the street, dusk was setting in, the streetlights coming on. He walked back to the Hotel Alfred and went up to his room. Filling a glass from the tap in the bathroom, he guzzled it.

A knock came at the door, and he pulled it open to find Charles, grinning at him.

"My cunning little weasel."

Slater waved him in. "I saw you at that café. You already know I went home with him."

Charles walked over to the windows and dropped into a lounge chair. "He was hardly in that bar for a minute before you left together. In the alley you and Leonov looked like *Dante and Virgil*."

"Who are they?"

"It's a painting. In the Musée d'Orsay in Paris." He waved a hand. "Look it up."

Pulling out his phone, Slater sat adjacent on the little sofa, and found the image. "That's pretty damn hot. Which one am I, the redhead or the brunette?"

"I think you know that."

"I've got better skin than either of these chumps. These guys are super pasty—ten minutes in Chania and they'd be sunburned as fuck." He tucked his phone away.

Charles was still grinning. "You slept with him, didn't you. I knew you were the guy."

"It's not like sex is an exceptional skill. We're kind of hardwired for it. Although I probably shouldn't say that, since you're paying me." He narrowed his eyes. "You are still planning to pay me."

He jutted his chin. "Tell me about your conversation."

Slater ran through it, and answered Charles's questions. He seemed most interested in Leonov's sex thing, about relinquishing power and being dominated.

Eventually Charles sat back. "What time is your dinner?"

"We're meeting at ten at the bar."

"Do you think he'll be up for round two? Maybe even tonight?"

"Probably. I think he enjoyed himself. I'll tell him I need to come back here because my meds are in my room, and I have to take my meds. What do people take after dinner?"

His eyebrows shot up. "That's so clever. Let's find out."

Digging out his phone, Charles tapped at it, and pursed his lips as he scrolled, his brow furrowing. Slater watched him. The guy really was handsome. Nerdy Boris had grown into a solid hunk of man, calm and competent and engaged.

"Statins," Charles said finally. "You're supposed to take those at night."

"What is it for?"

"Lowering your cholesterol."

"Would most people just wait until they went to bed?"

"You can say the meal was really heavy, and you're worried about it." He waved a hand. "You don't have to force the issue. I suspect he won't need more than a nudge. In the past he's often gone to hotels with his dates." Charles rose. "I'll let you do your thing."

Slater followed him to the door. "Will you be running the camera?"

"I don't know what you're talking about," he said, and walked out.

TWENTY-EIGHT

SLATER THOUGHT HE'D LEFT the hotel early enough to meet the guy on time, but Leonov was already waiting for him, standing in the street outside the bar, his hands in his pockets. All the tables at the little place were occupied now, as were the stools inside.

"I can still smell you on my skin," Slater said as he stepped up.

"You should have taken a shower."

"It's actually kind of hot."

"I know a good restaurant near the port." Leonov gestured up the block, and they walked together.

"Do you know the Russian writer Dostoevsky?" Slater said. "I keep running into one of his novels."

"You really do take me for a fool. Everyone in Russia knows this man. Which novel are you reading?"

"*Crime and Punishment.* I'm not actually reading it. I keep seeing it." He shook a fist in the air and growled, "Raskolnikov."

"Dostoevsky is sentimental, and religious." Leonov eyed him sidelong. "A relic of the nineteenth century. These days you have to be concerned with practical things. Your actions and their consequences. *Pragmatitchni.*"

"Pragmatic," Slater said. "It's the same word in English."

When they turned into a quiet street, Leonov paused and leaned back against the wall, pulling him close. The guy liked this, he realized, the thing about making out in public. Moving in, Slater pressed into him, leaning on him with the weight of his body. Kissing his neck, he tongued his jaw and his mouth. After a minute he pulled back to take a breath.

Leonov ran a hand through his hair and glanced up the street. His expression shifted, and he stood up straight. In a low voice, he said, "Run."

"What?" Slater followed his gaze. The only person visible in the street was a guy striding toward them. He knew the type—security or law enforcement, dressed in jeans and a black shirt, purpose in his stride, his hard eyes locked on them.

Leonov took a step back the way they'd come, but another guy with the same vibe was approaching from that corner. Glancing around, Slater saw a couple of doorways, but they were closed and gated. There was nowhere to go to avoid these two.

As the first one stepped up to them, Slater tried to sucker-punch him, throwing a fist from his waist. He caught the guy by surprise, and managed to strike his nose and turn his head. The guy reacted fast, with a counter-punch to the face. It landed on Slater's mouth and snapped his head back. In the same movement the guy lunged down to punch low.

Slater fleetingly expected a dick punch, but instead the guy struck the side of his thigh. A searing electric pain shot through his leg, and he instantly lost control of it, and collapsed onto his butt on the pavement. He hadn't seen a blade, and when he sat up to massage his thigh, there was no blood. What the hell had just happened?

The second assailant was on them now. Neither of them put hands on Leonov, but they stood close, and one of them spoke to Leonov in what sounded like Russian. Leonov didn't reply, but he walked away with them, with one on either side, heading up the street. Why wasn't he resisting them? They looked like three guys out for an evening stroll. Maybe Leonov knew he had no choice, knew they could seriously fuck him up, and he'd just surrendered to it.

Watching them until they turned the corner, Slater massaged his thigh. It had felt like an electric shock at first, and now it was tingling, like he might be getting control of his leg back. A straight couple walked into the street, dressed like tourists, and looked him over as they passed. The man furrowed his brow, and put an arm around the woman, and they both started to walk faster.

Gently tapping at his lip, it felt numb, and he saw blood on his finger. It was bizarre that he couldn't even stand up right now, and he felt kind of woozy. The guy had punched the edge of the muscle in his thigh with one knuckle—a precise blow. Maybe there was a nerve there. He could tell nothing was busted, but the muscle had basically been disabled. After a minute more of massaging it, he felt like he could stand.

Once he was on his feet, he took a few breaths and started to walk, heading toward the Hotel Alfred. He was limping a little, but after a minute it felt like his gait was almost back to normal. Whoever they worked for, those guys were pros. What the hell were they going to do to Leonov?

Pausing at a street corner to catch his breath, Slater looked absently at the carved stone fountain that stood there, water trickling down the front of it into a bowl.

The stone was all ratty and worn and crumbly. He'd seen this earlier today, and he'd read the plaque about it on the nearby wall. It was Roman. It had been sitting here bubbling for thousands of years. He was a little rattled, he realized. Forcing his eyes away from it, he set off walking again.

A thought struck him: he should call Charles. Pulling out his phone, he saw there was a text from TRAVEL AGENT, a single word:

Hotel.

When he got upstairs to his room, he found Alex inside, sitting on the sofa by the windows. She rose as he stepped in.

"Who were those guys?" Slater demanded.

"Save it until we talk to Charles. Come on."

He followed her out to the hall, and to the adjacent room, where Alex rapped on the door. Charles pulled it open and waved them in. It had the same layout as his own room.

"What the hell happened?" Slater said.

"I'm not sure." Charles nodded to Alex. "What did you see?"

"Two guys loaded Leonov into a van. They had his hands bound with zip ties."

"They were professionals," Slater said. "Not penny-ante local hoods."

"Why do you say that?"

"I know how to brawl, and I managed to land a punch on one of them. But only one. When he came at me, it was something else. He debilitated me with one precision strike. It didn't break anything, but I was sprawled out on the pavement. That's some kind of military or spy training. They also didn't look Greek. Too pasty, with the mousy brown hair."

"That's my assessment too," Alex said. "They were trained operatives."

"See what else we know," Charles said, and Alex stepped over to the desk, and sat down, and pulled open a laptop.

"It's almost certainly his government," Charles said. "There's been chatter that the regime has changed its mind about Leonov. They want to push him out of the inner circle."

"What are they going to do to the guy?"

"I assume they'll seize his assets and put him in a gulag." He waved a hand. "The situation has changed. He's no longer of concern to us."

Slater put his hands on his hips. "Can I talk to Irina? Maybe she knows something. Like why they came for him today specifically. She probably doesn't even know he's gone."

Charles shook his head. "No more contact with her. The job is over."

He stared at him for a moment. "So I'm here for nothing."

"You achieved exactly what I asked you to. The operation was interrupted, but in the bigger picture, things went the right way."

Slater rolled his neck. "Leonov is a threat to democracy and stability in Europe," he said flatly.

"Was a threat," Charles said. "And you don't need to feel sorry for him. These people are not your friends or your social acquaintances. They're targets. In this scenario, remember that you're one of the good guys."

He met his gaze. "You're wrong about that."

Alex called to them from the desk, still focused on the laptop screen. "They were definitely Russian. Mateo broke one guy's nose."

"How do you know that?" Slater said.

Alex glanced at him. "You know better than to ask.

They reported that they apprehended Leonov, after they'd found him in the company of an Emirati."

"Are they talking about me?" Slater demanded. "Do I look like an Emirati?"

"In a dark alley, sure." She looked up. "It's a logical assumption. Leonov has business relationships there."

"They send these goons directly from the motherland," Charles said. "They're not especially worldly. To them a brown guy is a brown guy." He waved a hand. "The misidentification is actually a stroke of luck for you. He temporarily disabled you rather than breaking your knee, or worse. They don't want to start a beef with the Emiratis."

"I need to sit down." Slater went over to the sofa and flopped down on it. "Maybe that knucklehead was being careful not to break anything, but he still hit me really hard. Do you have any ibuprofen?"

Charles stepped into the bathroom, and returned with a little bottle, and tossed it to him.

"Leonov ended up like Raskolnikov," Slater said. "He got shipped off to Siberia for eight hundred pages."

Watching as he opened the bottle and shook some tablets into his mouth, Charles said, "We need to debrief."

"That Russkie was supposed to buy me dinner. I could use some grub."

"We'll eat, but first we run through this."

He sat on the adjacent chair, and leaned toward him, and asked him a series of questions. It started to get repetitive as he had Slater explain the same things over and over—what the goons looked like, how they moved, how Leonov reacted. It was tedious, but this was just the way they did things. After a while Charles sat back.

"I think that's enough."

Slater took a breath and rested his head on the back of the sofa.

"I got Mateo a flight to LA from Rome in the morning," Alex said from the desk. "It's LA for him, correct, not New York?"

Not opening his eyes, Slater said, "There's no place like home, Auntie Em."

"You both leave here at six. I'll send the tickets to your phones."

"There's a vegan restaurant around the corner," Charles said. "Alex, will you join us?"

She rose from the desk. "I'd be honored, sir."

Slater just wanted to curl up on the sofa and crash, but his stomach was growling, and he forced himself to his feet.

They sat outside on a car-free street at the place Charles found. Slater had questions he wanted to ask about Leonov, and what was going to happen to Irina, but he knew they'd just shut him down. The pair of them pointedly talked about anything but the work they'd been doing—music and movies and pop culture inanities.

At one point Alex asked, "So do you ever see the celebs in LA?"

"Not really. I took some paparazzi photos of Artémise once."

"I love Artémise."

Slater waved his fork. "Oh—I found her dog."

"Rocky?"

"That's him. A gray pittie with a white chest."

"I know what he looks like. Everyone knows Rocky. What do you mean you found him?" Alex demanded.

"I was in a boat off the coast," Slater said, "and I saw this dog on a pile of rocks in the water. I have no idea how he got there. I grabbed him and took him to this lesbian dog rescue. They named him Rocky because I found him on the rocks. Apparently that's where Artémise adopted him from. He's really smart and calm. I hope she treats him well."

"Are you lying to me?"

"Why would I make that up?"

Alex looked to Charles. "Does that sound like a lie to you?"

He held up a finger and said, "Gurl."

Slater had to laugh. "You can believe it or not. Either way, it's true."

It actually felt good to talk about nothing, he realized, and to see Charles loosen up. It was satisfying to see his human side, to see that he could be authentic when he was off the clock.

He could understand now why people ate so late—it was finally cool at this hour. As they walked back to the hotel, Slater paused at a low retaining wall and ran his hand into the bush growing in the few inches of dirt behind it.

"What is that?" Alex said.

"Rosemary. A volunteer. It's kind of amazing that it just grows here like a weed."

She rubbed some of the leaves between her fingers and sniffed them. "Nice."

"You're a gardener?" Charles said.

"I'm surprised you didn't already know that. I need to get my hands in the dirt once in a while. Feel the earth. It counterbalances dealing with all the lowlifes."

"You have to get your hands dirty because you get your hands dirty."

"You know what I'm talking about." Slater plucked a sprig of the rosemary and chewed on it as they walked.

In the hotel lobby, Alex said good night and trotted up the stairs.

"That was polite of her," Slater said, "not to hang around to watch us go into the same room together."

"She knows we're going to. That's why she did it."

Slater followed him up the stairs, and they went into Charles's room. Pulling off his jacket, Charles tossed it on the bed, then sat on the sofa, draping his arm along the back.

"I wish you weren't with Pike."

"It doesn't mean we can't enjoy the moment. Like we've been doing." Slater put his hands on his hips. "You're not going to trash his career, are you? Get him arrested for seditious use of a government-issued stapler or something?"

"You're so paranoid. Why would I do that?"

Slater dropped into the adjacent chair. "I hate that there's no resolution. No one to be angry at, nothing to report to Elvaine."

He raised his eyebrows. "You're not going to tell her about Boris?"

"In my business my loyalty has to be to my client," Slater said. "I can't switch allegiance when I get a better offer. It's the fundamental rule."

"So you are going to tell Elvaine about me."

"There's always reasons to discard the fundamental rule. Extenuating circumstances."

"Like what?"

"It's been so damn long, Chuck. Half a lifetime. The only person who wants to know anything about Boris is Elvaine, and it's not personal for her—all she wants is the story to turn into a book. She doesn't give a damn about Boris. She'd be just as happy if they found his bones up in the San Gabriel Mountains."

Charles nodded. "So you're able to live with not being loyal to her."

"It's a drag that she'll never know her research was solid, that she came to the right conclusions. She basically figured it all out—the link between Professor Cameron and the military, and the theory that he hypnotized you into doing man-on-man spy stuff."

"I went willingly, but she guessed right."

"I'm going to give her money back, since you paid me. Technically I suppose that makes you my client."

"And if you do blab, I can always claw back that two hundred and twenty-nine grand of shut-up money."

"I get why you'd threaten me," Slater said, "but you don't need to. I just told you I'm on board. Elvaine doesn't even need a report from me. So far I haven't shared anything with her. Not even your name. I just told her I was tracking down a lead."

"What about Bettina?"

"Bettina's an idiot. She never really knew you. She claims you weren't gay." Slater scoffed. "More important, she's not the one paying me. I have zero incentive to tell her anything."

"So you're not going to blow up my life."

"You have a right to your privacy like everybody else." Slater sat up and leaned toward him. "If you really wanted to wrap up the whole issue, I can imagine a scenario where some national park archaeologists find a human femur under a pine tree in the San Gabriel Mountains, along with Boris's student ID card. That wasn't among the things he left behind, for some reason. And then lo, the DNA in the bone marrow matches Bettina's." Slater held his gaze. "Local PD closes the case, the coroner or Bettina shares the evidence with Elvaine, and Elvaine gets her story without anyone mentioning the feds, except those hard-working scientists at the National Park Service." He waved a hand. "It would make a much more poignant ending for the book she wants to write than anything to do with a bougie government linguist, don't you think? Everyone winds up happy."

"That's actually good," Charles said. "It's a lot of effort

to go through to get one journalist off my back, but I bet it would work. Maybe you're worth what we're paying you."

Slater rubbed his eyes. "I'll give you that one for free. You paid me to fuck the Russian, Chuck, and I fucked the Russian."

"We should crash." He rose. "Did you hear how early that flight leaves?"

"We're flying commercial, huh. Maybe if you summoned that G600 we could sleep in."

"Unfortunately that's not possible."

"But you let me get a taste for it," Slater said. "I'll think of that trip every time I'm stuck in the extreme economy cabin."

Slater peeled off his clothes and climbed into the bed. He'd planned to just sleep, but after Charles killed the lights, he felt his hands on him, and then his mouth on his, and his woody pressing against his thigh.

Shifting down the bed, Charles took him into his mouth, and he quickly got hard. Slater shifted position, and found his cock in the dark, and started to smoke him. It didn't take long for Charles to come, and Slater soon followed. He rolled onto his back and drifted off before he'd even caught his breath.

TWENTY-NINE

LATER KNEW HE WAS still jet-lagged when he woke, as it was dark out, and when he looked at his phone on the bedside table, it was over an hour until the alarm was set to go off. But he was totally awake.

Rising, he went over to the window and stood looking out at the lights of the neighborhood. His thigh was still sore, and his lip still stung where that idiot had split it.

A few minutes later he heard Charles get out of bed. Stepping up behind him, he wrapped his arms around his torso. His warm skin felt good.

Turning his head to him, Slater spoke softly. "Fresh."

"Are you OK?"

"It's been an odd couple weeks. One of my sources told me to look for coincidences. That synchronicities could guide me."

"That's from Carl Jung," Charles said, releasing his grip. "I'm not sure that's especially useful outside psychology."

"This guy talked about hermeneutics. Finding the meaning in the synchronicities. One of them actually led me to the connection between you and Boris. Or maybe it would have happened anyway. I can't convince myself it's real. If you stare at things long enough, you find connections everywhere."

"That sounds like what conspiracy theorists do."

"The truth is simpler, isn't it?" Slater said. "It's not supposed to be open to interpretation. Things are either true or they're not."

"I can't answer that. A huge part of my career has been about misinformation and disinformation. At this point I don't think I'd recognize the ring of truth if it was amplified at high volume."

"I don't love that about your world. All the layers. Mine is simpler—grifters and chiselers and lowlifes. The motives are usually pretty straightforward."

"So you don't want to work for me anymore?" Charles said.

"If you want to pay me that kind of scratch again for a couple days of my time, sure. But right now I really want my life back. My city. I even miss the May gray."

"Dysfunctional broken LA."

"LA is messy, sure," Slater said, "but anywhere that's not LA just seems kind of silly."

"I can give you your own phone now." Charles stepped toward the desk and turned on the lamp, and returned a moment later with a thick manila pouch, and pulled his phone out of it. "It should still have juice. Give me the other one."

Stepping over to where he'd dropped his pants, Slater fished it out and handed it over, then powered on his own.

"Are you not worried that my location history will show me abroad?" Slater said.

"That doesn't matter. You're not working for me anymore."

He walked into the bathroom, and Slater sat on the

sofa, peering at the screen to wade through his emails and texts. Elvaine had sent him a "what's up" message a couple of hours ago, followed by three question marks. He needed to talk to her. He texted back:

That lead was a dead end. It's not Boris. Let's talk this week.

A while later Charles came out, and turned on the room lights, and started to get dressed. A big smile was plastered on his face.

"You should get dressed too," he said. "We'll get breakfast at the airport."

"What's up with you, Sunny Jim?" Slater said.

"I saw what you wrote to the journalist."

"You're monitoring my phone? That seems snoopy, especially since I'm not working for you anymore."

"Snoopy is my job definition." Charles buttoned his shirt. "In my business nobody ever tells the truth. It just makes me happy that you did."

"I know what you people are capable of. If I blabbed your business, I know I'd soon be taking the long dirt nap." He pulled on the billowy low-cut shirt. "The bigger problem is that I've got some 'splaining to do to the boyfriend. Why did I need to switch off my phone? I'm going to have to come up with a reason. It'll have to be convincing—he's no dummy."

Charles pursed his lips for a moment. "Two ideas. One, tell him you went to track down your target in the radio-free zone around Green Bank, West Virginia. Everybody has to switch off their phones there because there's a sensitive radio telescope. The quiet zone covers a big chunk of land. Second, you could tell him you came to Europe to track your target, and you didn't buy a roaming plan for your phone, so you just switched it off. When it's closer to the truth, it makes a better cover story."

"I'm in awe of your ability to lie on the fly," Slater said, pulling on his capris.

"I've had years of practice."

"I'll meet you in the lobby," Slater said, once he was dressed, then walked down to his own room.

On the bed he found the shopping bag with his jeans and his boots, along with his satchel and the faux leather jacket. He thought those had been left behind in Charles's aerie. Retrieving his ring, he pushed it on his finger, then pulled on his jeans and boots, but decided not to change out of the billowy beach shirt.

Zipping open the black roller bag from the closet, he piled the clothes from the drawers into it, then folded up the suit he'd never worn and stuffed that in too, along with his leather jacket. Slinging on his satchel, he carried the bag down to the lobby.

Charles frowned at the sight of the suitcase. "You're planning to take that stuff?"

"It's more clothes than I've bought in years. I already know they fit me."

"That's not procedure."

"Think of it as part of my look. I'll draw less attention than if I were traveling overseas with nothing in hand." Slater tapped his temple with a finger. "Use your head, Chuck."

"I suppose it's better than just trashing them."

Alex appeared, looking tired. "The car's downstairs."

They surrendered their room key cards and trooped down to the garage, and Alex drove them to the airport. Climbing out at the curb, Alex stepped around to pull his bag out of the hatchback, and set it on the pavement.

"I'm not sure what to say," Slater said. "Have a nice life."

She smiled at that. "I already do."

He followed Charles into the terminal. The flight was

on a small jet, and when they deplaned at the airport in Rome, they walked directly into a concourse with shops and gates and crowds of people. It felt a lot bigger than Chania.

"Why don't we have to go through immigration?" Slater said.

"They don't monitor internal European Union borders anymore. It's called the Schengen system."

"Of course it is, because just saying 'unmonitored internal borders' would be too easy, so let's make up a new word that everybody has to memorize."

Charles stopped and stood facing him. "You're doing it again."

"Doing what?" he demanded.

"Acting like a dick to avoid your emotions."

Slater put his hands on his hips. "Thanks for the psych eval, Dr. Jung. Am I going to get a bill for that?"

"Your ticket is on your phone. Nonstop to Los Angeles in an hour or so. My connection is tighter. I have to board now."

"Well, Chuck, it's been an experience."

"I wish you could come to New York, and spend some time with me. It's beautiful in spring."

"I'd get vertigo in that apartment. It's too high up."

"Plus you hate my furniture."

"It's not your fault," Slater said. "Not everybody can have good taste. You just hired the wrong decorator."

He held his gaze. "Still, it's sad to be alone. I'm an empty man, Slater. A lonely shell."

"I can see why they recruited you." He raised his eyebrows. "You're really good. I almost believe you."

"I'm not playing you," Charles said, and frowned.

"Being alone is a choice. You can have any man you want. There's millions of them in New York." He waved a hand at him. "Look at you—you're gorgeous, even in your dotage."

"I'm not even sixty, you dick."

"Call me if you get out West to use that empty apartment. You should hit us up for a twofer. We do that sometimes. You'd like Pike. Everyone seems to."

"I like the sound of that." He flashed a sad smile. "Someone will contact you to pick up that passport."

"I'd like to hang on to it. It might be useful."

"No dice," Charles said. "Unless you want to work for me again."

"I suppose I wouldn't mind being whored out again to fuck some lowlife foreigner. But I don't like being told what to do."

He leaned in for a brief kiss, his hand on Slater's shoulder, and lingered in it, then pulled back.

Slater watched him walk away, then took a breath. Checking the boarding pass on his phone, he grabbed the roller bag and found the gate. It looked like it was already boarding. He dialed Pike.

"You're up late," Pike said.

"What time is it there?"

"Not quite midnight. It's always three hours earlier than New York. I was wondering where you were. It's been days."

"I'm coming back tomorrow. Can you pick me up? Around two at Bradley."

"Why are you coming in at Bradley?" Pike said. "That's for international flights."

"You're such a damn cop sometimes," Slater said. "You don't need to investigate me."

"That's not an answer."

"Things got complicated. I'm actually abroad right now. In Rome. That's why my phone was off. I didn't have roaming."

"Seriously?" Pike laughed. "You chased a lead there?"

"Something like that."

"I can't wait to hear the details. Did you track down Boris?"

"I found the linguist, but it wasn't Boris."

"That's odd. You had really solid evidence. I guess you can't crack them all."

"I'm not worried about it," Slater said. "I got paid."

He joined the line to file on board, and checked his seat number on his phone. It was up front, he saw, in first. As he stepped on board the flight attendant eyed Slater's phone screen.

"This is you," he said, and pointed it out for him.

"There's a lot of room here."

"The seats recline fully flat," he said. "It'll be daylight the whole way, but we close the shades. You might be able to sleep."

Slater looked over the seat. "Fuck me dead."

"Maybe later," he said, his expression deadpan. "Would you like pajamas?"

Settling into the seat, Slater had to grin. Charles was sending him back in comfort. It sucked that he couldn't tell anyone about this trip, or what he'd done, and that he'd actually found Boris. But maybe it didn't matter. Maybe it was enough that he and Chuck knew.

———·———